D1212593

THE
MIDDLE
OF
NOWHERE

THE MIDDLE OF NOWHERE

A Lenny Bliss Mystery

Bob Sloan

Atlantic Monthly Press
New York

Published simultaneously in Canada
Printed in the United States of America

FIRST EDITION

Library of Congress Cataloging-in-Publication Data

Sloan, Bob.
The middle of nowhere : a Lenny Bliss mystery / by Bob Sloan.
p. cm.
ISBN 0-87113-872-7
1. Bliss, Lenny (Fictitious character)—Fiction.   2. Police—New York (State)—New
York—Fiction.   3. Manhattan (New York, N.Y.)—Fiction.   I. Title.
PS3569.L5M53 2003
813'.54—dc21   2002033014

Atlantic Monthly Press
841 Broadway
New York, NY 10003

03 04 05 06 07   10 9 8 7 6 5 4 3 2 1

For Alice Jarcho and Tom Gallagher

FRIDAY

Bliss sat on the wooden floor of the yoga studio, his legs splayed indecorously in front of him while the rest of the class sublimely assumed Lotus position. Bliss was not in Lotus position. He was not anywhere *near* Lotus position, or half-Lotus, or an infinitesimal speck of Lotus. He couldn't imagine anyone being any more un-Lotus. He'd taken a wrong turn, missed his exit, and was miles away from Lotus, standing in a phone booth in the rain at a gas station reeking of beer and piss, holding a receiver without a dial tone. That's how far from Lotus he was.

As a present for his forty-third birthday, Rachel and the kids had given him a series of yoga classes. That was almost a year ago. He'd been putting it off, making excuses, citing his being busy at work, too many murders to attend to. But the coupon was about to expire. He didn't want to disappoint his kids. *C'mon, Dad. It was a present. You have to go.* So now here he was in the Serenity Loft, knee-deep in a squalid mess o'yoga.

Bliss pulled harder on his ankle, seeing if he could bully it closer toward Lotus, but it was as if there were an equally strong Lenny keeping his leg exactly where it was. Isn't this how saints were put to death in the Middle Ages? Burned at the stake, drawn and quartered, having their legs forced into Lotus. He was sure he'd seen a fresco of it in some church somewhere.

Suddenly, his hamstring cramped. He shot his leg out to relieve the pain and wound up kicking the back of an older woman in front of him. She didn't turn, didn't flinch, just stayed completely Lotus, the gentle swing of her long gray braid the only evidence of the collision. His muscle relaxed, but he didn't dare bend it yet. He left it out, to de-Lotus. Maybe someone would have pity on him.

Fucking yoga.

His family wanted him to go. The Girls—Rachel, Julia, and Cori. They wanted husband/dad Bliss to find more peace, to feel less stress, to be more at one with the universe. So he might be happier. More Om at home.

"It'll be good for you," Julia, his oldest, said. "I take yoga in school. It actually gives you *more* energy."

More energy for Bliss to pursue the depraved denizens of Gotham, the meanies who lurked in the shadows, who left the messes and spills he and his partner Ward were constantly cleaning up.

But he couldn't let the coupon expire. It was his birthday present. And, though it was probably the least yoga-esque reason for going, he went.

He had presented his coupon to a pretty, tattooed girl at the Serenity Loft front desk. She smiled and stamped it with some Japanese character that probably represented "balance" or "harmony" or "let's have fun watching the lumbering cop make a fool of himself."

He walked into the studio in his old, stained sweatpants and his Police Athletic League T-shirt and for a solid half-hour he tried gamely to be a yoga player. He tried Cobra position, the Cat pose, he tried Downward-Facing Dog until he could downward-face the dog no more.

The instructor, a woman about his own age, came over to him. Bliss tried not to notice the way her nipples poked through her leotard, sensing this might not be in the true yoga spirit.

She bent over him, her hand placed delicately, lovingly on his shoulder.

"It's okay," she said, her voice soothing. "Beginnings are always hard."

"I had a coupon," Bliss said.

"You need to stay with it."

"My kids gave it to me."

"Keep breathing."

"My present."

"Yes. Stay in the present."

"It was about to expire. I had to come."

"The next time will be easier," she said.

The next time, Bliss thought. That was what his first partner said—about the sight of death leaking from the hole in the neck of a livery cab driver hunched in the front seat of his cab, coffee and a donut in a little cardboard box next to him, the donut covered with blood, like cherry icing. *It'll get easier.* But he'd never been sure if easier was better.

"It's there," the instructor said with the gentle insistence of a Jehovah's Witness offering him a copy of *The Watchtower.* "It's inside you. You just have to find it."

But she didn't understand that Bliss expended most of his sentience trying *not* to find what was inside him.

He suddenly had an image of his father, Monty, walking in wearing his full dress blues (what he wore to police funerals), his shield festooned with the badges he'd earned in his twenty-two years of service in the Yonkers Police Department, staring in disbelief at his only son sitting on the floor as he did in kindergarten. And then Bliss imagined his father kicking him in the butt.

Let's get you out of here, son, before you get a rash.

Bliss grabbed his ankle in defiance and pulled it toward him, harder than he had before.

"Good," the instructor said. "Look at that."

He felt his father kick him again.

Let's get away from these nut jobs, Lenny. Queers. Lesbos.

He pulled his leg harder.

"Breathe into the stretch," the instructor urged him.

Bliss let out a groan.

He felt his father's foot, harder now. Relentless.

C'mon, son! This is no place for you.

It felt like his knee was going to snap. Almost forty-four years old and he was still trying to show up his father.

Lenny! Let's get the fuck out of here!

He gave one last protean effort and suddenly it was there, his left foot, resting atop his right leg.

"Yes!" Bliss said.

"Wow!" the instructor said.

He'd done it. Half-Lotus. He'd never get his other foot up, but he'd gotten *one*. He raised his arms in victory, making so much commotion that everyone's yoga-ness was shattered and they all turned to look at him, just in time to see Homicide Detective Bliss lose his balance, start to teeter, and then slowly, but inexorably, tip over until he lay on his back, one leg still crossed and the other sticking up in the air. Bliss heard stifled snickering from the class, until one woman could no longer restrain herself and, in a less than yogalike display, snorted and laughed heartily at the sight of Bliss lying helplessly on his back like a turtle.

You should have left when I told you, Lenny. You should have listened to your father.

Then his father turned his back on him and walked away. And his father was laughing, too.

*   *   *

Chantal ran into one of the stalls in the boys' bathroom, locked the door, knelt down and puked.

"Shit," said a voice. "You okay, man?"

She grunted as low as she could.

"Jesus, that stinks."

The boy flushed and left. Chantal flushed, too, then closed the top of the toilet, sat down, and took out the pregnancy tester and got the test started. The irony that she could be pregnant without having intercourse was not lost on her. Her own immaculate conception. She should just let Owen do it already, she thought. It would be tidier.

She followed the instructions on the package. She smiled, thinking how she was doing her pregnancy test in the boys' bathroom—Mecca of unwanted sperm.

She stared at the tester and prayed. *Please God, help me. No green. Please God. Don't let it turn green.*

In the commercials for the pregnancy tester, the woman waits with her husband in their cozy living room, staring at the strip together, both of them wanting her to be pregnant, wanting desperately for there to be a baby growing inside her. They had probably made love the night before by candlelight, moving together slowly like dancers, like people under water, the woman welcoming him inside her, *wanting* him inside her, completing each other. Not groaning and grunting like Owen did while he lay on Chantal's back, his weight pressing her face against his bedroom rug, leaving mottled marks on her skin, one of the ways he had of doing it without really doing it.

Chantal didn't think the tester company would be calling her any time soon for an endorsement: Close-up of girl in boy's bathroom stall. Wearing a shirt stained with tears, she holds the tester in her trembling hands, dread etched on her face, worried that her boyfriend's sperm had found its way from her thigh into her uterus, sneaking around where it wasn't wanted, trespassing. In the background, boys pee, a toilet flushes. It sounded more like a public service announcement from the Catholic church—see what happens when you have sex?

But the tester came up negative. She wasn't pregnant.

On the door of the stall someone had gouged a crude drawing of a penis and testicles. It had been painted over, but the outline was still there. If this had been in a novel they were discussing in English, she would have raised her hand and said that the author was trying to symbolize that even if you tried, you couldn't cover up the crude ugliness in the world, that it would find a way to show through. She was getting better at that kind of stuff. Finding the metaphors, the hidden meanings in the books.

She dropped the tester in the toilet and flushed, but it wouldn't go down. Another metaphor, she thought. She reached into the toilet bowl and pulled out the tester. The water was cold. She had never felt toilet water before. She wrapped the tester up in toilet paper as she did with her Tampax at school. That was kind of symbolic, too. Her period and her pregnancy both wraped up like a cocoon. *Another* metaphor. Metaphors, metaphors everywhere, but not a drop to drink.

Chantal discreetly deposited the tester in the trash basket in the hallway and went back to class.

She wasn't pregnant. She should be happy. But Chantal wasn't happy. She still felt nauseated and clammy. Maybe it was the flu. Or maybe it was just her, the way she was, the things she kept trapped inside her, the guilt, the shame, the secrets, churning inside her and making her sick.

She wondered if they made a test for that.

SATURDAY

They were in the kitchen. Together. Just the two of them. Their fifteen-year-old, Julia, was somewhere in the Village, hopefully not getting a tattoo or a piercing. Cori, their eleven-year-old, was at a friend's house, hopefully not getting a tattoo or a piercing. It was just Bliss and Rachel, husband and wife, sipping coffee, the way they'd started out almost twenty years before.

"You don't think I can take it, do you?" Rachel said.

"It isn't that," Bliss said.

"Then what?"

"It's just . . ." He trailed off.

A week earlier Rachel had announced she was finished with stand-up comedy. Three years doing the clubs had left her weary. She couldn't deal with any more vodka-hazed hecklers trying to impress their dates; or the dentists in town for their conventions, hitting on her, inviting her for drinks at their hotel, offering her drug samples, a free cleaning; or, most painful of all, the young comics mistaking her for a waitress, asking Rachel to get them drinks between sets. Clint Eastwood was still interested in the development deal about her life—stand-up comic wife of a homicide detective—but she just couldn't face the clubs anymore.

So Rachel proclaimed herself a writer of novels. Like the buffalo, his wife's creative impulses needed vast areas for grazing.

"What kind of novel?" Bliss had asked, as if he didn't know.

"About a homicide detective," she said.

And now, here she was again pressuring Bliss to take her with him on a case, to let her ride in the car with him and his partner Ward, to stand next to the victim, get some blood on her hands.

"Let's wait for 'Take Your Wives to Work Day,'" he said.

"No," she said. "Authenticity. That's what I'm after. Details. The details are the most important part of a novel."

"Who told you that?"

"*Everybody* knows that."

"Details."

"Yeah. Next case, I'm in the backseat."

Bliss wanted to tell her that certain details are not worth knowing, like looking at a girl's body on the floor of an abandoned building, her shirt bunched around her neck, her panties down at her ankles, her bare torso scarred, and suddenly your daughter's face replaces the dead girl's. Details like that can do permanent damage. He could attest to it.

"Sometimes the eyes on a corpse are black," Bliss said. "And not from too much mascara. It's the eyeballs themselves. Like a kid colored them in with crayons. Eight-ball eyes. It happens when someone gets shot in the back of the head."

Instead of making her wary, she seemed emboldened.

"Eight-ball eyes," she said, her voice giddy.

"Sometimes there is a mother by the body," he continued, remembering this scene all too well. "A mother, just like you. And she's begging me to make it go away—her son's death. She grabs me by the arm, her fingers digging into my skin. *Do something*, she says. *Please*. It's the 'please' that kills me. And I stand there helpless, trying to figure out why I can't do it. Get the bullet out of the skull of her son and back inside the gun. Such a simple thing, and her agony will go away. *I can make it go away. I'd be her hero. My photo will be by her bed. A place at Easter dinner forever saved for me. But I can't do it.*" He did his best Stanislavsky now, trying to get her to taste the fear. [quavering voice] "*Please,* the mother says, tears streaming down her cheeks [using his fingers to illustrate]. And I so much want to do it, [clenching fists] to put an end to her suffering [dramatic pause], but [opening hand, showing emptiness as symbol of failure] I can't."

He ended, waited for her to respond.

"I have to get my notebook," she said. "I *so* need to write this down."

He'd put his heart and soul into it, but it wasn't enough.

Then the phone rang.

"If it's Ward, I'm going with you," she said.

It was Ward.

"Floater," Ward said, his deep voice exuding its usual luxuriant calm.

Ward directed him to the bank of the East River, under the access ramp to the Harlem River Drive, near 128th Street.

"Be there soon, partner," Bliss said, then hung up.

"So?" Rachel's eyes were wide. There was no stopping her. In eighteen years of marriage, he'd never once succeeded. Why did he deal with homicides more easily than the needs of his wife? He wondered if the other detectives had the same problem. He'd bring it up at the next meeting of the Homicide Husbands Support Group. After the communal hug.

"Floater," he said. "Usually they're short a few facial features. Their stomachs are tidal pools, eels live in their lungs."

Rachel reflected, going to that mysterious place where women go to make the big decisions. When she came back, her face was perky, alert, like a kid about to get on the ferris wheel.

"What shoes should I wear?" she said. "I mean, to a crime scene—flats or pumps?"

Clara arranged the towels in the guest bathroom, folding them lengthwise in thirds so the monograms faced out the way the Missus liked them. All the women Clara had cleaned for had their own idea of tidy—towels folded just so, china stacked just so, clothes arranged in drawers just so. Some wanted the socks tucked together in balls and some wanted only the tops folded over, the rest of the sock hanging down like a dog's tongue on a hot day. *We like the socks folded just so, Clara,* the Missus said. *Our children are used to it.* And Clara had no doubt that if she didn't fold the socks just so, she would lose her job.

Because God forbid the children's socks should be folded differently than they were used to.

The Gelmans were the third family she'd worked for since coming to New York. She'd been with them for two months. She worked twelve-hour days, cleaning, shopping, making dinner. The Missus ate only minute portions of fresh fruit, steamed vegetables, and brown rice, as close to not eating as she could get. Sometimes she just had carrots. Still, Clara was the one who had to peel them and set the carrots on the gold-rimmed china. She wondered if someday the Missus would ask her to chew up her food like mother birds do, to reduce the strain on her delicate white teeth.

Clara filled the porcelain dish shaped like a large clam with tiny guest-bathroom soaps in the shape of seashells in the same pastel colors as the towels. Clara seriously doubted whether Mister Owen's friends at the party that night would care how the towels were folded in the guest bathroom or if there were enough seashell soaps. She just hoped they got the toilet lid open in time before they vomited. They didn't the last time Owen had a party. Not by a long shot.

Also at that party, the living room rug had been stained with red wine so badly it had to be thrown out, but not before the Missus had instructed Clara to spend an entire day lying on her stomach with a Q-tip and some industrial cleaning fluid in a futile attempt to clean each tuft individually. The next day, men were installing new carpeting.

"Clara!"

Mister Owen was calling her.

Mister Owen who, at seventeen, could not prepare a bowl of cereal himself, who didn't aim when he peed.

"Clara!"

His voice made her shudder.

There was a younger brother, too. The famous one. Fortunately, he lived in Hollywood. One Gelman child was more than enough for her.

Some children she had worked for were nice. Mister Owen was not one of these. He needed to spend a night on the sea in a leaking wooden boat pulling up fishing nets until his palms bled, the waves crashing over the side, filling his nose and mouth with acrid water, sending him reeling across the deck, only the iron grip of Clara's grandfather saving him from disappearing forever into the wild, black sea.

Clara returned the rest of the soaps to their place under the sink, and headed wearily upstairs to the third floor of the Gelman townhouse, to Owen's room.

She saw his hulking figure lying naked on his bed except for a small towel across his waist, sweating, breathing hard. He'd probably been working out, the weight machine in his room like some medieval torture device. Clara immediately turned to leave.

"Wait," Mister Owen said. She stopped in the doorway, kept her eyes averted, the way she had when her grandfather would club a fish to death in the back of his boat. "You put the beer in the fridge, right?" he asked.

"Yes."

"And the vodka's in the freezer?"

She nodded, inched a little further out of the room. But he wasn't finished.

"My mother said you were some kind of a nurse or teacher back in the Philippines."

"I was a teacher," she said, angry she allowed herself to tell him anything.

"What'd you teach?"

"History," she said.

"You could help me with my papers," he said. "But I don't think I'll be writing anything about the Philippines."

When was the French Revolution, Mister Owen? Who was Trotsky? What was the Marshall Plan?

She used to teach children this age. They would stand when she entered the classroom.

"Throw me a pair of boxers," he said.

She stood there, not sure what to do. She could feel the humiliation coursing through her body, like getting stung by a jellyfish.

"What color, Mister Owen?"

"The plaid ones."

"They're in the laundry, Mister Owen," she mumbled. She was close to tears, but held them back. She would die first before she would cry in front of him. But she knew that wasn't true.

Sending money home to the Philippines to take care of her own children was more important than any humiliation she suffered from this despicable boy.

"Then the red ones, Clara," Owen said. "If it's not too much trouble."

He's enjoying this, she thought. She found the underwear in his drawer and carried them in her thumb and index finger like they were something foul. She dropped them on the bed.

She turned and left, so she wouldn't have to see him changing.

She would go home now. She would sit on her couch surrounded by the framed photos of her own son and daughter. She would take them down from the wall and hold her children tightly in her arms.

Bliss drove under the Harlem River Drive toward the East River. This was no-man's-land. The dirt road was strewn with cans and bottles, broken strollers, wrecked shopping carts, a burned mattress, urban flotsam that had floated across the currents of the city, washing up by the water's edge.

Rachel sat next to him. Her silk shirt was open at the collar. He could see a little cleavage. His wife looked good. She smelled good. She might make the floater's eyes pop out of his head. Literally.

A novelist.

"Do you even know how to type?" he asked her.

"Is the floater male or female?" she asked, ignoring him completely.

"The fish have usually been nibbling," Bliss said, "so sometimes it's hard to tell."

"Black? Hispanic? Caucasian?"

"Floater," he said. "They have their own racial profile. Their skin color is often merely conjecture."

She wrote all this down.

Details.

"Shouldn't you turn on the siren?" Rachel asked.

"Why?"

"You're a detective."

"The floater's not going anywhere," he said. "Decomposition tends to cut down on your appointments. He'll wait. He won't start eating without us. Not that it matters. Once you see him, you won't feel like eating anyway."

Rachel nodded. She wrote more stuff in her notebook. Then she put the pencil to her chin and thought a deep thought, then she wrote that down, too. Then she looked at him, made some writerly observation, wrote *that* down, and closed the notebook as if it was her most precious possession, or if not her *most* precious, then certainly more precious than Bliss, her moribund husband.

Why a writer? Why couldn't Rachel get an overwhelming desire to dress up in a short, pleated, schoolgirl skirt and ask Bliss to help her with her homework? He wrote that down in his own notebook, a small dead-end alley in his head that had been covered with so many layers of plaint and remorse that the words had lost all sense of meaning, not even resembling words, rather the random scratches of an idiot. One day he'd let a Dominican kid loose inside his skull with a can of spray paint, let the kid cover up his brain with paeans to Sammy Sosa, wiping out everything else. Maybe it would set Bliss free.

"Isn't the novel supposed to be dead?" he asked.

"It depends who you talk to."

"What if I talked to people who read books? What would they say?"

"The siren," she said, "does it 'wail' or does it 'scream'?"

"Maybe it's appropriate," he said, "using a dead art form to write about dead people."

Bliss maneuvered around several large holes and moguls to where the police cars were parked, identifying the scene of a homicide like a willow grove marks an underground stream.

He jammed on his brakes to avoid a sinkhole as big as a bassinet. This was one of the few dirt roads in New York City. The East Side ladies could bring their SUVs up here, navigating their Navigators around the holes and moguls, using their four-wheel drive for the first time, get some mud on their tires.

He parked and turned off the motor. He watched Rachel, like a kid at a parade, gaze at the uniformed officers milling around, the police divers, the photographer taking pictures, the M.E. bent over what he assumed was the corpse. Rachel was happy. She had gotten her way. Big surprise.

He envied her. *It must be nice to just watch*, he thought. *To only have to watch.* You didn't have to put on latex gloves to type a novel for fear of picking up a virus; didn't have to rub menthol under your nose while you mused over your characters because the smell of decomposing flesh might make you gag. Yes, in his next life he would come back as one of the watchers—gazing from the sidelines, observing with a cold eye. He'd muse. He'd write poetry and wear a beret and live in the Village with some young, raven-haired grad student with librarian glasses and a tattoo of Proust on her shoulder and they'd do some mutual musing, watching all the poor, hapless people who had to actually spend their days *doing* stuff, like being a cop.

He got out of the car and stood by the garbage-strewn bank of the East River, from whose swirling, fetid waters the floater had been pulled like a toy from last night's bath.

"There are some rubber gloves in the glove compartment," he said to Rachel.

"You should call it the 'rubber glove compartment,'" she said.

"*You* can. In your book: Chapter One: The Rubber Glove Compartment."

"Maybe I will."

He joined Rachel on the other side of the car. She held her rubber gloves in one hand, her notebook in the other, finger wedged in the middle, ready to flip it open. It reminded Bliss of how he flipped the safety on his gun before entering a hairy situation.

Ward saw them, walked over.

"If it isn't Ozzie and Harriet," Ward said.

"This is Rachel," Bliss said, adopting an overly officious tone while they were in earshot of the uniforms. He didn't want anyone knowing she was his wife. "Rachel's a *writer*, doing research for her novel. To make it more authentic."

Ward shook her hand with mock formality; then leaned close to her ear.

"Ride back with me," he said. "I'll show you stuff, make your novel a *lot* more authentic. Especially if you keep your rubber gloves on."

"Sure," Rachel said, smiling, flirting, Bliss thinking he used to get those smiles all the time.

Still holding Rachel's hand, Ward led them toward the water and the floater.

Like the African kapok tree, floaters have their own eco-
system. The Museum of Natural History should make an exhibit,
Bliss thought. The Floater. In the display case, a prostrate body
in a permanent state of decomposition, the pus in perpetual leak-
age, ears flapping in the simulated plastic current. Hanging by
invisible wires, the fat eels and worms and odd creatures that
have mutated in the East River as a result of the toxins and general twisted New York karma that had seeped into the water—
high-strung, anxious, angst-ridden fish with bags under their
eyes, gills wrinkled with worry, swimming off with one of the
floater's fingers or toes in their greedy mouths, elated they'd
gotten there ahead of the other fish, that they'd found a bar-
gain. Bliss could be the museum guide, talking with the visiting
fifth graders, pointing out the cracks in the cranium where the
blunt object came in contact with the floater's head, the frayed
strands of rope that once tied the body to the cement blocks
(heavy object of choice among those in corpse disposal). *And
what do you think, boys and girls, was the last thought that went
through this person's mind, wriggling and twisting helplessly as the
cement pulled him down and the dirty water filled his lungs? Anyone
have any ideas? Kids?*
    The police divers stood on the deck of the harbor patrol
boat, peeling off their wet suits. That's one duty Bliss couldn't
fathom. This wasn't the Grand Caymans, after all. You weren't
diving for conch and lobster. If you went in the water, it was
strictly to search for death. Hunting around in the semidarkness,
the East River a Hieronymus Bosch painting come to life. There
was a *reason* this water was murky, Bliss thought. Whatever was
on the bottom was not meant to be uncovered; it was supposed
to remain hidden until it, too, liquefied and was absorbed into

whatever version of fluid the East River consisted of. And besides the dangers of being in contact with the water, while the diver was looking for a body, there was the chance he could be hit on the head by a gun someone was tossing away, or a bag of bloody clothes, or even another body, tied to cement, sinking quickly and joining the biodiversity at the bottom of the river.

They moved closer to the river's edge, where the floater was. Rachel started to slow down.

"You okay?" he asked.

She nodded, but didn't say anything.

"You don't have to do this," he said.

"I'm fine," she said.

We'll see, Bliss thought.

Cardozo, the medical examiner, bent over the body like he was lining up a putt. He stood when he saw them. Cardozo was their jester. Whether they were in the dark basement of a decrepit brownstone in the Bronx or at the Plaza Hotel studying the crushed body of a jumper, Cardozo played the room. He was indomitable, always composed, no matter who was decomposing around him.

"Detective Bliss, my favorite Boy Scout," Cardozo said. "Looking to earn a new badge today?"

"Cardozo," Bliss said. They didn't shake hands. No one shook hands at a crime scene. Hands shrouded in rubber belonged to the investigation, gathering clues, servicing the truth. At the crime scene, your hands were no longer your own. He wondered if Rachel noticed.

Bliss introduced her to Cardozo, saying nothing about her being his wife.

"She's a writer," Bliss said.

"Nancy Drew to your Hardy Boys," he said. "How quaint." Cardozo gestured to the body. "Well, I hope she likes Chinese food, because that's what a lot of this guy looks like at this point. Mostly subgum chicken in white sauce. I'm afraid this guy's fortune cookie came up on the grim side."

The floater lay in the dirt. It looked out of place, like a floater out of water. It resembled a compost heap casually arranged in the shape of human being. Limbs loosely organized around the rotting hulk of the torso. Cardozo pointed to it with his toe.

"Howaya, pal," Cardozo said to the body, "Give me some skin." He turned to Rachel. "This is where the expression 'How's it hanging?' comes from," he said. "In case you were wondering."

Rachel stared at the body. He knew what she was feeling— the sickness, forcing herself to deal with it, pushing past the revulsion, desperate not to look weak.

"He trusts you, Rachel," Cardozo said, gesturing to the corpse. "He's only just met you and already he's opening up to you, spilling his guts."

Rachel swallowed hard, then lifted her eyes to Cardozo.

"How long has he been dead?" she asked.

Cardozo's face transformed into a mask of shocked dismay. "He's *dead?!*" He turned to the corpse. "Oh My God, you're right! Say, I'll bet you're a hell of a novelist, the way you interpreted his inner feelings like that."

"Knock it off, Cardozo," Ward said.

"Sorry. Actually, it's a good question. Glad *someone* asked. I would say by the advanced state of decomposition that he stayed in the bath just a little too long. Maybe three or four months."

"Any signs of trauma?" Bliss asked.

"There are *only* signs of trauma. What we need is a spot that doesn't look like it should be served with chopsticks."

"How about the cranium?"

"How about it?" Cardozo said, acting coy for Rachel's sake.

"Any dings, dents, blows, bullet holes?" Bliss asked.

"The stuff that dreams are made of?" Cardozo shook his head. "This guy's mind is like a sieve." He dismissed himself from Bliss and zeroed in on Rachel, eager for the new audience. "These detectives, they always want magic. They think I can gaze on a corpse, put my hand on a too-poor piece of rotting flesh and tell them everything they need to know: cause of death, the weapon, the motive—vengeance, inheritance, double indemnity, drugs. Like all this is discreetly tattooed on the dead body's skin and only I can decipher it—maps to missing evidence, X marks the spot."

"We want justice," Bliss said. "And if the murderer was waiting next to the dead body, doing a crossword puzzle until we arrived, his gun in a Ziploc, a confession typed and double-spaced, holding his own set of handcuffs and a stack of magazines to read in prison, then we wouldn't need you, Cardozo. But the murderers don't do that. So tell us, what do you see?"

Cardozo looked. For the moment, he saw nothing.

Then Rachel broke the silence.

"Hey, guys," she said, "is that a belt?"

And they all looked down and there, wrapped loosely around the floater's wasted waist, was the remnant of a belt and the dull metal of what was once the buckle.

And because Bliss had been so focused on Rachel, *she* was the one to notice the belt. Making Bliss look foolish. If the floater had any eyeballs left, they would have been rolling.

"Check those initials on the buckle," she said to Cardozo. The medical examiner obeyed at once, just the way Bliss did when she instructed him to pick up an errant pair of his socks.

Cardozo bent closer. "'F-H.' Ring any bells?"

Before Bliss could say anything, Rachel said, "I bet that's Felix Hernandez."

"Who?" Cardozo said.

"That guy that's been missing," she said. "You know, the landlord wanted him out from that rent-controlled apartment and he wouldn't go and then he disappeared."

"I knew that," Bliss said.

"It was all over the *Post* a few months . . ."

"I *remember!*" Bliss shouted. He had, after all, worked the case.

But the damage had been done.

"You should keep her around," Cardozo said. "She realized this guy is dead *and* she figured out who he is."

Bliss ignored Cardozo, wanted to ignore the whole thing.

"He have teeth enough to make an ID?" Bliss asked.

"I think he's got the minimum."

"See what you can do," Bliss said.

Then he grabbed Rachel by the arm and walked her to the car. She started to apologize. Bliss cut her off.

"Don't say anything."

He knew they were watching: Cardozo, the divers, the police photographer, the uniforms, all looking at them, but mostly at her, at Rachel, his still-alluring wife. He'd forgotten just how alluring she was until he saw other men admiring her.

It would all be in her novel. He knew that. A year from now he'd be reading the manuscript and it would all be in there.

"They're all staring at you," he said.

She ran her fingers through her hair and put just a bit more wiggle in her walk.

"Well, then I'm glad I wore my heels to the crime scene," she said. "Out of respect for the dead, of course."

Rick Purdy stood outside Ben's door, his hand resting on the knob that, he knew without trying, was locked from the inside. His son Ben was in there, getting ready for a party. Soon Ben would leave. Rick would say good-bye, receive no response.

His son had become a shadow, passing in and out of the doorways of his house.

That's why Rick wanted to talk to Ben now. Just for a few minutes. Talk to him in some kind of meaningful way. Or if not meaningful, then maybe some banter. A little friendly banter. He'd settle for banter, because at least it acknowledged that Ben knew he was alive.

But Ben was inaccessible. Locked in his sanctuary. His son, but not his son. Rick turned the door knob. It didn't move.

Consequences. That was the key. Repercussions. He'd read about it in magazine articles his wife Ellen had shoved in his face, as if it were a kind of punishment for peeing on the rug.

You don't set limits for Ben, she told him, again and again. *You don't establish consequences. You need to read this article. This book. You have to speak with a therapist.* Rick was floundering as a father. *You have to speak with a therapist right away!* Rick was failing. Rick was getting an F. F for father.

Rick picked at his nails.

Ellen hated it when he did that, picked or bit his nails. It reminded her of his weakness, of the fact that he never really accomplished anything on his own. *If it weren't for my father, we would be nowhere.* They *were* nowhere. Just nowhere in a penthouse.

Rick directed the retail operation of Ellen's father's luggage business in the Northeast. Rick almost never left his office—which was just as well. Rick hated luggage. People buying luggage were traveling, had a destination. People buying luggage had plans, were excited about going somewhere.

Rick had no plans, no itineraries. Rick was merely in luggage. In luggage.

He hadn't thought of that before, but it was the perfect description of him. In luggage. Crammed in, packed tight, locked down, something that had to be taken along, dragged or carried by the person going somewhere, the one doing the actual traveling.

He picked at his cuticle.

He picked and picked and picked.

Rick wanted to break down the door to his son's room. Run into it enough times with his shoulder so the wood buckled and the lock snapped. He knew he could do it. He'd done it so many times in his head, at night, lying in bed unable to sleep, thinking about his son.

His son, but no longer his son. A phantom.

Ben's friends could come and go as they pleased. Like Owen. Owen only had to knock once and Ben's door would open right up. But not for Rick.

So Rick had to break the door down.

But what would he do then? Standing in the doorway, his shoulder throbbing, what would he say? His son smirking, sitting on his bed smirking. Thinking about how he would tell his friends later, how his pathetically weird father broke down his door.

Rick backed away, retreated down the hall to the study, sat at his desk.

He had to come up with something to say.

After the wood cracked and buckled and he was standing face to face with his son, Rick had to think of what he would say.

And then he'd do it.

He'd break down the door.

He would.

Ben! he screamed. But the sound never left his head, just echoed there, like someone calling for help in a canyon in the middle of the desert, at night, and completely alone.

Ben!

Ben rang Owen's bell again.

"B.D.F!" he shouted. "Open the door!"

In fourth grade they had read a book by Roald Dahl called *The B.F.G.*—the Big Friendly Giant. Now, years later, Ben had adapted the acronym to suit his friend—B.D.F., Big Dumb Fuck. *Same as that book we read, Owen, about the giant.* Owen didn't realize the initials weren't the same. Sometimes their friendship reminded Ben of the two guys in *Of Mice and Men*, which they read last year in English. Only unlike Lennie in the book, his friend Owen had been getting laid regularly since ninth grade.

He rang the bell again. "Clara!" Ben shouted. No answer. She'd probably quit already. Some kids liked to shoot squirrels with BB guns. Owen's hobby was tormenting housekeepers. It was one of the few things he was actually good at it, the big dumb fuck. There was likely some support group back in the Philippines where all the housekeepers who had worked for the Gelmans would go and comfort each other, throw darts at Owen's picture hanging on the wall.

Finally the door opened. Owen stood there in a pair of red boxers, muscles taut, shoulders wide, wearing his usual mawkish grin.

"Chantal like it when you have those on?" Ben asked.

"She likes it better when I have them *off*," Owen said, putting extra emphasis on the word, so that Ben would be sure to know he was telling a joke. Then he gave his dumb laugh.

Ben walked in, then pushed the button on the side of the door so it would stay unlocked for the party.

"Good idea," Owen said.

"Let's go upstairs," Ben said.

"Yeah," Owen said. "C'mon. I have something to show you."

Ben led the way. Owen followed. As usual.

"Check this out," Owen said when they got to his room.

He turned on the TV and VCR. He hit "play." It was a surveillance video. The Gelmans had recently installed security cameras. A few weeks ago, they had watched a video of Owen's father coming home in the middle of the day with his secretary. Ben told Owen to hold on to it, save it for when he got himself in deep shit, like a "Get Out of Jail Free" card.

"This one stars yours truly," the B.D.F. said, barely able to contain his toothy grin.

There were two cameras, one aimed at the front stoop, one at the backyard. The video cut between them about every ten seconds. A grainy black-and-white image appeared on the screen, Owen and Chantal in the backyard, sitting on the bench; cut to a shot of the front door of the house. Cut back to Owen and Chantal, kissing now.

Ben had a sense of where this was going.

"I don't need to see this," Ben said.

Owen let it play.

Cut to the backyard, Chantal unzipping Owen's fly. Cut to the front door. Cut to the backyard, Chantal maneuvering Owen's cock out of his pants. Cut to the front door.

"I said I don't want to *see* this!" Ben ripped the remote out of Owen's hand and turned it off. Owen grabbed it back and they started wrestling. Owen could have crushed him in a second, but he let Ben pin him, the way he usually did. Ben squeezed Owen's thick wrist, digging his thumb hard into the pressure point until Owen's hand opened and the remote fell on to the rug.

Ben got up. Owen rubbed his wrist.

"What's your problem?" Owen asked.

"Nothing," Ben said. "Maybe I'm jealous."

"Yeah?"

Ben didn't let on whether he was joking or not. He wanted Chantal so bad. It pained him every time he thought about her with the B.D.F.

But tonight he had a plan. He put his hand in his pocket, found the small vial filled with white powder. Magic powder. A pinch in a girl's drink and you get the thing you're dreaming about. One little pinch takes a girl down the rabbit hole to Wonderland. It's where they want to go anyway, right? Isn't it where everyone wants to go? Wonderland?

The doorbell rang.

"You should get it," Ben said.

"You get it," Owen said.

"It's your party."

For some reason this seemed very funny. They both cracked up. The bell rang again.

"We'll both go," Owen said.

They walked down the two flights through the empty house to the front door. Ben opened it.

Standing there on the stoop, a cigarette in his mouth, was the last person Ben wanted to see, Billy Dix. Behind Billy was his friend T-Bone.

"Ben Purdy," Billy Dix said, smiling, the cigarette bobbing between his lips. "Just the man I'm looking for."

Ben didn't say anything. Ben owed Billy Dix some money for some drugs. Not a lot, but enough. He knew T-Bone was staring at him, hoping Ben would start something. T-Bone was always hoping someone would start something.

Billy Dix took a deep drag from the cigarette and flicked it over the railing.

"I hear your friend Owen's having a party," Billy Dix said to him. "Aren't you going to invite us in?"

Finished with the floater, his wife in the car buried in her notebook, Bliss took a moment alone by the water's edge. The sun was starting to go down. A cool breeze came across the water. Bliss had a clammy feeling, as though he was taking a bath in tub full of the East River, getting more soiled instead of clean.

Ward came over, stood next to him.

"Felix is back," Bliss said.

"As the song says, *There's got to be a morning after*."

And Felix was the toothless slattern he now found sharing his pillow in the cruel light of dawn.

Behind him, Bliss heard the distinctive sound of the body bag being zipped shut. Cardozo had a name for it. "Wrap this

one up to go," he said. Bliss had to hand it to the guy—keeping a sense of humor in the face of what was often faceless. He wondered if Cardozo did yoga.

A tugboat passed by, pushing a barge the size of a football field packed with yesterday's garbage. A dull, dusky smell accompanied it. The evening sun was glistening on the black plastic bags mounded like a sinister chocolate icing. It was only about twenty yards away.

"If we each grab an end of the body bag," Bliss said, "we could toss Felix onto the barge."

Felix would be dumped somewhere far away, wherever they took the garbage now that the Fresh Kills landfill was closed (and seeing how long Felix had been dead, Fresh Kills wasn't the proper place for him, anyway). He'd be buried along with the other bags under a ton of waste. And that would be that.

"We're homicide," Ward said. "Not sanitation."

"It's still waste management," Bliss said.

Waste of life, waste of time, a wasting of his soul.

The barge headed out under the Triborough Bridge to the harbor—another lost opportunity.

"You okay, Lenny?" his partner asked.

"I thought we were done with Felix."

"We'll reinterview. Go over the leads again." Ward said.

"There are no leads."

"We know it's a homicide now."

"We knew it was homicide then. We just didn't have a body."

"What else can we do?"

"Once I visited Cori's second grade class," he said. "It was Dad's Show and Tell Day. I brought in my handcuffs, my badge, a spent Uzi cartridge from that shooting on 112th Street."

"I remember. Uzi cartridges everywhere," Ward said, "like rice after a wedding."

"I told the kids some stories," he said. "I let them hold the nightstick I used back when I was in uniform."

"I remember that stick."

"Cori said all the kids agreed I was the coolest dad. The other dads brought in boring stuff—X rays, law books, floor plans of skyscrapers, genuine stock certificates. But Cori's teacher said I was probably the bravest. She said Cori should be proud of me."

"So what's the problem?"

"I don't know. I'm thinking maybe being one of the boring dads might not be so bad. Sitting behind a desk instead of dealing with floaters before dinner."

"That could be the title of your memoirs. *Floaters Before Dinner: A Life in Homicide.*"

He turned away from his partner, looked out over the water. There was supposed to be solace in a river as it flowed out to the sea. Didn't poets write about it?

Just a few yards away, by the water's edge, a father and son were fishing, using surf casting rods to send chunks of bait into the swift current of the East River. Bliss couldn't help thinking working homicide was much the same, waiting for a bite, day after day, hoping for a nibble, yet knowing that whatever they pulled from the water would be unclean, unnatural, and much better off left where it was.

Chantal was with her friend Julia in the cab on the way to the party.

"Owen wants me to let him do it tonight. It's his birthday. He wants it to be his birthday present."

"What's wrong with a tie?"

Chantal started laughing.

"Or taking him out for a sundae? Hot fudge."

"Stop," she said, catching her breath. She and Julia used to laugh all the time. They only had to look at each other and laughter happened.

Not so much anymore. Not since Owen.

Chantal could hear the party as soon as she and Julia got out of the cab. Blink 182 was playing through an open window. She recognized a couple of kids smoking on the front stoop, beer cans tucked behind their backs.

"Hey," she said as they walked up to the front door.

"Hey, Chantal, Julia," came the unison response. Chantal rang the bell.

"It's open," one of the kids on the stoop said.

Chantal turned the knob and walked inside. Julia followed. In the foyer was a huge blow-up of Owen's brother Holden on the cover of *Seventeen*.

The lights were low; the smell of pot hung in the air.

Then Ben, Owen's best friend, descended the staircase wearing what must have been Owen's mother's fur coat—inside out, the mink next to his body, dressed only his boxers.

"Come into my lair," he said, spreading his arms wide. He reminded Chantal of one of the demented creatures in *The Island of Dr. Moreau*—half man, half beast. "Come into my furry lair." He wrapped the coat around Chantal, drawing her into the fur. He knelt down in front of her.

"Let me kiss the ring," he said, putting his lips up to her belly button, pierced with a silver ring. "Ah, your holiness—no pun intended—bless me."

Chantal put her hands on Ben's head.

"Bless you, my child," she said.

"What are you wasting your time with Owen for, when you could be with me?" he said. "Don't you know I love you?" He stuck out his tongue and buried it in her stomach.

"Cut it out," she said, and playfully pushed him away.

"But I love you, Chantal," he said.

Julia grabbed her arm, started pulling her toward the front door.

"Let's go," Julia said.

"We only just got here," Chantal said.

"Stay, oh fair Chantal!" Ben moaned.

"Then at least let's go upstairs," Julia said.

Julia led her up the steps. Chantal looked back to see Ben still on his knees, his arms reaching up, like he was praying.

"I love you, Chantal!" he cried.

Then Julia yanked her around the banister and into the living room on the second floor.

When Julia and Chantal were out of sight, Ben rushed into the kitchen to make them drinks. He put them on a little tray, but before heading upstairs, he ducked into the bathroom and locked the door. He moved the fake clamshell with the stupid shell soaps and rested the glasses on the sink. He carefully measured a pinch of the powder into each drink, stirring them until the powder disappeared.

One for Chantal and one for Julia.

Cheers, ladies.

Then Ben would just sit back and let the fun begin.

The fur felt smooth against his skin. People should walk around with fur next to them all the time. Maybe some people did. Later, he might try laying the coat on the bed when he was screwing Julia. Or Chantal. He wasn't sure which. He'd have to see how things developed. Maybe he could get some play from both of them. You never knew what could happen, once they got to Wonderland.

Bliss sat on the living room couch listening to "Green Onions" by Booker T. and the MGs with his twelve-year-old daughter Cori. Julia had left already to go to some party. Rachel was at the comedy club. Her last set ever, she said, now that she was a novelist.

Cori probably should have been in bed, but since they were home alone, Bliss was breaking rules. As many rules as he could.

"Another soda, Sweetie?"

"Two was enough," she said.

"Let me know."

"Is that his real name?" she asked. "Booker T.?"

"Yeah."

"What's he play?"

"The organ. That's Steve Cropper on guitar."

Cori nodded. "He's good. Funky."

This was no casual session, but an integral part of his calculated scheme to protect Cori from listening to pop music. The plan was to inundate her with classic blues and soul which, like a vaccine, would fight off any kind of Top Forty infection. So far it was working. Cori preferred Aretha to Britney, the Coasters to 'N Sync. She knew all the words to Wilson Pickett's "In the Midnight Hour." Bliss only had a few cc's of James Brown and Sly and the Family Stone left before he felt his treatment was complete.

Let her listen to what she wants, Rachel had said. But he'd done that with Julia and the results were devastating. One whining Joni Mitchell wannabe after another. Like they all came from some island, like a place Gulliver landed on his travels— a country where all the women carried guitars and sang in self-important contraltos about what they did that morning and everyone worshiped them. He wondered if the tickets to their concerts had little white strings attached to them.

Bliss was determined that Cori wasn't going to be corrupted.

"Nice groove," Cori said.

"Down home," said Bliss. "Classic Memphis soul."

"It's getting late, Dad. Mom said . . ."

"It's okay."

"I just don't want you getting in trouble."

"It's okay. Really."

When Bliss first thought about having kids, he dreamed of moments like this, sitting on the couch playing one record after another (CDs hadn't been on the scene when he first had the dream); the two of them just listening, not saying anything, just tapping their toes. The moment had never been right with Julia. But Cori had responded, and with Rachel preoccupied with her comedy, Bliss had more time to shape and mold Cori into the kind of cool, hep chick he had in mind.

"I wish Julia was here," Cori said.

"When she's home, you fight. When she's gone, you miss her."

"We're sisters."

"Tell me about it." He hit the remote and changed the CD. Aaron Neville's ethereal tenor filled the room.

> *If you wa-a-a-ant*
> *Something to play with*
> *Go and find yourself a toy . . .*

"Aaron Neville, man, no one can sing like him."

"That's a boy?"

"Yeah. With arms like tree trunks. Tattoos and everything."

"Weird."

"But beautiful."

"Did Mom ask Julia to get me a picture of Holden Gelman tonight?"

"The boy on TV?"

"Yup. That's where the party is and I wanted Julia to get me a picture."

"Maybe Mom told her."

"I never got to hear Mom perform." Cori said. "And now she's not doing comedy anymore."

"You're too young."

"Did it ever bug you that she made fun of you?"

"She doesn't make fun."

"She makes jokes. About your job. I know *that* much."

"What I do, being a detective, sometimes it's dangerous. People like to laugh at things that are dangerous. They need to. That's why so many comics do routines about flying. It's something everyone gets nervous about. Scared. So they laugh."

"Do you get scared?"

"In airplanes? No."

"What about when you're looking for bad guys?"

"No. Not then, either."

"Because you're tough, right, Daddy?

He nodded. He thought about Felix's decomposing corpse, how it didn't bother him, how death hardly ever bothered him anymore. Maybe *that's* what he should really be scared of.

Then Cori did this thing, she put her hand up in front of her, fingers spread open, like she was a mime doing the old invisible wall trick. And Bliss lightly pressed his fingertips up to hers. They stayed that way, their hands meeting together in a gentle touch and they listened to Aaron Neville on the living room couch.

> *Tell it like it is*
> *Don't be ashamed*
> *Let your conscience be your guide.*

"I love you, Cori," Bliss said. It just came out.

"I love you, too, Dad. Even though you lied to me."

"About what?"

"About not being scared."

Chantal and Julia walked through the second floor, looking for Owen. A couple was making out feverishly on the couch, his hand under her shirt. A group of three girls were dancing together. A cluster of kids hovered by an open window passing a joint around. Julia recognized most of them from school.

But then a boy she didn't know began staring at Chantal. There was an unsettling stillness about him. He took a drink

from a bottle of vodka. He turned to the boy next to him, someone else she didn't know, said something, then he looked at her
again.

The boy walked over and stood directly in front of her,
studying her, like she was behind glass.

"I'm Billy Dix," he said.

"I'm going to the bathroom," Julia said. But Chantal knew
Julia just wanted to get away from these boys. Sometimes she
wondered if Julia even *liked* boys. "You coming, Chantal?"

Billy Dix kept her fixed in his gaze.

"You're Chantal, right?" he asked.

She gave a furtive nod. Where was Owen? It was supposed
to be the two of them together. His birthday. This wasn't the
kind of party she expected.

"Ben told me all about you," Billy Dix said.

"You know Ben?" she said.

"Oh yeah," Billy Dix said. "Ben and I are good pals. We go
way back." Billy Dix put his hand on her shoulder.

"Oh," she said.

"Speak of the devil," Billy Dix said.

She eased out from under his hand and turned to see Ben
coming toward them, still in the fur coat. He carried a tray with
two drinks.

"Where's Julia?" he asked.

"She'll be right back," Chantal said.

"I hope so. Here's yours."

Chantal took big gulp of the vodka and orange juice. She
needed it. She wasn't sure anymore that she wanted to let Owen
do it tonight. He should be there, now, *with* her, his arm around
her shoulder, so she could look into his eyes instead of those of
this freaky stranger.

"Where's Owen?" she asked.

"Upstairs," Ben said. "He'll come down for you when he's ready, he said."

She took another drink. Billy Dix was watching her the whole time, staring at her breasts, not even trying to hide it.

"Nice," he said.

Julia came back. Ben handed her a drink. She took a tiny sip. She never drank much.

"Not thirsty?" Ben said.

Julia ignored him. "You ready to go, Chantal?" she asked.

Then Chantal heard a voice that made her smile.

"Chantal's not going anywhere before she dances with me."

It was Malcolm Marcoux. Even though he was a senior, he had taken a liking to Chantal. He told her she reminded him of some French actress in some French movie Chantal had never heard of. Malcom was improbably handsome. Everyone in school knew he was gay, except Malcolm himself.

"Hey, Malcolm," Chantal said.

Ben and Billy looked disgusted.

Someone put on some disco. Malcolm let out a whoop. "It's Hustle time!"

She finished the rest of her drink and happily let Malcolm whisk her away. He was a great dancer. Instantly they were twirling around the room.

Ben and Billy Dix stood together, staring at her. Once, when they moved close, she heard Ben's voice.

"Fucking faggot."

He said it loud enough for Malcolm to hear, but Malcolm never stopped, never looked over, as if Ben wasn't even there.

* * *

Bliss lay in bed next to his wife, waiting for the front door to open and his daughter to walk in. It was almost 12:30. Still a half-hour left before curfew.

This whole curfew thing was new to him. Bliss didn't have a curfew growing up. The concept hadn't occurred to his parents. His mother would stroke his cheek before he went out, not saying anything, just touching him tenderly, perhaps fearing she might not see him again. There were a couple of kids in the neighborhood who didn't make it back from a Saturday night, arrested after robbing a store or mugging someone. Or both. Others wound up wrapping their cars around telephone poles. *Be careful, Lenny,* her eyes would say. *My only son.*

His father, the cop, offered him words of caution, some fatherly advice. *Don't come home dead, Lenny,* his father would say. *I don't want to be working your fucking case tomorrow.*

He wondered what he would do if Julia didn't come home before her curfew. Wondered how he'd handle it if it got to be three in the morning and she still wasn't back, Bliss still lying there in bed, eyes bugging out of his head with worry. Would he go to the party and pick her up, barge in, his badge out, combing the apartment for his daughter—calling her name, embarrassing her for the rest of her life? And what if he found her in the arms of a boy, her tongue in his mouth, his tongue in hers? And what if they had gone further? What would he do if they were lying together in bed, the boy on top of her . . .

He flung off the covers and got out of bed, going to the kitchen for a beer, trying to drive the image out of his head, the boy on top of Julia and what Bliss would do to him, this poor, pimply fifteen-year-old who dared invade the sanctity of Detective Lenny Bliss's daughter.

He sat at the table, drank one beer, then opened another. He wasn't sure if he was up to this daughter thing. He wondered if it was too late to get her into Spence or one of the other all-girl schools. He wondered if there was a Jewish equivalent of a nunnery. If not, he could start one.

He finished the beer, dragged himself down the hall back to bed, knowing sleep would not come easily.

"Chantal."

She thought she heard someone calling her.

It must have been Owen. She hadn't seen him yet, she was so busy dancing.

She followed the voice upstairs. On the way, she suddenly felt dizzy. She had to lean against the wall to keep from falling. She loved him. She really did. But she didn't want to do it to-night. Didn't feel like it now. Maybe in the morning. She could stay with him. They could spend the whole night together in each other's arms and then make love in the morning, like the couple in the pregnancy tester commercial.

"Chantal."

He seemed far away, like he was calling to her across huge dunes, the sound distorted by swirling winds.

"Chantal."

Now his voice was right in front of her. Surprise.

She walked in. Darkness. Candles.

Cool, Chantal thought. She took the last sip of the vodka and orange juice Ben had given her and set it down on the table, only there was no table so the glass fell on the floor. It made her laugh.

He was curled up in bed, turned away from her, doing something to make the bed wavy, like she was seeing it through waves of shimmering heat. Wavy bed. Wavy wavy bed. She giggled.

"Hi," he said in a whisper, like they were in the library.

"Shhhhh," she whispered back. "No talking in the library." Her voice sounded strange, like it wasn't her own. She wasn't even sure she was talking out loud or if these were just thoughts.

"It's my birthday," he said.

"I know."

"Close the door," he said.

She turned. Or maybe she stood still and the room turned. Her hand found the door and she shoved it closed. She turned back to the bed, but someone had moved the bed and it wasn't where it was just a second ago. It was like a game. Now it was on the other side of the room, so she went there.

She wanted to tell Owen about her idea. That they would spend the whole night together just holding each other.

"Take off your shirt," he said.

She could do that, she guessed. She crossed her arms and grabbed on to the bottom of her shirt and lifted it up, but her arms somehow got tangled and the shirt was stuck in front of her face. It was kind of funny, stuck inside her own shirt, like being a little kid. She tried again and this time it came off.

"Come into bed," he whispered.

She did. He didn't have any clothes on. His body was warm. She grabbed him and rested her head by his shoulder and closed her eyes. This is nice, she thought. She drifted off to sleep. But then she was on her side and his arms were around her.

"It's my birthday," he said.

He started kissing her, kissing her all over, burying his mouth in her neck. It tickled and she began to laugh but someone was already laughing for her, someone on the other side of the room laughing. *I love you,* he said, his mouth close to her ear. It made her smile hearing him say it. *I love you, Chantal.* Finally saying it. She was floating in the air. But also she was under water. In the air and under water at the same time.

Then he moved on top of her, using his knees to spread her legs apart, which was okay because her pants were on, but then she felt a sharp pain in her vagina and she realized somehow her pants weren't on and he was inside her and she knew she should be afraid, that she should push him off her, but *that* Chantal, the one who was terrified, *that* Chantal seemed far away, behind thick glass, thick frosted glass, just a hazy silhouette of a little girl trying to get someone's attention, flapping her arms, banging on the glass, trying to get someone's attention. The glass was way too thick but still the little girl tried to tell someone that something was horribly wrong. Who was she trying to warn, Chantal wondered, this poor girl pitifully banging on the glass like that?

Chantal closed her eyes and drifted away, wondering what the girl behind the thick glass could possibly have to say to her that was so important?

Bliss woke up with a start. He checked the clock. 3:18. He got out of bed and looked in Julia's room. It was empty. He checked the sofa. Both bathrooms. She wasn't there.

Her friend Chantal's number was posted in the kitchen. He called. No answer.

He remembered where Cori said the party was, the kid with the brother on TV, and looked the number up in the school directory. He called, got an answering machine.

He should go back to bed, he thought. He hit redial, got the machine again.

It was 3:18. His daughter should be home.

He wrote down the address. He threw on some pants and a sweatshirt and put on his sneakers without bothering to hunt down some socks. He stuck his gun into the back of his pants and headed out the door.

There was no traffic going across the park and he was on the East Side in minutes. He found the address, a townhouse off Park Avenue.

Bliss took the front steps two at a time and rang the bell. Nothing. He rang again. No one came. He tried the knob. It turned. He went inside.

"Hello," he called out. "I'm Julia's father."

No answer. An eerie silence.

"Hello?!"

It seemed over. Nothing left but the distinctive smell of cigarettes, beer, and pot.

A few hours ago, Julia was here. Having fun. Laughing. Talking about stuff that was important to her. Flirting. Dancing. Commiserating. Being alive. Being very much alive. The real Julia. Full of feeling and vitality. It wasn't fair that he couldn't see any of that. As Dad, he only got the sardonic Julia. The jaded, weary Julia. Why didn't he get the laughing Julia? Where was the justice in that?

It was his fault. He didn't get her listening to Aretha early enough. Didn't blast Brother Ray singing "Hit the Road, Jack" into her crib, Otis doing "Try a Little Tenderness" as her lullaby. He had only himself to blame.

Something, some kind of animal was lying on the floor. It took him a moment to realize it was a fur coat. He headed toward the back of the house, not sure where to start, only knowing he wanted to find Julia before he went upstairs, where he assumed the bedrooms were.

He did not want to find her in one of the bedrooms.

The house was like the scene of some natural disaster, some plague that wiped out everyone at the party, then caused their bodies to disintegrate. Like Pompeii. Evidence of the chaos was everywhere. Ashtrays, plastic cups, planters filled with cigarette butts. Bowls of chips, half-eaten sandwiches, nuts, and popcorn littered the floor. This was some of the most expensive real estate in the world. Now it looked as if squatters were living here.

Julia wasn't in the library, curled up in one of the leather chairs with a book, some dusty old volume, *Great Expectations*, which she started and couldn't put down. *Oh, hi, Daddy. Is the party over? I was just reading about Mrs. Haversham.* No, that was too much to ask for. On the floor, an oddly shaped bottle, one of those expensive single malt Scotches. Empty. Daddy wasn't going to be happy.

He walked back to the hallway. He would have to look further.

He went up one flight.

He felt a twinge of pain in his hands and realized his fists were clenched tight. This was a foolish venture. Unnatural. He shouldn't be there. But he wanted to find his daughter. What was unnatural about that?

She probably went to a friend's. Chantal's house. She must have gone there, put on their pajamas, made hot cocoa, and watched reruns of *Bewitched*.

Then he went up one more flight, to the bedrooms.

"Hello. Julia's father. Police."

Father. Julia's police.

"Hello."

He pushed on. He opened the first bedroom door, just a crack. From the dim glow of the streetlight through the window he could see a boy in his bed. Alone. Trophies on the dresser, clothes on the floor. Batman on the bedspread. Sleeping alone. Good.

In the other room, another boy. Also alone. Very good.

What would he have done had he found Julia in there?

He took the stairs two at a time to the top floor, to the parent's bedroom, the blankets twisted as if people had been wrestling. Oh, but they weren't wrestling. Teen lust running rampant. *Reefer Madness!*

He should be looking for clues. He was a detective. From the shards of residue he would piece together some kind of story, a likely scenario, recreate the party in its entirety and figure out what happened to his daughter, why she wasn't home.

But he wasn't sure where to start. There was so much chaos. And where were the parents?

He went back downstairs. Julia wasn't in the house. There was nothing more he could do. He went out the way he came, feeling more unsettled than when he arrived. He knew if he wasn't a cop he wouldn't be acting this way—*Julia's father, Julia's police*. But he had seen too much. His wasn't some abstract sense of evil, the "bad things" that happened to "other people." His knowledge was firsthand, and that hand might be bloody, might be missing fingers, might be frozen in death begging for mercy that would never be granted.

He drove back home. He called Chantal again. Still no answer. He got out of his clothes and grabbed another beer from the fridge to drink in bed in bed, hoping sleep would claim him for a little while.

As he was walking to his room, Cori's door opened and Julia emerged in her pajamas, staring at him, her father and protector, in his tired boxers, holding a half-finished beer.

She didn't say anything by way of a greeting.

"When'd you get home?" he asked.

"I don't know. Hours ago." She yawned. "I was being quiet. I thought you were sleeping."

"How was the party?" he asked. "You drink a lot or a little?"

"Nice try, Dad," she said. "I only stayed about ten minutes."

"Oh."

"It was stupid," she said. "When I got back, Cori was up. She had a nightmare. About you. That you were behind a wall calling for help but she couldn't help you because the wall was too high."

"I know that wall," he said.

"I stayed with her for a while. I guess I fell asleep."

Bliss nodded, scratched his belly, realized what he was doing, then stopped. Good thing he hadn't scratched his nuts.

"I'm going to go to the bathroom now," she said. "Then I'm going back to bed."

"Okay," he said.

She stood there a moment longer, perhaps waiting for her father to say something wise. He thought for a moment about telling her where he'd just come from, but that would have been too reckless, even for him.

She sighed and walked past him down the hall, but just before she went in the bathroom, she stopped and turned.

"Good night, Lady Bliss,'" she said.

He smiled. Once he told her that his favorite jazz player of all time, Lester Young, called people he cared about "Lady," his own unique term of respect. It was where Billie Holiday got her nickname "Lady Day."

He watched her close the bathroom door. He took a long swig of his beer and thought that maybe his daughter might just love him after all.

SUNDAY

It took Clara a few moments to realize that the hairy mass lying on the living room floor Sunday morning was the Missus's fur coat. It lay there like a dead animal, the sleeve stretched out, as if it had been beaten to death as it tried to crawl away.

How did children become like this?

The house was a shambles. Beds distressed on every floor, lamps tipped over, bottles and cans of beer everywhere. Clusters of crumbs in corners that looked like the work of raccoons, an alarming design on the coffee table made entirely of green olives—some kind of portrait, perhaps, or maybe a message to Clara, warning her to leave this house, this family, now! Before she got in any deeper. She should probably heed the advice. A person got only so many warnings.

In the master bathroom a bottle of shampoo had been tipped over and had leaked into the corner. The dark red shampoo the Missus used to color her roots between visits to the salon. Sienna. Clara knew. She'd once come back with the wrong shade from the drug store and had to go back for the right one. There was a puddle of Sienna pooled in the corner of the bathroom, like fish blood on the deck of her grandfather's boat, to be washed away at the end of the day with buckets of sea water.

She got down on her hands and knees and used one of the damp towels to clean up the shampoo. Then she went to Mister Owen's room, opened the door a crack, saw him asleep. *When was the Louisiana Purchase, Mister Owen? What was the Rosetta stone? Who was Charlemagne?* Ignorant child. She closed the door.

She opened the brother's door but stopped when she saw the bare feet sticking out under the blankets. Owen's friend. He often slept over. She would clean these bedrooms tomorrow. Let sleeping dogs lie.

Clara went downstairs to deal with the fur coat. It was wet, incredibly heavy, soaked with beer, like someone had used it as a mop. She grabbed a sleeve and dragged it to the back of the house, leaving a damp smear on the carpeting like a trail of blood. She opened the door and swung the coat out. It fell with a loud splat on the·flagstone in the garden. Maybe the sun would dry it out. She really didn't care one way or the other.

The cost of that coat was probably equal to all the money she would send back to the Philippines over the next five years— money for her children to go to school. She tried not to think about how much of their lives she was missing. Annie would be eleven soon. Jimmy, six. They lived with Clara's mother. She kept in touch as best she could, photographs and phone calls her only connection to the changes in her children's lives— tricycles giving way to two-wheelers, hair growing longer, teeth lost or gained.

She shook her head, checked her watch, then fought off the wave of tiredness that brought her near tears. But she refused to let these people make her cry. She had to keep moving, so she could get home and write her daily letter to her children. She would nap later, on the subway, hopefully not sleeping past her stop.

Clara trudged to the basement and put the sheets in the washing machine. With any luck she would finish before Mister Owen woke up.

* * *

Every fight tells a story. That's the way Dom DeMoro saw it. Every round a chapter. It wasn't about any one punch, any single combination. He'd fought a kid from Red Hook once who Dom hit a dozen times a round. Solid right hands. Pummeled him. The kid's third-generation Red Hook Italian blood splattered across Dom's own back, a wide red streak down his arm where the kid rubbed his face against him in the clinches, the way a puppy nuzzled against you when it wanted to be scratched. The kid took everything Dom had. Soaked it up, each punch just drizzle in the desert. At the end, Dom's arm was raised, Dom got the decision, but the story of that fight belonged to the kid from Red Hook.

Every fight told a story and you either made it *your* story or you wound up on your back in the center of the ring. It's what Dom enjoyed. Not hurting someone, but manipulating them, making them do what you wanted, forcing them into your story. Ali could do that. Make the other guy think he was in control, but really he was just a pawn, a minor character in Ali's script. Disposable. And he doesn't realize it until he's lying on his back, not knowing his name, not knowing anything except that the bell is ringing and the fight is over. Maybe not even knowing that.

Dom DeMoro thought about this while standing on the sidelines of the baseball field in his black Canali suit and shades, watching Jonah play T-ball. Dom had never known about T-ball before he started working security for Jonah's family. It struck him as about the most ridiculous thing he'd ever seen. Kids whacking a ball off a post and running around the bases while the team in the field swarmed around the ball, practically fought over it like hyenas over fresh kill. Jonah's parents were in Bermuda for the weekend. Rosa, Jonah's nanny, stood next to Dom, cheering Jonah on, shouting to him in Spanish.

Dom liked this kid Jonah. Why not? It was the parents who were screwed up. The kid was just a kid.

Dom could have waited in the limo for the T-ball game to be over, but he liked standing on the sideline, his dark presence an intrusion on the bright green field, dressed in his suit and turtleneck on a warm spring morning. Jonah's dad liked having Dom around, the little lawyer with his very own pet goon on a leash driving his limo, opening doors for him, keeping tabs on his kid. Retaining muscle like Dom made the lawyer feel important, that he had a reason to fear some kind of menace. Like anyone would actually give a rat's ass about him.

Dom scoped the rest of the parents lining the first and third base lines, cheering for their kids, as if hitting a ball off a tee was actually an accomplishment of some kind. This being the T-Ball league for the Upper East Side, they were driving Jaguars and Navigators to the field, decked out in their Ralph Lauren shorts and sweaters, the women in fancy workout clothes, all with cell phones, maybe keeping the grandparents posted on the score. Maybe not.

Though they looked trim and healthy, Dom didn't think there was anyone on the sidelines that morning who could take a punch. Not even from a flyweight.

Eleven decisions—ten KOs. One loss. Every fight a story.

You didn't beat a man simply by knocking him out. Any boxer can knock out any other boxer of the same weight with one clean, solid punch. That was a given. So to win, you had to give the fight your ending. You fight your opponent's story, you lose. It was that simple.

Jonah stepped up to the tee to bat.

"Heet the ball!" Rosa shouted. "*Arriba,* Jonah. *Arriba!*"

Jonah swung and missed. Jesus. The kid missed a ball sitting on a tee. The father was in Bermuda instead of teaching his son how to bat. Jonah looked over to Dom for encouragement. Dom made a fist. Jonah nodded, like he'd seen some athlete do, some guy on the Yankees probably. The father had season tickets. The father ate perfectly aged steaks from exclusive butchers. The father drank wine that was a hundred dollars a bottle. But his kid couldn't hit a fucking ball that was resting on a tee.

Jonah dug in and swung. He missed again.

A hush fell over the crowd. A strikeout in T-ball was pretty rare, humiliating for everyone concerned. Maybe that's why Jonah's dad was in Bermuda.

Words of encouragement rained down on Jonah from parents on both teams. *C'mon, Jonah. You can do it.* But instead being spurred on, Jonah looked like he was about to cry.

Dom decided to help the little guy out.

"Time," he shouted, and sauntered toward the batter's box. Jonah's coach looked at him in wonder, but Dom didn't give a shit.

"Only coaches on the field," someone yelled from the other team. Dom glanced up, found the source of the voice, a guy with a matching pastel cap and T-shirt proclaiming him Team Parent. Dom gave the guy The Look, the one Dom had perfected in center ring before a fight, for the stare-down, the look that said *I'm about to pummel you senseless and then kill you by driving your nose into your brain.*

The Look shut Mr. Team Parent up.

Dom approached Jonah. The kid was practically trembling.

"Howaya, Jonah?"

"Okay," Jonah said.

Dom pointed at a spot in the dirt with the toe of his soft leather loafer a few inches in front of the tee.

"Put your left foot here," he said. Then he pointed to another spot just behind the tee. "Your right foot here," he said. Jonah obliged. Dom then moved Jonah's hands so they touched, so there was no space between them as he gripped the bat.

"Bend your knees," Dom said.

Jonah bent his knees.

"Now hit the shit out of the ball," Dom said. He walked back to the sidelines, taking his time, adjusting his sunglasses. He smiled at one of the moms. They didn't look like the moms he remembered growing up. These moms had the fat sucked out of their thighs, their tits surgically adjusted toward the heavens. They didn't necessarily look real, but they looked good, especially with their clothes on.

He turned as Jonah ripped a liner past the third baseman.

"*Muy bien*, Jonah!" Rosa shouted. Jonah smiled proudly. But as Dom was bending down to wipe the dirt from his loafers, he saw Jonah still standing in the batter's box.

Dom shook his head. He forgot to tell the kid to run to first.

They sat at the breakfast table, just the two of them, both girls still asleep. He held the typed pages of Rachel's novel. Three so far. More to follow. Like a virus, multiplying.

He read.

The floater wasn't floating anymore, Mae thought. It lay now on the hard ground, ~~doleful~~ *sad, like a human puddle.*

"Mae?" Bliss said, looking up.

"Mae Stark—Homicide," Rachel said.

"Mae Stark." Bliss mulled it over. "The 'Stark' part sounds tough. But 'Mae'? That's what you say when you're asking permission."

"I may change it."

"What about 'human puddle'?"

"What about it?"

"It's a little . . ."

"What? He was human, he was lying on the ground. Puddles lie on the ground. He was useless, unwanted, a remnant, just like a puddle is a remnant of the rain. Hence, *human puddle*."

"Oh."

"It's called *writing*," she said. "It's what writers do. We *write*."

Beginnings are always hard, he thought.

He read on.

What had once been a life now resembled Chinese food—what had once loved and laughed and held someone close in moments of deep passion now looked like subgum chicken.

"That was Cardozo's line."

"Not exactly."

"But close enough."

"Just read," she said.

He read.

But it still had a story to tell. Every corpse did. A secret hidden in its bones. Someone did this to me, it said. It called out to Mae with its rotten, toothless mouth. Imploring her. Please, find out who it was who killed me.

Mae felt a presence. Her new partner ~~Julius Hank Seymour~~ Rock . . .

"Rock?"

"What about it?" Rachel said.

"No one's actually named 'Rock,'" he said.

"Of course they are. Anyway, it doesn't matter. It's evocative. You hear 'Rock,' you immediately think 'swarthy,' 'rugged.'"

"I think porn star."

"Read."

". . . *new partner Rock sauntered over and stood next to her. Mae slid her left hand behind her back to hide her wedding ring, then remembered she wasn't wearing it. As of last Friday, she wasn't married anymore. She had to keep reminding herself. And what a* ~~joy~~ *relief that was.*

"'Relief?'"

"I knew you would say something about that," Rachel said. "If you're going to get bogged down in the trivialities, maybe it's better you don't read it."

"I guess one person's 'triviality' another person's getting kicked in the nuts."

"Is that what you call them?"

"What do you mean?"

"Is that the word cops use? When you're by yourselves, in the locker room, getting changed." She opened her notebook, her pencil poised. "Do you say 'nuts' or 'balls' or 'cojones' or 'jewels' or what?"

"Different guys say different things."

"So there's not one standard cop word." She wrote something down anyway. "What about for the penis—'cock' or 'dick'?"

"We say 'weenie,'" Bliss said. "But usually we're too busy knitting sweaters to be thinking such dirty thoughts."

Rachel wrote more stuff in her notebook, then closed it. She was in love with her notebook. Her husband was just another human puddle.

"You ever talk to Julia about sex?" he asked her.

"A little bit," Rachel said. "She gets it in school."

"Sex?"

"No. Information."

"Putting the condom on the cucumber and stuff like that?"

"The condom on the cucumber is later," Rachel said. "Why? You think she's doing it?"

"Have you noticed any cucumbers missing lately?"

"Very funny."

"For the little kids," he asked, "you think they use a Kirby cucumber?"

"I *mean*, Lenny, do you think she's doing it with a boy?"

"She'd say something to you, wouldn't she?" He looked over at her. "I mean, she'd say something to her mom."

"Why should she say anything to me?"

"I just thought she would," Bliss said.

"Did she say something to you?" Rachel asked him.

"No," he said. "So why does Mae feel so relieved that she's not married?"

"I haven't decided," she said. "Maybe he stopped fascinating her. He couldn't compete with the excitement of her job."

"Oh," Bliss said.

"It's just a book," she said, yawning. "It's made up."

"I'll read the rest later." He handed it back.

"Okay."

They sat in silence for a few moments. Then Rachel turned to her pages, reading them intently. She smiled, she bit her lip, she shook her head and crossed something out, she took a sip of coffee, swallowed, got an idea and wrote something down, looked at it, closed her eyes, opened them and wrote something else, bit her lip again, took another sip of coffee, then smiled with satisfaction.

This is what it would be like when the girls are gone, Bliss thought. Just the three of them. Bliss, Rachel, and Mae Stark. And sometimes Rock.

Bliss scoped the *Daily News*. He'd been hoping Reagan or the pope might have died in the night and usurped the front page, but no, there it was—"Felix Floats."

Felix Floats.

Dom stared at the *Daily News* lying next to him on the front seat of the limo. "The light's green, Dom," Jonah said.

He pulled forward, focused on the street. A taxi swerved in front of him and he had to hit the brake and turn sharply.

Felix Floats.

Felix Hernandez, whose windpipe Dom had constricted in such a way as to sufficiently impede his breathing so that Felix strongly considered getting dead.

Fucking Felix.

Maybe the knots came undone. Dom should have paid more attention in Boy Scouts. Or maybe the rope had rotted away.

He should have buried Felix out in Jersey somewhere. But it was hard to find a spot to bury someone if you didn't know of one already. People didn't realize that. Burying takes time, and then leaves freshly dug earth in the shape of a grave. Kids find it playing hide-and-seek. Hunters stumble on it. Teenagers making out. Dom had heard about a case just like it when he was a rookie cop—kid and his dog just knocking around in the woods when they stumbled on what looks exactly like a spot where someone buried another human being. The kid was only seven, but he knew just what it was. *Jeepers, I bet that's a grave,*

Spot. It looks freshly dug. We gotta call the police. Not a flower bed. Not an animal digging for food. Not the landing site of a small alien spacecraft. But a grave. *Gee, Spot, I guess someone got killed and the murderer buried him here. Boy, was that guy stupid!*

So the river seemed like the right decision at the time. Tie Felix up to a pair of cement blocks and dump him in the river.

"You missed the turn," Jonah said from the back.

He had passed Jonah's street.

"I thought you wanted some ice cream," Dom said, quickly covering up. "After your big hit."

"I forgot to run to first," Jonah said.

"Yeah, but you'll never forget that again, will you?"

"No way."

"You got to learn from your mistakes," Dom said.

Like the mistake Dom must have made, allowing Felix to float. The case would be reopened. A new spark of interest. Before, they only suspected Felix was dead. Now they knew for sure.

Now it was a homicide.

He double-parked in front of the Ben and Jerry's store and waited as Rosa took Jonah inside to get a cone.

He'd gone over the scenario hundreds of times in his head, looking for loose ends, the way he would have when he was a cop. Nothing came to mind. Because Dom hadn't planned it, and sometimes *not* planning works out better. No discernible motive, nothing to go on. Felix just went all Humpty on him and Dom dumped him in the river. But Felix didn't stay down. He came back.

Just like the Dominican.

The Dominican—on his back in the eighth round. Out. Motionless. Dom standing over him, staring down at him.

Knowing he had done it. He had told the story of this fight ex-actly the way he wanted, setting the Dominican up, leading with his left, straight left-hand jabs for seven rounds, opening the eighth with a solid right, then another, then another, then a left uppercut that came from nowhere, that the Dominican hadn't seen all fight, the punch Dom had been saving, that put the Dominican down and out. Out.

Dom stood in the corner, watched the ref start the count. At three, Dom saw the Dominican blinking his eyes. At five, he had a glove on the rope. At seven, he was on one knee. And at nine, he was on his feet. Like a bad dream he was back on his feet. He wouldn't stay down. Then, before Dom could charge in and pummel him, the bell rang.

In Dom's story, the Dominican stayed down. The End. But now the Dominican was back, smirking at him across the ring. And Dom wasn't sure he had enough left to write a new end-ing. The bell rang, and Dom stepped out into the center of what he feared most—not the Dominican, but the uncertainty.

And now Felix was giving him that same feeling.

He wouldn't stay down.

A knock on the front window startled him. His alarm must have scared Jonah, who stood holding out an ice cream cone with a look of trepidation. Dom smiled and lowered the window.

"I got this for you," Jonah said. "Thanks for teaching me how to hit."

Jonah turned back to Rosa who smiled approvingly.

"He pay with his own money, Mr. Dom," Rosa said.

Jonah nodded, and pushed the cone toward him.

"Thanks," Dom said. "You're a good kid, Jonah."

"Back at ya," Jonah said, something Dom had taught him.

Rosa grabbed Jonah's glove from the back seat and told Dom they were walking home. That left Dom free for the rest of the day.

He tossed the ice cream cone out the window and headed toward the FDR, which would take him to the Brooklyn Bridge, which would take him home.

You have to learn from your mistakes.

He thought about Felix's wife Celia, her dark eyes, her glistening skin, stopping by before leaving for her mother's house in Puerto Rico, spending the afternoon with him. It was then that Dom realized you've never had sex until you've had it with a woman whose husband you popped.

But as Sonny Liston once said: *Life a funny thing.*

Felix had been the consequence of his first job after leaving the force. He contacted the lawyers he'd met at trials where Dom had to testify, let them know he was free for any kind of work they needed—security, surveillance, just being around in places where it was good to have someone like Dom around.

His first job involved getting a handful of tenants out of a building on the Lower East Side. Five old people and one Puerto Rican. Dom would get ten grand for his troubles. Cash money. No paperwork. No accountability. And soon, no more crossing the bridge. He could already taste his apartment in Manhattan.

Dom approached his new job like one of his fights. He worked the ring. Every fight told a story.

Round one, he'd wait until the old people left their apartments, then let himself in with the passkey. Each apartment had that certain old-person smell. *Eau de Old.* Not any one specific aroma, but a combination of a whole lot of things dying all at once. These weren't classy old people. These were forgotten old people, waiting to go to nursing homes until they died. They didn't need their own apartments anyway. They'd be happier somewhere else, someplace bright and clean where someone else cooked their meals. They'd have to be. Anyone would.

So Dom helped them along to the next phase of their lives. But with savvy, on his toes, always on his toes.

Once in their apartments, he'd empty their milk containers, hide their hair brushes, toothpaste, shaving cream. He'd take the batteries out of their radios and remote controls, tear pages from the books by their beds, put photo albums in the freezer.

He changed the locks. One of the women went out to the pharmacy to pick up her prescription and came back to find her key didn't work. She tried for an hour, but it was no good. Dom watched through the keyhole from the empty apartment across the hall. Watched her wringing her hands, wondering why this was happening, if she was going mad. Then pee started dripping down her leg and Dom had to turn away, disgusted.

This was just to soften them up. For the middle rounds, the construction started. Dom hired a Polack, fresh off the boat, hardly spoke any English. He gave him a hammer, some two-by-fours and showed him what he wanted: bang the wood. Not building anything, not constructing. Just banging. Constantly. Put the two-by-fours against the wall and wail away. Make the house vibrate. The Polack must have thought Dom was crazy, or that this was some kind of strange American custom. A few days later, the guy showed up with his cousin and made it clear with gestures and a phrase book that for fifty dollars a day, his cousin would be happy to bang on wood, too. They kept it up for twelve hours each day. After the first week, the two old ladies were gone.

That left two old men and the Puerto Rican couple.

Dom thought he was making good progress, but the lawyer said the landlord was getting antsy. Every month they were in there he lost thousands in rent.

So for the late rounds, Dom got the landlord to give him some cash. He grabbed one old guy in the hallway, just as he was putting the key in his door. Snuck up behind him, threw his arm around the guy's neck and started tightening it, just a touch. He felt so fragile, Dom was afraid he might break, like the guy was made of balsa wood.

"Take my wallet," the old man said. "Just don't hurt me."

"I'm not going to hurt you," Dom said. "Just don't say anything. Don't call out. Just listen. I'm going to let you go and you're going to walk in your apartment and close the door. You're not going to turn around. You understand?"

A barely perceptible nod.

"Good. I'm going to put a bag in front of your door. It's going to have a thousand dollars in it. If you pick up that bag and take it inside, it means you are going to move out of your apartment by the end of the week. If you don't take the bag, I'll sneak up behind you one day just like I did now and I'll throw you down the stairs headfirst and if you're not dead, I'll pick you up and throw you down again. You understand?"

The nod was stronger. Fear gives you strength, even if you're ancient.

"All right, now walk inside and don't turn around. However many mistakes you've made in your life, you turn around now, it will be the biggest one you ever made."

He slowly let go. The old man did as he was told. Dom left the money. Ten minutes later, it was gone. The next day, the old man was gone, too.

One old man down, one to go. Dom felt good. So far, no one had gotten hurt.

The last old man was easy. Dom used the passkey to let himself into the apartment while the guy was asleep. He took a half-dozen eggs out of his refrigerator and put them in a pot on the stove. No water. Then he turned the heat on high. After ten minutes he called the fire department. The stink from the burnt eggs was horrible. Dom did it again two nights later. The next day, the guy's son came and took him away, fearing his father would burn himself up.

By this time contruction had started, apartments were being renovated, Andrej, the Polish guy, and his cousin turned out to actually be carpenters and were working for the landlord. Everything was going according to plan.

That left the Puerto Rican couple—Felix Hernandez and his wife.

Felix drove a livery cab during the day, then he'd drink and play dominoes until late. When he'd finally made it home, he'd either pass out or slap his wife a few times and *then* pass out. Dom wasn't sure what story he wanted to tell in his bout with Felix. The banging didn't seem to bother him. He was out all day and his wife went to a relative's or something until it quieted down. Dom turned off their power for a few days, turned off the heat even though it was the middle of winter. The guy was oblivious.

The wife's name was Celia. Maybe it was some kind of ar-ranged marriage because she was at least fifteen years younger than Felix. She had a childlike face that was just beginning to harden around the edges. Dom had remained invisible to the other ten-ants, but for Celia he revealed himself. He hung out with her, told her jokes and made her laugh. He brought her food and they had lunch together. She hated Felix, she told him. When he touched her, she felt sick. When he hit her, she wanted to kill him.

"He cheats at dominoes," she told him. "The other drivers think he's a fool."

Dom was in the basement when he heard a loud smack and Celia's scream. He came up, not caring now if Felix saw him. He opened their door with the passkey and saw Felix whaling away at Celia in their living room. Before Felix had time to react, Dom threw a thick arm around Felix's neck and crushed his windpipe. He lifted him off the ground and jiggled him a few times. Felix's legs twitched and then he hung limp.

Dom dropped him in a heap. The wife used the wall to help herself up. Her eye was purple and already swelling. They both stared at the body.

"You have family in Puerto Rico?" Dom asked.

"Yes," she said.

"Go there. I'll give you money. Don't come back for a year, at least. You understand?"

"Yes."

Every fight told a story. This one he was telling after the final bell.

"Felix beat you one too many times. You ran away. The last time you saw him, he was trying to hit you with a hammer. You don't know anything else. You understand, Celia?"

"I understand."

She stared down at her husband, took a long, hard look at the man who had tormented her.

"*Adios*, motherfucker," she said. Then she spit on her husband's lifeless body.

She turned and walked out without looking back. She didn't say thank you. But then her husband had just died, so Dom figured she was too bereaved.

Chantal woke up. She didn't recognize the bed. She didn't recognize the room. Her head hurt. Her vagina hurt. She had a vague memory of something happening. Something bad.

She bolted up, but a sharp pain tore through her head and she had to lie back down.

She started to cry. She wanted her mother, but her mother was still in the Hamptons.

"Are you okay?"

She recognized the gentle lilt in that voice.

"Malcolm."

"You're finally up."

"Did you take me home?"

"I gave you my silk pj's. I had to sleep in flannel."

"I guess I had too much to drink."

"Or something."

She closed her eyes. She tried to remember last night, but couldn't get it clear. She had gone upstairs and Owen called to her and she dropped her drink and she got in bed. She couldn't wrap her mind around anything else.

"Help me," she said, reaching out to Malcolm. "Get me to the bathroom, I have to . . ."

But it was already on its way up. She clamped her mouth shut on the bitterness and Malcolm practically carried her to the bathroom. She got most of it in the sink, but some landed on the floor, splattering the white rug.

"I'm sorry, Malcolm. I'm really sorry."

But then her head started spinning again and she lurched back to the bed.

"It's okay, baby," Malcolm said. "You didn't hit the silk."

She wanted to smile, but she was overcome by a wave of exhaustion and she curled up and closed her eyes. But just before she fell asleep, something flashed in her mind. As she was vomiting, she remembered seeing her hand, braced against the sink, seeing it clearly in the bright light of the bathroom, her hand seemed to be stained with blood.

Bliss sat at his desk at the precinct, the Felix Hernandez file open in front of him. Four months had passed since the initial investigation. Then Felix floated. Cardozo said the frigid winter waters kept Felix from rotting so fast. But then he heard the birds chirping and he decided to pop up to the surface, one more bud flowering in these early days of spring, only Felix was a vile blossom.

Fucking Felix. Why couldn't he have stayed put?

Bliss looked at the file. The names brought back memories, none of them jolly:

Celia. Felix's wife. Twenty-two years old, her tender, dark eyes showing the strain of living with Felix. He'd beaten her. Friends had confirmed it. Finally she had enough. She told Bliss she left him, went home to her mother in Puerto Rico. She knew nothing about Felix since she walked out the door. Bliss remembered her golden skin.

He flipped to the next page. Andrej, the building's super. Spoke broken English. Wore cheap running suits, looked like he was waiting for some Eastern European dictator to come back to power. Any dictator, it didn't matter. Bliss remembered asking Andrej where the last tenants went. He didn't know. *They move, I throw their shit out. They get old and die, I throw their shit out.* Now Bliss would have to go back and ask him if he threw Felix out, too.

Then there were the tenants—two old woman and two old men. None of them lucid. One old guy been convinced someone was playing tricks on him, telling Bliss that an imp was changing his locks, pouring out his milk. Then he recapped a Dodgers-Braves game from 1958 pitch by pitch, down to the final at-bat when Ralph Kiner hit a game-winning double off Warren Spahn.

He flipped to the next page. Empty, except for a note to himself: $4M.

He remembered the phone conversation with his father-in-law, Anton.

Bliss had called him about the building where Felix lived. Not only was his father-in-law in real estate, but he knew everything there was to know about making money in New York.

"Lower East Side?" Anton said, speaking in his usual staccato bursts. "Hot neighborhood. How many units?"

"Sixteen."

"Right. Some units likely rent stabilized. Rent—a thousand a month. Some rent controlled. Those, five, six hundred a month. Total rent, maybe eleven, twelve thousand a month. From that comes maintenance, heat, taxes. Get the tenants out. Renovate to eight two-bedroom condos—half-million each. Four mil total."

Four million dollars was definitely a motive.

Then Anton made his usual pitch for Bliss become his head of security.

"Not as a favor, Lenny. You know I don't do favors. This is a *need*. Security. I have to hire someone. Might as well be the best."

Bliss said no. He always said no. He was a detective. He had wrongs to right. He had Felix's killer to find.

Bliss closed the file. It reminded him of studying for a test in high school. He would talk to Felix's relatives and friends again. They would all say the same thing. Everybody would say the same thing. Reopening a case without new, substantial evidence was an exercise in futility. Or whatever was one notch below futility—watching Madonna try to act. Or Bliss visiting his father in Florida.

Iron Butterfly, Ward would say. Which meant they had nothing to go on, no clues, in the middle of nowhere—in a gadda da fucking vida.

It took only ten minutes on the Bruckner Expressway to completely undo the last three days of relaxation and massage and Pilates and aromatherapy and poached fish at the spa. The limo inched forward in fits and starts, horns bleating around her. Nedra Gelman sat in the back and attempted to relax, to embrace the Bruckner, which had become a river of ire, and let it flow through her, but an unexpected stop sent her lurching forward, and suddenly her neck hurt again.

She dug her phone out of her purse and called her son Holden in L.A. If talking with him didn't relax her, at least it might take her mind off how *un*relaxed she was.

"Hello?"

He sounded groggy, even though it was already eleven o'clock on the Coast.

"Did I wake you?" she asked.

"Who is this? How did you get my number?"

"It's your mom."

"Yeah?" He didn't believe her. "What was the name of our dog when I was a kid?"

She thought for a moment.

"We never had a dog."

"Hey, Mom. What's up?"

"It's Sunday. I'm calling to say hello."

"Oh." He yawned loudly into the phone and made clicking noises with his tongue. "So thanks for calling. See ya."

"Wait."

"What?"

"You keeping up with your studies?"

"Yeah."

"How's the new tutor?"

"Cute."

"I'm serious. Is Arnie taking care of you?"

Holden was staying with her brother, who supposedly directed commercials, but seemed to work only on occasion, surviving now on the money they sent him to watch Holden. Arnie had a large house in the Hollywood Hills that he bought when he was working steadily.

"Yeah. We went out on a double date the other night. Two sisters. Arnie took the younger one."

"Are you serious?"

"Mom, this is Hollywood. Everyone's always serious, except when they're not."

It was like one of those riddles you had to solve in order to get past the wizard who guarded the bridge. Nedra decided it was better to not try to figure it out. She'd get the story from Arnie later, though it would probably be just as vague. She should have known better than to trust her son with the man who had the last ponytail in L.A.

"Did you call your brother Owen on his birthday?" she asked.

"Not yet. Did you?"

"Not yet. Did you?"

"Did *you?*"

"Did *you?!*"

She giggled. Sometimes it was like talking to her best girlfriend with her youngest son.

"Listen, Mom," Holden said, "tell Owen happy birthday *for* me. Will you?"

"Fine. You're probably too busy anyway."

"It's true. Tell him for his present I'll get him a picture of Heather Graham topless. Listen, gotta go, Mom. Love you."

"Love you, too, baby. I'll be out to see you next week. Bye."

He was all grown up. *Beyond* grown up. She sighed and looked out the window.

There was a slowdown on the Triborough Bridge. There always seemed to be a slowdown on the Triborough Bridge. It wasn't fair. They should have a separate lane for the limos. The Limo Lane. She'd pay more. It was worth a hundred bucks to get through this traffic. Plenty of her friends would do the same. The city could use the money for repairs. New orange cones. Longer lunch breaks for the toll collectors. She didn't care.

She closed her eyes, trying to relax, trying to find the flow, but in her heart Nedra knew there weren't enough mantras in the whole universe to deal with traffic on the Triborough.

Dom parked the limo in front of the gym and walked up the three flights. The dull sound of fists hitting leather mixed with the rapid patter of jump ropes greeted him at the top landing. He hadn't put on his gloves in a while. But Felix floating seemed like a sign that maybe he should sharpen up his reflexes.

Learn from your mistakes.

Every fight told a story, and he felt the thread of this one starting to slip away.

The gym was crowded. Most fighters kept full-time jobs, so Sunday evening was a popular time to work out. He changed, putting his shoes in the bottom of the locker and carefully placing his neatly folded suit on the shoes, so the wool wouldn't have to come in contact with the locker itself, which was rusted on the bottom and smelled from fifty years of sweat.

Once in his shorts, he went to Solomon, one of the trainers, to tie the laces on his gloves. It always struck him as odd how helpless a fighter was once he had his gloves on. This engine of destruction couldn't tie his own shoes. All he could do was punch.

"Good to see you back, Dom," Solomon said.

"Thanks."

"Take it slow."

And he did. He went through his regular routine, ten minutes on the speed bag, ten on the heavy bag. Then Solomon put on the thick pads and Dom worked on his combinations. Solomon would call out the combination he wanted Dom to throw, then move his hands to the exact spot so the pads took Dom's blows— left jab, left hook, straight right; straight left, right hook; right hook, straight left, straight right. They worked together this way for twenty minutes, Dom not throwing the punches as hard as he could, but working the combinations, over and over, to get them deep into his body. So there was no more thinking. You think in the ring, you lose. Like what happened to Joe Louis.

After twenty minutes, Dom was tired. He got some water and sat on a bench, his head leaning against a locker. Two black kids were sparring; Solomon and Ollie, another trainer, stood on opposite sides, leaning on the ropes, shouting instructions. Neither kid had much stuff. Both were thick-armed, tightly muscled with ferocious grimaces behind their headgear. But neither was a boxer. On the street, they were probably feared. Kids in the neighborhood might run out of the borough, might jump off a roof rather than take punishment from either of them. But in the ring, they were only to be pitied. No jabs. Right hands thrown from too low. Telegraphing every punch. Dom wrote a story where he knocked out the shorter one in round two. Knocking out the other guy required four rounds, but no more.

Then Dom saw a face from the old days, off in the corner, shadowboxing by himself. Arturo had been a rising middleweight, maybe the one hope the gym had for a contender. But then, in a tune-up in Jersey City, Arturo killed a guy in the ring. A Korean kid, twenty-one years old. Arturo had him against the ropes, hitting him at will, but the Korean wouldn't go down. Arturo stepped back, waiting for the ref to stop, *begging* the ref to stop it, but the ref gestured to keep fighting. Arturo knew it was over. That the Korean's will was all that was keeping him up.

The ref yelled at him, the crowd booed. So Arturo moved in. The Korean instinctively threw a right hand and, just as instinctively, the way he'd done for fifteen of the twenty-eight years of his life, Arturo slipped the punch and threw a combination that started with a right to the kidneys and ended three punches later with a left uppercut to the chin and the Korean fell in a dead heap and that's what he remained until three days later when his cousin cremated his body and sent the ashes to his family back in Seoul.

Arturo never fought again. He kept training, but when the time came for him to fight, he disappeared and didn't show up at the gym for six months. Solomon and Ollie kept working with him, as if Arturo was their best hope, their one chance for a champion and some long green. Arturo would probably have jumped off a bridge if they hadn't.

Dom got Solomon to snip the tape off his gloves and untie them. Then Dom slid a jump rope from the hook on the wall. He hadn't done any rope work in a while, but soon the rope was a blur and Dom was losing himself in the rhythm. He was still light on his feet. For a big man, he'd always been light on his feet.

He showered and changed and got back in the limo and headed home. But the sense of ease only lasted until he caught a glimpse of the newspaper on the front seat; *Felix Floats*.

The bell rang. Round one was over.

Walking back to his corner, Dom knew he was already behind on points.

"You promised you would do the alto players tonight," Cori said.

"It's late," he said.

"Can't you just read her a book before she goes to bed like everyone else?" Rachel said, standing in the doorway.

"How about the adventures of Mae Stark, Homicide," Bliss said.

"You think you're so funny, flatfoot," Rachel said. "Good night, Cori. I love you."

"Love you too, Mom," Cori called out, then turned to him, waiting for Bliss to begin.

"Sidney Bechet was the first," he said, "even though he didn't play alto. He played soprano sax, but he influenced Johnny Hodges, who *did* play alto. His nickname was Rabbit."

"How come?"

"Nobody knows." Which may or may not have been true. But Bliss needed to keep up the appearance of his expertise.

"Who was next?"

"Benny Carter. He also played sweet, like Rabbit, but he had slightly more complexity."

"Did he have a nickname?"

"No. But Charlie Parker did."

"Bird!"

"Right. Bird was next. He took the alto and all of jazz to a whole new place. Bird was like electricity," he said.

"What do you mean?" Cori asked.

What *did* he mean? Speaking to her, he came up with stuff he didn't know he knew.

"It was like once electricity was discovered," he said, working it out, "no one lived their life in the same way. Once Bird started playing, it was like electricity had been discovered in jazz and no one could play like they used to."

"Who's that lady you were talking about?"

"When?"

"Before," she said, impatient that he didn't know exactly what she was talking about at all times. "The lady in the story you were going to read me," she said.

"Oh. Mae Stark."

"Yeah."

"She's the hero of the book Mom's writing."

"She's a detective, too?"

"Mmm-hmm."

"Oh," Cori said, taking this in. "Mom's writing a book about being a detective."

"Yes."

"She probably wants to be just like you," Cori said.

"Who, Mae?

"No," Cori said. "Mom."

"You think so?" Bliss said.

Cori nodded. "Who else would Mom want to be like?"

MONDAY

Clara saw the note the Missus had left for her about taking the fur coat to the cleaner. It was too heavy to carry. She would have to take a cab, though she might have a hard time convincing the driver to let her put it in his trunk.

The buzzer on the dryer sounded and Clara went down to the basement to retrieve the sheets. She trudged up the three flights to the Missus's bedroom, where she folded them and put them away in the linen closet. On the way back downstairs, she decided to poke her head into Mr. Holden's room, to see what kind of nasty damage Owen's friend had done in there.

She opened the door. Feet were sticking out from the Batman blanket. The same as yesterday. She pushed the door further and walked in. It was then that the smell hit her and she knew what it was. Though she'd never seen a dead person before, she knew this was the way death smelled. Moving further into the room, she saw where the blood had stained the far side of the pillow and had soaked into the rug, which was now a deep crimson. She crossed herself and prayed the Missus wouldn't make her try to clean it.

Then she called the police.

"What are you going to say to him?!" Ellen shouted. "He never called! He never came home! He missed his curfew! He didn't do his homework!"

Her eyes were wide with anger, her voice like a scalpel. Rick bit the corner of his nail until it bled. He looked at the corners of all his nails, the tips of his fingers, gnawed and ravaged. It was like he was at war with himself and this was the battlefield.

"What are you going to say to him, Rick?! What are you going to do?!"

Rick wasn't exactly sure what he was going to say or do.

"He's grounded," Rick said. "I'll ground him."

Ben cursed Rick and gave his father the finger.

Rick grabbed Ben by the shirt and shoved him against the wall, going eyeball to eyeball with his son. Rick spoke in a low, measured tone, without faltering. Rick was in command.

"I do not expect my son to act this way. There will be repercussions. There will be consequences! No exceptions! I am unwavering!"

"How long will you ground him?"

"A week."

"And that's how you're going to say it? Like that?"

"Like what?"

"Like it's a question? Like he has the option?"

"Why are you doing this, Dad?" Ben asked, his voice quivering.

"Because I'm your father!" Rick shouted. "This is how a father's supposed to act. Consequences! Repercussions!" Rick spat these words in his son's face.

"Rick."

Ben's face softened.

"I'm sorry, Dad," Ben said, tears welling in his eyes.

"What are you going to say, Rick?!"

"From now on, Dad," Ben said, emotion cracking his voice, "I'll be the son you want me to be. Thanks for showing me the right way."

And Rick opened his arms and his son walked into them. And Rick hugged his son tightly.

"Rick!"

"What? What the hell do you want?"

"You're getting angry at me?" she said, her eyes wide, incredulous. "Your son is out of control and you're angry at *me?* Use it on him! Take that anger and use it on your son." She shook her head in disgust. "You stupid, stupid man. You have no idea what's going on around you, what's happening to the people you supposedly love."

In her dream, the floater appeared to Mae dressed in a fancy tuxedo and top hat, tap dancing like Fred Astaire. He sang a song that revealed his killer. When the phone woke her she was smiling. The case was solved. It took her a moment to realize it was only a dream, which was somewhat of a relief, because the name the floater gave her as his ruthless, psychopathic murderer was her soon-to-be ex-husband.

"Again with the husband," Bliss said, throwing the pages down on the table.

Rachel could barely contain her smile as she sipped her coffee.

"What's funny?" he asked.

"I think it's cute that you're upset."

Bliss didn't want to be cute. He wanted to be indomitable.

"You ever dream about your cases?" she asked.

"Yes."

"Why don't you ever tell me about them?"

"They wouldn't make sense to you. They're dreams. The one Mae had, that's a book dream. Characters in novels have dreams like that. Homicide dreams are more like the dreams Indians deep in the Amazon rain forest have, dreams that go back to the beginning of time, serpents entwined, wrapped together, tails in each other's mouths, impenetrable."

"Oh," she said, contrite now. "I see, Mr. Margaret Mead."

Bliss was glad to see she hadn't taken out her notebook, hadn't written anything down.

Then the phone rang. It was Ward.

"We got a Bob Crane," he said.

"Yes," Bliss said, thinking this could be what he was hoping for, a case to take priority over Felix. Invoking Hogan of *Hogan's Heroes* meant someone had been mysteriously bludgeoned to death. Possibly in a motel room, but that part was not essential. There weren't that many motels in Manhattan.

"Where?" Bliss asked.

"Triple L," Ward said. (Location, location, location.) "A townhouse. Lieutenant says we're working this together. Garcia will take over the Felix case."

Bingo.

Ward gave him an address, where to meet him, so they could alert the parents of the dead boy, see if they were calm enough to talk.

Bliss hung up the phone, started to get his gun. Excited. A case worthy of his time and energy.

"I'm going, too," Rachel said.

"We have to notify the next of kin."

"Can't I notify them with you?" she said, following him into their bedroom. "That would be incredible."

"No," he said.

"Please," she said.

"Stick with Felix. He's your case."

"This one sounds better," she said. "It's fresh."

"Sorry."

He put on his holster, took out his piece, checked the clip, checked the safety, put it back in his holster. He grabbed his jacket and headed to the front door, his lovely novelist wife right behind him.

"Can't I just watch?" she said.

"They'll be sad." He turned to her. "That's the way next of kin get when they find out someone they love is dead. Put it in your notebook: Next of kin—Sad."

"I want to see how they react."

"Make it up," Bliss said walking out the door. "Isn't that what writers do?"

Fuck fuck fuck fuck fuck fuck fuck.

Fred Gelman was in his hotel room in London when the phone rang and some reporter was asking him what he thought about Owen's friend being dead, about Owen's girlfriend going missing.

Fred told the guy he had no idea what the fuck he was talking about and hung up. How did the reporter know where he was staying?

Two seconds later, Nedra called.

"What's going on?" he asked her, while with his free hand he was dialing his cell phone to see if his girlfriend Sheena could come right over, sensing he might soon be leaving unexpectedly for New York.

Nedra started telling him about the party, how Ben was found naked in Holden's bed with his skull crushed.

"And Chantal is missing," Nedra said.

Who was Ben? Who the fuck was Chantal? What did this have to do with him?

"The police want to know what happened."

He held the cell phone to his other ear, listening to it ring, hoping Sheena was home.

"You there, Fred?" Nedra asked. "Are you hearing me?"

"Hold on, Nedra," he said.

Sheena answered. He put his hand over Nedra's receiver and whispered to Sheena to get right over, he might be leaving soon. He clicked off, got back on the other phone.

"Call Douglas," he told Nedra. Douglas was his lawyer.

"I did," she said.

"So why do I have to come back?" he said. "Douglas will deal with everything whether I'm there or not." His cell rang. He checked the ID. It was Douglas. "Nedra, I'll call you right back."

Douglas told him that a dead boy in his house took precedence over whatever deal or tryst he had planned and that he should get on the next plane to New York.

He called Nedra back, but the new housekeeper, whose name he couldn't remember, said that Nedra was "having massage" and couldn't be disturbed. Fred imagined her on the bed surrounded by candles, all that aroma bullshit she was into. Listen, if it made her happy. All he wanted was to make her happy. He hung up.

Isabella, the masseuse, was one of a small legion of people Fred employed—math tutors, English tutors, S.A.T. tutors, karate instructors, piano teachers, interior designers, nannies, housekeepers, carpet cleaners, window washers, dog walkers, more tutors to tutor the other tutors, soothsayers, jesters, whothefuck knew who they all were. He had enough to put on his own Broadway show—half of them were out-of-work actors anyway. But he needed them to make Nedra's life easier, to make her happy. Fred was vaguely aware of their passage through his house. He of course didn't mind when the young and exotic Isabella came over. Fred shared his fantasies with his friends whose wives also got their massages from Isabella. Because what made Nedra's friends happiest was to do everything the same—exactly the same. So-and-so went to Costa Rica or bought an espresso maker or got her lips thickened, now Nedra has to do it—with the same doctor at the same time of day, probably wanting to use the same needles if she could—the ones you used on Laura's lips, Doc. Just wipe them off. That's the difference between men and women, he thought. His friend got something he wanted, Fred wouldn't settle for the same, he'd have to get the one that was bigger and better.

Fred poured himself a drink. He didn't want to get on a plane, leave London a day early, missing the closing on the hotel, his last night with Sheena. But despite Fred's best efforts, he couldn't undo the fact that seventeen years ago he had copulated with his wife and the resulting procreation meant he had a son named Owen whose friend wound up dead and whose girlfriend was missing.

Fuck fuck fuck fuck fuck fuck fuck.

Sheena arrived late because of London traffic, which was even worse than New York's, so he told her to hop in the limo. They could get in a quick screw on the way to Heathrow. Sheena wasted no time, sitting on his lap, pressed herself against him, her tongue doing the hully-gully in his mouth. She slid down to the floor and maneuvered his joint out of his pants. She did this with great dexterity. He wondered if it was a trait of all Scottish girls. He wondered if there was a way to find this out.

She ran her tongue around the tip of his cock and then took it in her mouth. After a minute, she lifted her head and looked up at him, batting her eyes.

"Hello," she said. "My name's Sheena, what's yours?" Which is what she always said whenever she fellated him, a reminder of when they'd first met.

She raised herself up, hoisted her skirt and eased herself onto him. Her warmth and wetness surprised him. She wasn't wearing her Marks and Spencers. She came prepared. He came inside her, quickly. She didn't mind. She never seemed to mind. Good thing, he thought. A woman he slept with once told him he fucked like he was double-parked.

Sheena slid off him and sunk back on the seat. He pulled up his trousers.

"I'll miss you," he said.

"How come you have to go back?"

"A boy was found dead in my house."

"It's always something with you," she said, but with a smile.

"I'll buy another building quick," he said.

At the airport, the ticket agent informed him they didn't have room for him in first class.

"My son's friend has been brutally murdered!" he shouted at the prissy young man behind the counter with those permanently pursed putty lips like Hugh Grant's. "The boy was like another son to me! And you can't secure me a decent seat?!" The wanker worked it out. They always worked it out whenever Fred went ballistic. Fred could run rampant over these stolid English prigs anytime he wanted. He wished they put up more of a fight.

He boarded the plane, gave his jacket to the flight attendant, who he noticed had a trim figure under her uniform. He took his seat and closed his eyes.

Douglas would be waiting for him at Kennedy when he arrived. Douglas would have things under control by then, assembled the necessary people, his conduits to the cops, his well-connected thugs, like the ex-boxer who put in the security cameras.

Then Fred realized he should have asked Douglas if Owen was under suspicion. Whether his own son might be a suspect in the murder.

Fred should definitely have asked Douglas about that.

Fuck fuck fuck fuck fuck.

The flight attendant came over to make sure everything was okay. She was in her late thirties, very classy.

"Can I get you anything?" she asked in her elegant English accent, her voice soft and soothing.

"Another Scotch," he said. "Neat."

"Of course," she said, smiling, Fred trying to figure out if that was her official smile or one meant especially for him.

He closed his eyes.

Why couldn't Owen get his shit together like Holden? It would be harder then for people to see Fred's fatherly fuck-ups.

Holden. Fred could never forgive himself for allowing Nedra to call him that ridiculous name. Cost him a thousand bucks, too. Nedra had consulted a "prenatal spiritual counselor," some fragile orchid of a woman (*she has a degree in prenatal spiritual counseling?* Fred had asked) who came to their house and lit a shitload of scented candles so the room smelled like a taxicab and laid her hands on Nedra's ballooning belly. The woman closed her eyes and listened for something she called a "prenatal vibration" in Nedra's womb and declared that their child was going to be a "free spirit." Fred made some joke about needing tie-dyed diapers. Neither woman laughed. Conceiving free-spirited progeny was apparently a serious business.

So Nedra came up with two "free-spirit" names—Holly (if it was a girl), from *Breakfast at Tiffany's,* and Holden (if it was a boy), from *Catcher in the Rye.* Fine, Fred said, as long as Nedra was happy.

Fred's failures weren't in such acute focus in his younger son, whose fame overshadowed Fred's long absences, his preoccupation with his work, his lack of intimacy, his using money to replace himself with his family. Fred Gelman wasn't stupid. He read articles about parenting. He *knew* he was a lousy father. It wouldn't surprise him when he got home to see his son Owen being dragged away in handcuffs. And in some future interview with John Stossel, just before his execution, Owen would put the blame squarely on Daddy's shoulders and John would nod sympathetically, handing Owen a tissue as the memories of a childhood scarred by paternal abandonment and a lack of intimacy caused his tears to flow freely.

Fred tried to remember the last time he and Owen had a real conversation. The only image that came to mind was Owen sitting in the principal's office, his face contorted with panic as his history teacher asked him questions about a final essay Owen claimed he'd written, but had really been composed by his tutor for a hefty fee. Fred remembered thinking how dumb his son was—hating himself for thinking it but thinking it anyway— his own kid, not smart enough to do the work, not smart enough to cheat without getting caught.

The flight attendant returned with his drink. She placed it down on his tray.

"You look troubled," she said.

"Yes."

"Try to get some rest."

She laid her hand on his for a brief moment. It was warm. Her fingers were long and delicate.

"I'll try," he said.

"That's a good boy."

This time when she smiled he knew it was meant just for him.

Ward drove. Bliss thought about how he would break the news to the parents. There was no easy way. He had to hope for help, backup, usually from the father. If the father stayed strong and in control, it was possible to get through it easy, even get some answers. But you never knew. Sometimes it was the men who crumbled in front of him, like the string that held them up had been cut. It was never easy. Maybe he *should* have let Rachel do it.

He wondered how his father handled it, informing the next of kin. Monty Bliss was probably not the person you wanted telling you someone you loved was dead. *Mr. and Mrs. Wilson, it's about your son. Well, let me put it this way, that bike with the training wheels on the front lawn? Well, you won't be needing to take those training wheels off.*

It was probably his father's partner Alphonse who was the one to inform the next of kin. Lenny remembered Alphonse clearly—balding, stains on his lapels, eyes permanently down-cast, as though he had just found out he'd placed second in a talent show, that he wasn't going to be invited back to the pro-gram next week. Alphonse would have been more gentle, more discreet than his father with the next of kin. He could see Alphonse embracing someone if he needed to, letting a grieving widow cry on his shoulder. His father would be thinking about copping a feel.

Bliss remembered how sweet Alphonse always was to his mother, and how gently she spoke to him, so much more tender than when she talked to Bliss's father. It felt good to hear her voice that way, not afraid to say the wrong thing. His mother would offer Alphonse coffee, and he would hold the cup with both hands, like it was the only nice thing someone had done for him all day, maybe in his whole life. He would ask her what she was cooking, curious about the Eastern European smells, the sweet-and-sour aroma coming from a pot of simmering stuffed cabbage. *There are raisins in there? You put 'em right in with to-mato sauce?* And then Alphonse would say that would have to bring his own wife Angelina over so Lenny's mom could teach her a few things about cooking. His mother smiled. Flattered.

Bliss wondered if his father brought Alphonse around on purpose, like some kind of puppet, to talk to his wife, his partner saying what Monty could never say himself. One hour with Alphonse was more conversation than she got from her husband in a month.

Once, when he was home from school with an ear infection, his father and Alphonse pulled up in the cruiser and stopped in to see him, brought him an Orange Julius and the latest Fantastic Four. They were all in the kitchen and Alphonse made his usual comments about his mother's cooking. She offered him a taste, cutting him a thick slice of brisket. Alphonse wound up dripping sauce down his tie. Lenny laughed. Next thing he knew, his father had smacked him across the head. *Who do you think you are?* Alphonse put out his hand in protest. *It's okay, Monty.* But his father smacked him again. *That's my* partner, his father said. *You never laugh at my partner.*

Later that night, his father had come into his room.

"What'd you make me do that for?" his father said.

It was as close to an apology as Bliss ever got.

Don't come home dead, Lenny. I don't want to be working your case tomorrow.

But maybe he'd never given his father sufficient credit. Maybe, in his own way, his father was reaching out and Lenny hadn't given him a chance. *Don't come home dead*—his father saying that to him, it could have been the beginning of something very close to resembling love.

Rick opened the door and saw the two policemen standing in the hall. One black, the other white. They each held out their badges so Rick could see them.

He instantly knew that his son was in big trouble—*Consequences! Repercussions!* And if Ben was in big trouble, it meant he was, too. Ellen was going to kill him. Or worse, make him live under her wrath, blaming him for whatever happened to Ben for the rest of his life.

"Mr. Purdy," the white policeman said, "I'm Detective Bliss."

Rick noticed how comfortable they were with each other. The way they stood, shoulders touching, watching, listening, together. They had badges. They were the kids with badges, who started a secret club that Rick couldn't be part of, a club that was formed just so Rick would be left out.

"This is my partner, Detective Ward."

His *partner*.

Rick wanted a partner. Someone to stand next to, shoulder to shoulder. Someone to help him deal with stuff. They could have badges, too. A special code only known to the two of them.

"You might want to get your wife, Mr. Purdy," Bliss said. Detective Ward didn't say anything. He just watched.

"Go ahead, Mr. Purdy," Bliss repeated, stern now, as if there might be repercussions if he didn't. Consequences.

Rick nodded.

He stopped in front of Ellen's door. In a moment he would let her know there were policemen at the door and then they would walk down the hall together. Then the policemen would tell them something bad had happened to their son, maybe even that Ben was dead.

And then there would just be the two of them. Rick and Ellen.

It wouldn't be good, just the two of them. They didn't get married so it would be just the two of them. Ellen had gotten pregnant the first night of their honeymoon. They planned to have lots of children, Ellen staying home to take care of them, her father giving them whatever money they needed, a bigger apartment if they needed, more nannies if they needed. And though they tried, no more children came. Then they stopped trying. Without Ben, it would be just the two of them. That would be hard under the best of circumstances. *This is my husband. He works for my father. He sells luggage. He's not even good at that.*

But now it was going to be even worse.

He knocked on their bedroom door. His hand was trembling. He told Ellen detectives had arrived and needed to speak with them. He couldn't bear to look at her.

They walked back to the foyer. Ellen reached for his hand. That's when he had a premonition it was going to be really bad.

"We're sorry for your loss," Bliss said.

"I knew it," Ellen said. She grabbed on to him, her fingers digging into his arm. "Before you came, I knew he was dead."

Rick couldn't say anything.

"How did you know that, Mrs. Purdy?" Detective Bliss asked, his voice low and soothing.

"I just knew," Ellen said, speaking with an amazing clarity. It must be the grief, Rick thought. Making her world for once clear and in focus. With Ben alive, there was only chaos and pain. Now that Ben was dead, everything made sense. "The school called," she said. "The secretary asked why B-ben hadn't shown up for school. Where was he? *You have no clue where your son is, Mrs. Purdy?* that bitch cunt asked me." Ellen's voice rose, the pain taking over. "Yes, I wanted to say. Yes, you bitch cunt, I *know* where he is!"

"Ellen," Rick said. She yanked her arm away from him. He moved to hold her, but she put up her hand like an irate traffic cop.

Here it comes, he thought.

But she said nothing. Her mouth moved, but nothing came out. She rushed to him and he held her.

Rick thought he should definitely be asking how it happened. But maybe because he imagined Ben dead so many times, the real circumstances didn't really matter. Ben had ownership of the thing they both cherished more than anything else—the life of their son. Ben tormented them every chance he had, jeopardizing their son's life with drugs and drink and there was nothing they could do. Because Ben wasn't really their son anymore. The Ben they had was just some kind of punishment. Their real son, the son capable of love and compassion, the son who needed them, was buried deep inside this Ben. The precious, delicate, wondrous child Rick had once loved so much was buried deep inside this Ben/Thing, this wreck. Their real son had been kid-napped, the evil Ben/Thing holding it hostage, until now, when he had finally destroyed it.

"I'm sorry," Bliss said, "but I need to ask you, did your son have any enemies that you knew of? Anyone who might have wanted to do him harm?"

"Yes," Ellen said, abruptly pulling away and pointing to him. "My husband."

Bring it on, Ellen, Rick thought.

"My husband did my son harm every day of his life."

That's right. Pack me away. Sit on the lid of the suitcase so you can get the clasps shut tight. *You have to excuse my husband. He's in luggage. He works for my father.* Rick nibbled on his thumb.

"What do you mean, Mrs. Purdy?" Bliss asked.

"Can't you see?" she shouted. "Can't you see just by look-ing at him??!"

Then Ellen stopped, her bottom lip quivering uncon-trollably.

"W-w-what will we do about the C-c-christmas c-card?" she said, her voice shaking. Their skiing trip, the one thing they did together as a family, and each year they would take a photo of the three of them for the Christmas card, smiling on the slopes, arms around each other, together as a family—Greetings from the Purdys.

"The Christmas card," she said in a whisper, and then her knees buckled and she sank down to the floor.

Ellen made a sound he'd never heard before, some kind of deep, seal-like bark.

The detectives looked at him, waiting for Rick to move, to come to the aid of his wife.

You try it, Rick wanted to say to him. *You* go over there. If I had a partner maybe I'd do it. But alone? By myself? I know better. If Ellen needs me she'll say something. But I'm not going over there only to be pushed away, have my face rubbed in my comfort like a bad dog.

Well, she wouldn't be treating him like that much longer. This was all going to change. And soon.

Rick was going to make a point of it.

Then he cleared his throat and asked the detective how it happened.

Dom sat in the waiting room while Jonah was in with the doctor. The kid had felt "sinusy" and the school nurse said he should see the pediatrician. It happened about once a week. Jonah never seemed very sick to Dom, but what did he know. You had to piss blood before Solomon would consider scratching you for a fight. Actually, you had to piss a lot of blood.

The doctor had games and puzzles for the kids to play with while they waited. Dom watched one kid with a truck, sneezing on it, wiping his snot with his hand and then driving it around the rug until his appointment, at which point he passed the truck on to another kid. Dom had an uncle with a replacement glass business in Canarsie who would have his son go around the neighborhood breaking car windows. Same deal.

Dom scanned the coffee table where some magazines and newspapers were laid out, relieved to see no mention of Felix. He picked up a *Highlights*. Goofus and Gallant were still doing their thing, Goofus never holding the door or saying thank you or please or looking at someone when he shook their hand.

In this installment, the boys were eating dinner at a friend's. Goofus blurts out, "Got any more?" But Gallant politely inquires if there "might possibly be seconds available?" They should make it more realistic, Dom thought. Goofus drinks the friend's father's booze without asking. But Gallant shows the friend how to pour water into the bottle so the father won't be upset. They were a pair of pissants—Goofus and Gallant both. That was the problem with *Highlights*—telling kids you had to be one or the other, when really you had to be *both*. Goofus *and* Gallant. Otherwise, you wound up stuck forever in the neighborhood, working at Tommy DeTolo's restaurant, a waiter if you were Gallant, asking the customer if they wanted their linguini *al dente;* a cook if you were Goofus, cursing the waiters, the bus boys, Tommy DeTolo, cursing the entire world as you stood in front of the stove trying to keep your cigarette ashes from falling into the marinara.

He was interrupted by the nurse.

"Are you Jonah's daddy?"

"No," he said. "What's the problem?"

The nurse looked over at Rosa and decided she was not Jonah's mommy. The nurse sighed and shook her head wearily, as if to say, *Where are the parents?*

"Jonah has strep," the nurse said.

"You mean he's actually *sick?*"

"Yes."

"He need a shot?" Dom asked.

Last time Jonah needed a shot, Dom had to pin him down on the table while the doctor plugged him, Jonah furiously kicking and wiggling, letting out piercing screams like an animal being slaughtered. No wonder the mother was at the manicurist whenever Jonah had to go to the doctor.

"No, he doesn't need a shot," the nurse said. "He needs antibiotics."

"No pills," Dom said. "Jonah can't swallow pills."

That had been another ferocious bout, Jonah screaming while Dom held him and Rosa popped in the pill. Then Jonah had started gagging, flailing his arms and legs, his foot connecting with Dom's nuts. *Low blow, ref, for fuck's sake.* Dom would rather go ten rounds with a Panamanian on methamphetamines than try to get another pill down Jonah's throat. Sometimes Jonah really pissed Dom off. He knew it wasn't the kid's fault, that no one had ever taught him how to behave. Still, occasionally Dom felt like breaking Jonah's finger, just to shut him up. But then that would have meant another trip to the doctor's.

"It's not a pill. It's a liquid," the nurse said. "He has to take it twice a day. But I'd really feel better if one of his parents were here."

So would Jonah, Dom thought.

"I make sure he takes it," Rosa said.

The nurse sighed again. "I'll have the doctor call in the prescription."

In the limo, Dom was thinking some of the bodyguard shit was starting to get to him. The candy after school, for one thing. Jonah *had* to get candy after school and the mother said Jonah absolutely had to get it at this one particular deli. Dom didn't see why the candy at this particular deli was different from any other candy. Dom could buy several pounds of it for the same money on Atlantic Avenue in Brooklyn, but that didn't matter. Jonah had to get his candy at the deli where every other kid went. So Dom had to fight through a throng of sugar-starved seven-year-olds, whacking him in the shins with their book bags, stepping on his toes, shoving him out of the way as they clawed to the candy racks. It reminded him of working the St. Patrick's Day parade as a rookie cop.

And then there was all the waiting. Hanging around outside school every afternoon in the limo, as if Jonah's dad was actually important, a sheik, a Japanese banker, some big-time rock star. Dom would unbutton his coat so he could get to his gun, knowing that the worst thing that could happen was some older kid trying to extort lunch money from Jonah. Might be good for him. Build his character.

But Jonah's dad liked to pretend he was important enough that someone would actually want to kidnap his son. Like this is Brazil or Mexico City. Like anyone in America even *knows* how to kidnap someone anymore.

Dom started the car, ready to drive strep-infected Jonah back home, when his cell phone rang. The ID came up Douglas Lipper. Last time he spoke to Douglas it was to install the security cameras at that fancy East Side townhouse.

"Dom," Douglas said, "I need you."

"When?"

"Now. Pronto."

Douglas liked to make things sound dramatic, like an episode of *The Untouchables*.

"What'll I tell Jonah?"

"Who?"

"The kid I'm protecting."

"Just get over here."

Douglas obviously didn't have time for Dom's problems.

"It's serious?" Dom asked.

"Murder," Douglas said. "A kid was murdered at the Gelmans'. Where you put in surveillance."

"The real estate guy."

"Yeah."

"You told me he could help find me a one-bedroom in Manhattan," Dom said. "That was part of the deal."

"We'll work it out."

"But we didn't work it out," Dom said. "I still live in Brooklyn. I still live on a street with four body shops."

"I said we'll work it out."

"How many body shops you have on your street?"

"Just get over here."

"I want a terrace, too," Dom said. "And make sure it's a *real* one-bedroom. Not a studio with a wall down the middle."

He hung up.

He drove Jonah home and parked the limo. When he got up to the apartment, Jonah was in bed, watching cartoons. Dom sat down next to him.

"So what do you do after you hit the ball?"

"Run to first."

"What if you think it's going foul?"

"Run to first anyway."

"Right. Listen, I may not be at your next game."

Jonah looked grim.

"Why?"

"Something's come up."

"You going to start boxing again?"

"No. Something serious. I've got to do some serious work. I'll try to get to your game. If not this week, then next week."

"I'll hit a home run for you, Dom."

"Thanks, kid. Hey, maybe you'll come to my new apartment. We'll watch the Yankees, have some hot dogs on the terrace."

"Okay."

He left the room and took the elevator down to the lobby. He felt bad walking out on Jonah. Then he remembered the kid had two parents and more money than God and what kind of world was it where you wound up feeling sorry for a kid like that? There were plenty of other people for Dom to worry about. Someone like Arturo, for one. Himself, for another.

Bliss drove now, Ward next to him.

"She said she knew he was dead," Bliss said.

"She's prescient," Ward said.

"The husband never moved to help her when she fell. Just let her lie there."

"Maybe he'd been waiting a long time to see her like that," Ward said. "You never know with people."

But Bliss had notified too many next of kin, borne the initial wave of their grief, not to know that something was amiss with the Purdys. Strange how he could make an assessment about this. His was a rarefied knowledge. Arcane, like being able to read hieroglyphs or play the theremin. He actually had enough experience notifying next of kin to judge their response—8.5 for the spontaneous display of grief; 9.0 on her fall to the floor—it would have been a 10 but she didn't nail the landing.

"It's the penthouse," Ward said. "The air is always foul on the top floor. Rots out your soul. If we looked we would have found a stash of Perry Como records. Vic Damone. Jim Nabors' *Greatest Hits*."

Bliss saw the police cars on the corner, the yellow tape. He slowed and turned off Park Avenue onto the side street. It was quiet. Staid. Different from the rest of New York. More like a small town. The trees were blossoming. If you dropped a dollar on this street, someone might actually give it back to you.

On the corner, by Park Avenue, the media vans were getting their big antennas in the air, like giant erections, aroused by the prospect of a big story. A "live feed," they called it, because that's what the people in the story became, live feed for the ravenous media sharks.

A few housekeepers and nannies from the neighboring townhouses were watching from their stoops. Some were in uniform. Bliss remembered when he and Rachel had interviewed nannies, spending a whole day talking to a steady stream of Haitian, African, Filipino, and Jamaican women, all trying desperately to make a good impression, willing to do anything for the job, work six days a week, twelve hours a day, clean, cook, shop, walk the dog, their *neighbors'* dog if they didn't have one. Bliss wanted to hire them all, find some place in his house for each of them to stay, take care of *their* every need.

They got out of the car. Bliss saw where the uniforms were congregating at the crime scene, and realized it was the same townhouse he was in the other night.

"What's the name of the boy?" Bliss asked.

"Ben," Ward said.

"No. The kid on the sitcom, he lives here, right?"

"Holden," Ward said.

His mouth went dry.

"This neighborhood doesn't know what's about to hit them," Ward said. "They'll be under siege for a week at least. Maybe longer."

But Bliss wasn't listening. He was still putting it together, that this was where the party was, where he went to look for Julia.

Ward headed to the building.

"You coming, partner?"

He shouldn't go any farther. He had to say something now. Anything. As long as he didn't go inside,

But he followed Ward. It was his job. And his partner needed him.

A dapper guy in a swanky suit emerged from the front door and stood on the landing, surveying the scene with a regal air, every hair in place, cuffs elegantly displayed below the sleeves of his suit jacket. He walked down the steps, in no rush, met them at the bottom, introduced himself.

"Douglas Lipper," he said, "counsel for the Gelmans."

"Isn't the house sealed off?" Bliss asked.

"The bedroom is."

"Not the whole house?"

Douglas shrugged.

"I guess it is now," Douglas said. "Anyway, fifty kids were at that party. That's a lot of fibers and prints, don't you think?"

Plus mine, Bliss thought.

"We're going to go inside now," Bliss said.

"Do what you have to do," Douglas said.

Bliss was about to enter when the doorway filled up with a size forty-six-long Italian suit packed to the brim with Dom DeMoro.

More surprises.

"Dom," Bliss said, thinking if Dom's neck got any thicker, it would break off and start a new body on its own.

"Bliss and Ward," DeMoro said, hunching his shoulders just a bit, to call attention to their breadth, which made about as much sense as Mick Jagger pursing his lips. "The Lone Ranger and Tonto. I was hoping you'd catch this case."

DeMoro used to be a cop, but had opted for less stress and longer green working security. Judging by his fancy loafers, Dom wasn't too concerned about dealing with any floaters on the muddy banks of the East River.

"Been a while, DeMoro," Bliss said.

"Yes, it has." They didn't shake hands. DeMoro turned to Ward. "And how are *you, kemosabe?*"

Ward stared at him. Dom stared back, probably the way he did in the ring before a fight. They kept at it, trying to stare each other down on the stoop of the six million-dollar brownstone. Bliss put his arm on Ward's shoulder.

"C'mon, partner," Bliss said. Then he turned to the lawyer. "Keep your behemoth in line, Mr. Lipper."

Bliss pulled on his rubber gloves and went inside the crime scene, retracing his steps from the night before, when he went to rescue Julia. Some Rubicons are wide. This one was just a few feet, the length of the front foyer, between the street and the house.

Then he was inside.

He rested his hand on the newel post. Had he done that the other night? Had he held the banister? Which doorknobs had he turned? Had he picked up a glass? Evidence of his presence in the house was everywhere, minute traces that, under a microscope, would loom as large as Times Square neon—*Bliss Was Here*—flashing red, lighting up the lab.

And what had he taken with him? How many Gelman carpet fibers had clung to his clothes, nestled in his cuffs?

The housekeeper sat on the sofa in the living room, a small Philippine woman, hands in her lap. Bliss had to hope she was good at her job, that her rag was soaked through with Lysol to pick up every drop of his DNA-riddled sweat. That she was Willie Mays with her vacuuming, catching everything that came her way—strands of his hair, carpet fibers from his rug at home. That she had then changed the vacuum bag, so all traces of Bliss were gone.

So far the signs were good. The house was unrecognizably clean.

He had to hope.

"Lenny," Ward called to him from the second-floor landing.

"Yeah."

He started up the steps, then felt a presence behind him. He turned, saw Dom, seemingly intent on following him upstairs.

"Where are you going?" Bliss said.

"Douglas wants me to help you out," Dom replied with feigned innocence. "See if I can throw some light on the subject, clear up any confusion that might arise."

"Stay outside," Bliss barked.

"Okay, detective," Dom said, raising his hands in surrender and flashing a grin.

"And let me know when Owen gets here," Bliss said.

"Oh he's here," Dom said. "He's with Douglas."

"We want to talk with him now."

"As soon as Douglas says it's okay, we'll come find you."

Bliss knew he wasn't talking to the boy until Douglas went over everything with him first.

"Just get him upstairs soon."

"Whatever you say, detective," Dom said, a twinkle in his eye. "We want a good, clean fight. And may the best man win."

Rachel was writing in her head as she approached the crime scene.

Mae pushed her way through the crowd surrounding the house where the murder had taken place. People had always done this, she thought, *cramming into the square in Paris to see someone guillotined, or slowing down on the highway in hopes of seeing bloody tangled limbs in the car wreck. She should be used to it by now, but it bothered her, how ~~prurient~~ depraved most people were.*

Then again, Mae thought, *if they were different, she'd probably be out of a job.*

Rachel spoke to the uniformed officer at the barricade, mentioned Detective Bliss, and he let her through.

On the stoop, another uniformed officer stood talking with a large man in a black Italian suit that made him look like he was auditioning for *The Sopranos*. The uniform stopped her.

"I'm with Detective Bliss," she said.

"I still can't let you in," he said. "Sorry. Right now, the whole house is considered a crime scene."

Then the Sopranos wannabe stepped toward her.

"Anything I can help you with?" he asked.

He stuck out a large hand for her to shake. He had a silver chain around his wrist, a diamond ring on his pinkie. She wondered if he ordered everything from some catalogue—J. Mob.

"Dom DeMoro," he said in a surprisingly soft voice. She took his hand. It felt like it was made of bronze, like a Rodin.

"Mae Stark," she said. "I'm a novelist."

"You doing research or something?" he asked.

"Yes, in fact," she said.

"No kidding. I could tell you all kinds of stuff," Dom said. "Murder. Mayhem. A pocketful of malfeasance."

"Authentic?"

"One hundred percent. You don't want to hang around with Bliss. He's old. Tired. Me, twelfth round and I'm still on my toes."

"You're working this case?" she asked him.

"I used to be on the job. Now I do security. Maybe you should run home and get your typewriter. Whattaya think, Mae?"

She smiled, held up her notebook.

"I'm covered," she said.

He reached into his pocket, handed her his card. Dom DeMoro—Security. "That's my cell number," he said. "Call me. Old guys like Bliss, they get philosophical. You don't want that. You want nitty-gritty."

"You've got nitty-gritty?" she asked.

"The nitty I got doesn't get any grittier."

"Sounds good," she said. She waved his card, showing him she wouldn't lose it. She turned and walked down the steps of the townhouse. Dom intrigued her. She needed another perspective. Dom seemed like he might provide a little color. Some menace. Some very gritty nitty.

Mae just might have to give Dom a call.

Bliss looked at the body of the boy, all tucked in bed, dead tired, stiff, skin glazed like a donut, eyes empty, starting to rot. The feet still hung over the edge of the bed, just the way they had the other night when Bliss thought he was sleeping. He definitely wasn't sleeping now.

Bliss had his reverie interrupted by Cardozo.

"The floater, and now this," Cardozo said, clicking his tongue with disapproval. "You see a pattern?"

"No," Ward said.

"What about you?" he asked Bliss.

"It escapes me, Cardozo."

"Try harder."

Bliss didn't see it. Except for Douglas Lipper the lawyer, there was nothing in common.

"Both of them are dead," Cardozo said. "*That's* the pattern."

"You're the best, Cardozo," Ward said.

"Case closed," Bliss said.

Bliss scoped the room. Bookshelves. Window. Television. Glossies of the movie star kid were framed and hung on the wall. A basketball in the corner. Trophies. It didn't feel like anyone lived here. It was more like a shrine.

Forensics was just packing up the crime scene kit. Olson, pink-cheeked, freckled, looking like he escaped from a Norman Rockwell painting.

"We're lucky," Olson said. "The housekeeper hasn't been in this room since the party. She thought the kid was sleeping."

"How long has he been here?" Bliss asked Cardozo.

"Two days," Cardozo said. "I wish I lived in a place big enough to have a dead body around for two days and not notice. If there was an extra pair of socks in my apartment I'd know it in a minute, never mind a whole body. My apartment is so small, even the mice are hunchbacked."

Cardozo waited for the rim shot. None was forthcoming.

"Well," Cardozo said, "as long as I'm here in my capacity as medical examiner, I might as well speak to you about some forensic evidence that could perhaps be germane to your investigation."

"What is it?"

"His head," he said. "It's been cracked open. Either by a light object with incredible force or a heavy object with less force."

"Okay."

"But there's something else."

Bliss detected the touch of excitement Cardozo felt when he made a discovery.

"What?"

"Another mark," he said, "on his forehead. Made by something sharp."

Bliss and Ward bent down to look. A small dent, dried blood leaking out, blending into the general carnage at the back of his skull.

"What do you make of it?"

"Trial run," Cardozo said. "Whacked him once, but it didn't have the desired effect. He needed something more substantial." He gestured to the ravaged cranium. "Clearly he figured out what that more substantial thing was."

Bliss looked around for something in reach. If I wanted to crack someone's skull, what would I use? He saw the set of free weights in the corner—a barbell and three dumbbells. There should probably be four.

That was easy.

He got on his radio, told the uniforms to start looking for a gray dumbbell, ten pounds. Check the garbage cans in a three-block radius. Later that night, Bliss would stop by Lexington Avenue off 85th Street, the block where the homeless men set up blankets laid out with goods they'd pillaged from the garbage during the day. Maybe the dumbbell would be on display.

"What made the other mark?" Garcia asked.

They looked around the room together. It could have been any number of things. Or something the killer brought with him, even, that didn't serve the purpose.

"Get the housekeeper up here," Bliss said. "See if she notices anything missing."

"Something else, too," Cardozo said.

"What?"

"There was blood on his penis," Cardozo said. "And it wasn't his."

"How'd it get there?" Bliss asked.

There was a moment of silence, then Ward and Cardozo simultaneously burst out laughing.

"Cute," Bliss said. "So there was someone in bed with him."

Cardozo lifted a long, blond hair from the pillow with his tweezers and held it before them. Olson bounded over, bagged the hair and marked the bag.

"I guess it would probably be a good thing to find out whose head that hair belongs to," Bliss said.

"And whose blood is on Ben's shlong," Cardozo added.

Chantal sat on the edge of the bed. She was groggy, but at least her head wasn't spinning anymore. She was still at Malcolm's. She hadn't gone home.

But then memories of the party came back to her and forced her to lie down again. She put a pillow on her stomach and held it tightly.

I love you, Chantal.

She had lost her virginity. Owen had found a way to get her pants off and force his way inside her. She must have wanted it to happen. What did she expect, climbing into bed with a naked boy. That he wanted to discuss Dostoyevsky? And not just any boy. It was Owen. Owen, who discharged his semen so recklessly it was bound to get inside her eventually, like those monkeys typing *Hamlet*.

So maybe now she was really pregnant.

She started crying—just a little bit, too tired to weep.

Then another memory jogged her brain. She looked at her hand. She remembered blood there. Now it was clean. She put it to her nose. It smelled of flowers.

The door opened and Malcolm waltzed in.

"Rise and shine," he said. "My dad and I have a big day planned and we want you to come."

"What about school?"

"School?" he said, incredulous. "It's the first day of spring. There is too much rapture in the air to go to school."

She should call her parents. They'd be driving home from the Hamptons, like they did every Monday morning once it got warm, her father wanting to spend every possible minute out there. *What's the point in owning a house in the Hamptons, on the water no less, if you don't use it?* She heard him say it a hundred times, then that little laugh—how proud he was—on the *water* no less.

"Chantal."

"Yes."

"Are you coming with us? I guarantee you a good time."

She smiled. Malcolm, her savior.

"Okay."

"Good. Let's go. My dad will have the Impala out front. And the top will be down."

Bliss waited while Nedra, her son Owen, and the housekeeper stood in the doorway of Holden's room. He had asked them to look for something missing, something out of place.

"Did you have to put this yellow tape across the door?" Nedra asked with a petulant whine. She was dressed in a black workout outfit, skintight. There didn't seem to be an ounce of fat on her. "It's not like we're going to go in there. We don't *want* to go in there."

"I need to preserve the integrity of the crime scene," Bliss said.

"Can't you use anything else besides that tape? Some ribbon, maybe. Or even a different *color* tape. Something with earth tones."

"Sorry," Bliss said.

She rolled her eyes. Obviously Police Yellow didn't go with their color scheme. Then again, it wasn't supposed to. On the door was a sign Holden must have put up when he was a little boy. "Warning," the sign said. "Disaster Area."

Douglas, the lawyer, stood behind them, ever watchful, listening to every word.

"Clara," Nedra said, "I'll need you to light some candles, lots of candles, to get the smell out, bring in some better karma."

"Yes, Missus," Clara said.

Then, almost as an afterthought, Nedra said under her breath, "maybe I'll just renovate the whole house."

"Yes, Missus," Clara said.

The Batman bedspread had been pulled down to the end of Holden's bed.

"You used to make a Batcave," Nedra said.

"I remember," Owen said. "We stretched the bedspread across to the desk, weighed it down with encyclopedias. I was Batman, Holden was Robin. We'd hide and watch under the bed for the feet of our enemies."

"You were nice little boys," she said, loud enough so Bliss could hear. "Never hurt a soul."

Bliss saw Owen reach for his mother's hand and hold it tightly. Nedra seemed surprised, like it was unexpected, her son holding her hand. Like maybe he hadn't done that for a long time.

"See anything yet?" Bliss asked.

"It's kind of an oxymoron, isn't it, detective?" Owen said. "Looking for something that isn't there."

Nedra was now even more astonished—as though her son knowing such a long word like that was an unprecedented accomplishment.

"In a way it is," Bliss said, trying to make Owen feel good, keeping things upbeat, despite the bed sheet bearing the vague outline of Ben, where he lay dead for two days. Bliss could just make out the shape of Ben's legs, the indentations of his arms. The pillow was stained a dark brown with the blood from his head. A smaller bloodstain graced the middle of the sheet, about where someone's groin might have been, resting there like a fallen petal.

"I can't tell what's missing" Nedra said. "I'm not good at these things. Puzzles. They give me a headache."

"Please try," Bliss said.

"I hardly ever go in here. Clara does all the cleaning and . . ." She started to wobble, like she was going to fall down. Douglas the lawyer immediately sprung to her side like a cat or an obsequious lawyer, and held her up.

"I feel nauseous," she said. "Puzzles give me a headache."

Douglas flashed him a look of lawyerly contempt. *See what you've done to this poor, innocent woman?*

"You all right, Mom?" Owen asked.

"We'll do this later, Nedra," Douglas said.

"I'm okay," Nedra said. "We want to help them, don't we?"

She was starting to sound like Norma Desmond in *Sunset Boulevard.*

"Maybe you're thirsty," Bliss said. He handed her a glass of water. Owen and Clara, too. He hoped he didn't think it odd that he had water there, in glasses, ready for them. Nedra took a sip.

"Are these our glasses?" she asked the housekeeper. The housekeeper shook her head no. Nedra shrugged and finished the water. So did Owen. Before Douglas could catch on, Bliss took the glasses back, holding them carefully by the lip and base, and handed them to one at a time to Ward. Now he had prints of the mother and, more importantly, the son.

"We're looking for something out of place," Bliss said, urging them on, like a game show host. "Something missing, something that's not there." *Survey says?*

"Take your time," Bliss continued. "I know none of this is easy for you."

Holden's face watched them from a framed poster for his TV show.

Then the housekeeper spoke up.

"There's a trophy missing," she said.

"How do you know?" Bliss said, getting out his notebook. He flashed to Rachel doing the same thing.

"He had four," she said. "Now there are only three. I know. I have to dust them."

Bliss wondered if that was a dig at the mother.

"What was the figure on it?" he asked.

Clara studied the three remaining trophies.

"It was a baseball player," Owen said.

"He was good at baseball?" Bliss asked.

"Who? My brother?"

"Yes."

"No," Owen said. "Holden sucked. Everyone in the league got a trophy. Just for showing up. It's the Upper East Side."

Owen let go of his mother's hand. She turned to him with a look of longing, like it might take the death of another friend for her son to seek out her hand again.

"I have to lie down, Douglas," Nedra said, "I have to rest."

"That's all for now, detectives," Douglas said. "You got what you wanted."

Douglas took her arm and led her upstairs. Like a gentleman caller.

Bliss had seen those trophies the other night. He couldn't be sure how many. But his testimony was useless, unless he wanted to make it the last thing he said as a cop before being dismissed from the force and going to work for his father-in-law.

Owen started to wander off.

"Don't go far," Bliss said.

"Where do I have to go?" Owen said.

And it occurred to Bliss that Owen's best friend was dead and behind the bluster and the muscles and the spoiled petulance was a fragile, frightened little boy who was very, very sad.

Maybe.

The reporters surged toward Fred like Morrocan begger children as soon as he got through customs, shoving cameras and microphones in his face, shouting questions. He immediately understood why movie stars were prone to breaking cameras, punching out photographers.

He caught a glimpse of Marjorie, the flight attendant, wheeling her bag toward the exit. She saw him and gave him a look of pity. He hoped his being hounded by the media would help his chances with her—maybe she'd think of him as a kind of Princess Di. He had her phone number in his pocket.

The first torrent of questions was about *Holden*—How does *Holden* feel? Will his show keep shooting? Did he know the dead boy? Did he know the missing girl?

Then, almost as an afterthought, they asked about Owen.

Was it true there was cocaine at the party? Was it true Owen taught Holden how to act? Was it true the boy was Owen's lover? That the girl was under age?

Fred realized he couldn't answer most of these questions if he wanted to. He didn't know anything about the dead Ben boy or Owen's missing girlfriend. He didn't know who was at the party, didn't know there *was* a party. He didn't know the names of Owen's teachers or his favorite cereal. So what were they asking him all these questions for? Shouting at him, as if he *knew*.

Then one voice rose above the others.

"Why did Owen do it?"

Fred moved directly toward her.

"What did you say?"

She was accusing his son of murder.

'What's your name?" he shouted at her, right into her face.

"Adelaide," she was practically whimpering.

"Who the fuck do you work for?!" She was too shocked to respond. The herd of reporters grew quiet, watching, waiting to see what would happen, if a story was developing, a story within the story, like an etching by Escher. They were probably hoping he'd hit her, break her jaw. He wondered if any of them would come to her aid if he had her on the floor and was punching her face bloody. Or would they be too busy maneuvering for a better angle.

"I asked you who you worked for."

She mumbled the name of one of the local networks.

Fred reached into his pocket, pulled out his cell phone, found a number in his directory, hit the call button.

"It's Fred Gelman. Put me through to Ross. It's very important."

In a moment his friend Ross was on the line.

"Fred," Ross said, "Howya holding up? This news. About the murder. I'm . . ."

"Ross, you still own that TV station?"

"Fred, you know we do."

"Well listen, I got a cunt reporter here works for you, asking me some questions which are a little out of line. Thought maybe you could straighten her out."

"The network's just one of our divisions, Fred. I don't know if I . . ."

"Just fire her, Ross," Fred said, loud enough for the girl to hear, for them all to hear. "Her name's Adelaide something. Tell her she's fired, you'll find a reason later."

He handed the receiver to the reporter, watched as she listened, nodded, handed it back.

"I know all your bosses," Fred shouted to them. "I have their numbers right here." He held up his phone for them all to see. "Their *private* numbers, the ones they answer. They're friends of mine. Our kids go to school together. So don't fuck around with me."

Bliss found the dumbbell under the bed in Owen's room. Traces of blood were on one side, covering up the number 10. Olson bagged it and marked it to take back to the lab.

"Maybe we'll find a print," Bliss said to Ward.

"A print is always nice," his partner replied. They would match it against the print they got off Owen when he took the drink of water.

"We'll have to ask Owen how it got here," Bliss said. "The murder weapon. Under his bed."

Ward nodded. He didn't speak much during an investigation. This led others to fill in the silence, often with remarks that led to their demise.

They didn't find the trophy.

"We're going to have to talk to all of the kids who were at the party," Bliss said. "Find out what they saw, or at least what they remember."

Julia wouldn't be much help there. Still her name would come up—the daughter of the lead detective.

Bliss picked up the VCR remote.

"Let's see what Owen liked to watch," he said. "Maybe there will be a clue. Like in Agatha Christie."

"I like her," Ward said. "The detective always finds the killer in Agatha Christie."

The television came on—a surveillance tape. The front stoop of this very house.

The tape cut from the front stoop to the backyard where a young girl had her hand on a boy's cock. Cut to the front stoop, cut to the boy and girl. Bliss hit fast-forward, speeding past the jerky motions of the boy, who they recognized as Owen. Then the girl and he got up. Then the front stoop, empty. Then the girl alone on the bench, head bent. Then the front stoop—the housekeeper carrying groceries. Then it went to static, which must have been when Owen removed the tape from the recorder.

Ward turned it off.

While he was watching, it occurred to Bliss that there would also be a tape of him, appearing on the front stoop, in clear focus, entering the house, leaving a little while later. His heart was pounding.

Tell your partner everything, his father always said.

"Are you a voyeur if you like to watch *yourself* have sex?" Ward asked him.

Bliss said nothing.

Tell your partner everything.

"That must be the girlfriend," Ward said. "Chantal."

Bliss nodded.

"There should be a tape from the night of the party," Ward said.

Starring Bliss.

Douglas the lawyer would be ecstatic. *What were you doing during that time, Detective? Your prints were found on the third floor, where Ben was murdered. How do you explain that?* Douglas would have a giant litigious hard-on—a pro boner.

"You okay?" Ward asked.

Tell your partner everything. Lie to your wife if you have to. Your mother, your rabbi—whoever. Even me—your father. But always tell your partner everything.

"I'm good," Bliss said. "Let's go find the tape. From the night of the party."

"I already looked," Ward said.

"And?"

"'96 Tears,'" Ward said.

Which meant question mark.

"Gone?" Bliss asked, trying not to sound too hopeful.

"Purloined," Ward said. "The wife showed me where the recorder was. Empty."

"What did Douglas say?"

"He was as confused as I was. He said he'd talk to the guy who installed it. But it seems anyone who knows where the recorder is can have access to the tape."

"Some security," Bliss said. "Maybe it's in here somewhere." Referring to Owen's room. "Maybe he's starting a collection."

They looked, but came up empty.

"I think we need to have a little talk with Owen," Bliss said. "And with his girlfriend, Chantal. I think we need to find out whose bed she slept in that night."

The entire block of Park Avenue around Fred's street was lined with TV vans. Reporters were standing in front of video cameras, talking bullshit into their microphones, no doubt spreading misinformation about his family. Fred wanted to tell his driver to ram the cameras, knock over the vans with their antennas, but he knew more would come, to cover *that* story. It was like Lennigan versus the ants—there were too many. He couldn't kill them all.

A cop stopped his limo at the entrance to his street. Fred rolled down his window.

"I live here," Fred said.

"I'll need to see some ID," the cop said.

"What do you mean ID?" Fred asked. He looked at the cop's name tag. "Patrolman Carter," Fred said, "move the barrier and let me through."

"I need to see proof of your address," the cop said. Like a robot. "A driver's license. Then I can let you through."

"Not only do I *live* on this street," Fred said, "but these fucking trees that everybody thinks are so pretty with their purple blossoms, I *paid* for them."

Fred showed him his driver's license. Patrolman Carter told another cop to move the barrier. Everyone needed someone to boss around, Fred thought.

The limo stopped in front of his house, and as soon as the driver got out and went to open Fred's door, frenzied screaming erupted across the street, from young girls assembled behind some barricades.

"It's him!" they screamed. "It's Holden!"

The television crews and photographers aimed their cameras—flashes went off, TV lights flooded the street. The police had corralled them all at the end of the block, as they did for parades. Some held their cameras at arm's length above the crowd, no eye connected with them, pointing at Fred. That was cheating.

Fred got out of the car and shouted at them.

"He's not here, you scavengers. Look! See!" He opened the door wide so they could all look inside. "It's just me." The cameras started clicking anyway, focused on the empty car. They shouted more questions at him, like at the airport. All at once, like pigs squealing.

The limo driver rushed to the trunk to get the bags, but Fred was in no hurry. He leaned against the car and stared at them—the reporters and photographers and Holden's coterie of fans—gathered behind the barricade like animals in the zoo. He should feed them, he thought. He reached into the limo and grabbed the jar of nuts the driver kept on the bar. Fred opened it and poured some into his open hand. "Here," he shouted. "You look hungry." He flung the nuts toward the crowd. Again the cameras clicked, the voices rose. He knew Douglas would be upset with him about his behavior. He knew it would cost him a couple of grand extra in spin control. He didn't care. *Fred! Hey*

Fred! They kept calling to him, shouting questions. He threw another handful of nuts. It was like when he was a kid and used to go to a pond near his house, a clear shallow pond that was home to a large school of sunnies. Fred would stand on a rock and spit in the pond. The sunnies would swim over all excited, thinking his spit was bread.

Stupid fucking fish would think his spit was bread.

"Fred."

He heard his name and turned to see from the other side of the street, away from the reporters, a man walking toward him, waving, a big smile on his face. No camera. No notebook. Just a guy in a nice suit, like he'd just gotten off work. Someone he knew, but couldn't place. A neighbor, probably. Fellow brownstone owner, curious about the crowd. A cop stopped the man, but Fred said it was okay, and moved toward him, around the front of the limo, away from the commotion.

"I'll take these up, Mr. Gelman," the driver said, holding the bags. Fred nodded. He'd had enough fun with the crowd. He wanted to go inside his house.

The guy who called his name came closer, was now just a few feet away, still smiling.

"It's like a circus," the guy said.

Fred nodded in agreement.

"They all need to get a life," Fred said.

Fred was about to apologize for the chaos when the man punched him hard in the face.

The fucking guy punched me!

Fred covered up, but the guy was all over him. "Help!" he shouted, but then a sharper pain overwhelmed him—the man's knee in his stomach—and he couldn't get any words out and he was bent over gasping for air. The man hit him again and again, randomly, on the shoulder and back and head, just pounding away. Where were the cops? Fred tried to lurch forward to get free but the man moved after him and pushed Fred into the road and started kicking at him, kicking wildly, missing sometimes as Fred curled up in a ball and tried to spin away, using his feet to kick back, trying to keep the man away, feeling blood on his face. A searing pain ran through Fred's arm as the point of the man's shoe connected with the hand that was covering his head. And then it was over. The blows stopped. He peeked through his fingers, saw the cops holding the man, lifting him off the ground, because his legs were still moving, still trying to connect with him, flinging out madly, like a broken machine. Fred uncurled from his protective ball, realized he was on the street, he was lying on the street, his face in a small puddle of his own blood. He got to his knees and only then did he actually hear the voice, which had been there all through the onslaught but Fred hadn't registered it. A wild furious voice.

Your son killed my son! the voice screamed, at *him*, at *Fred*. A high-pitched unearthly sound. *Your son killed Ben and now I'm going to kill you!*

Bliss watched quietly as the housekeeper came in the living room with a Ziploc full of ice. Douglas the lawyer jumped out of his chair to take it from her. He brought it to Fred, wanting to place the ice on the lump now bulging from Fred's forehead. Bliss wondered how Douglas would bill him for this service.

Fred grabbed the bag away from his lawyer and held it to his own head.

"Fucking guy tried to kill me," he said.

"We'll press charges, Fred," Douglas said.

"Did you arrest him?" Fred asked.

"No," Bliss said.

"The street is swarming with cops. You couldn't catch him, get him in cuffs? Dom would know what to do with the little prick."

"His son was murdered," Ward said. "We cut him a little slack."

"He sucker-punched me."

Douglas put a soothing hand on his client's shoulder.

"We'll deal with it, Fred," Douglas said.

"You bet your ass we will."

They were in the Gelman living room—all the men. Fred and his lawyer sat on the plush sofa, Owen in a leather armchair, Dom in a small antique chair, dwarfing it as he leaned forward, elbows on his knees. Bliss and Ward stood by the fireplace. They could have been there to discuss a merger, or launching young Owen's career. Instead, they needed to talk to about a murder, specifically to find out what Owen knew.

"Can we start?" Bliss asked Douglas.

"Go ahead," Douglas said. "Just remember, the young man has only just discovered his best friend was murdered."

"I will, Douglas," Bliss said. He turned to Owen. "When was the last time you saw Ben alive?"

Owen turned to Douglas with a questioning look.

"Go ahead," Douglas said. Clearly they had worked this out already.

"He was talking to Chantal," Owen said in a soft voice. "He . . ." Owen looked over at his father now, worried.

"Say it," Fred said.

"He was wearing my mother's fur coat. Just his boxers and the fur coat."

Bliss noticed the father was chuckling, perhaps enjoying the image of Ben in fur. Maybe Fred liked to do the same thing when he was a kid. Maybe he still did.

"Where were Ben and Chantal when you saw them?" Bliss asked.

"On the ground floor. I was on the stairs, looking down. They didn't see me. They were talking. Actually, Ben was . . ." Owen faltered for a moment, sorting this memory out, either trying to remember what actually happened, or what Douglas had told him to say. "Ben was on his knees. He was kissing her stomach."

"Were you jealous?"

Owen looked at Douglas. Douglas cleared his throat.

"They were all friends, Detective," Douglas said. "You know how kids are these days."

"Did Ben often get on his knees and kiss your girlfriend's stomach?" Bliss asked.

This was apparently too much for Douglas.

"Detective," Douglas said, scolding him.

"Okay," Bliss said. "So what did you do then, Owen? Did you come downstairs?"

"No. I went to my room. I was waiting for Chantal."

"You didn't go downstairs to find her?"

"No. She was supposed . . . I wanted her to come up on her own. It was my birthday."

"And did she?"

"No," he said. "She . . . I must have fallen asleep or something. I don't know. I felt pretty tired. The next thing I knew it was Sunday morning."

"Did you have a lot to drink?" Bliss asked.

Owen looked at Douglas. Douglas put up his hand to wait. Douglas was thinking. Then Douglas spoke.

"It was a party, detective," Douglas said. "A certain amount of drinking takes place. Owen might have had a beer, to feel part of the group. But not more than one. Isn't that right, Owen?"

"I guess I had a beer," Owen said. "It's sort of what you do at parties. Like what Douglas said."

"And that was the last time you saw Ben?"

"Yes."

"On his knees, in front of your girlfriend, kissing her navel. Dressed in your mother's fur coat and his boxers."

"That's his statement," Douglas said.

"Do you think the reason Chantal didn't come to see you was because she was with someone else?" Bliss asked.

Owen's eyes flashed. But before he could speak, Douglas was up, in front of him, shielding him from the evil detectives.

"Enough." Douglas said. "The boy is grief-stricken over the loss of his friend. Let's try not to make him feel even worse."

Douglas made a show about leading Owen out of the room. But Bliss could see the idea that Chantal was with someone else had struck a nerve.

Bliss wanted to press it, but thought he'd better wait.

He would talk to Owen again, mention to him the blond hair found in the bed where Ben was murdered, the blood on the sheets, on Ben's penis. Yes, he would talk to Owen very soon. From the size of him, Bliss thought, Owen would have no problem wielding a ten-pound dumbbell. Especially if sufficiently provoked, like discovering Chantal was sleeping with his best friend.

Dom DeMoro sat on the bench in the backyard and listened while Fred ranted at Douglas.

"How could you let them get away with that shit?" Fred said. "Letting him talk to Owen like that."

"It's okay, Fred," Douglas said. "No harm done. It was bound to come up. Better now than later."

"Fuck them," Fred said.

Dom liked this backyard. No sagging clotheslines, no TV antennas or dead trees or broken radiators or deformed plastic swimming pools like the backyards where he grew up. He first saw it when Douglas called him in to revamp the Gelmans' security system. He'd been back a few times since, to set up the cameras. And now this.

Fred threw the bag of ice he was holding to his head against the fence.

"This isn't from when he hit me," he said, making sure they knew he could take a punch. "I banged it on the street when I fell."

Dom nodded. The guy wouldn't last twenty seconds with a flyweight from Veracruz who, for a measly two-hundred-dollar purse, wants nothing more than to see you lying unconscious in the center of the ring with blood coming out of your ear. See how in control he would be then. Punches coming at you so fast the pain from the first one hasn't registered before the next one connects; head butts in the clinches, eye gouges, shots to the kidneys the ref never sees. Let Fred deal with *that* for a few rounds.

"Whattaya think, Dom, you like that bench?" Fred asked him, his voice more rough, now. Like he was from Brooklyn. Trying to impress Dom, commune with him.

"It's comfy," Dom said.

"Good. Because that bench is the *third* fucking bench we got," he said. "My wife didn't *like* the first two benches. They didn't go with the *feel* of the yard. I bet you didn't think a back-yard could have a *feel*. But they do. Or at least that's what the backyard designer said. For ten grand a week they've got to say something. Not the right feng fucking shui!"

Fred started pacing across the flagstones, working himself up. The guy was starting to unravel, Dom thought. It's a good time to get what you want from someone when they're starting to unravel. A good time to put them down on the canvas. Dom was thinking about his apartment, the terrace, setting up a grill, making some steaks, maybe having that writer over. Mae Stark.

Douglas made a big deal about checking his watch.

"Don't worry, Douglas," Fred said, getting nasty, "you can bill me for this."

"It's not that, Fred," Douglas said. "It's just I promised Katja . . ."

"Unless you were stupid enough to put her name on the checking account, Katja isn't going anywhere," Fred said.

Katja was Douglas's second wife, a potter, twenty years younger than he was. She made pots in a studio Douglas rented for her. Douglas had bragged to Dom about how she liked to take her shirt off while she did her pottery, trying to impress him, so Dom wouldn't think he was washed up. *Great tits*, he said to Dom, all excited, rubbing his hands together, as if she would be anywhere near him if he wasn't paying for everything.

"I want this prick," Fred said.

"We do too, Fred," Douglas said.

Fred held out a tightly closed fist. "I want to make him suffer."

Dom felt himself smirk just a little. He couldn't help it.

"We'll find him, Fred," Douglas said. "Then the system will do the rest."

"What are you talking about?" Fred asked.

"The guy who killed Ben. We'll make sure we find who-ever did it."

"Fuck Ben. I want that prick who hit me. I want him on his knees."

Now this was getting interesting, Dom thought.

"The guy was upset, Fred," Douglas said.

"It's no excuse."

"We've got to focus on Owen," Douglas said officiously. "To make sure he's not implicated. Frankly, I feel that should be our principal concern."

"What's he doing?" Fred said, pointing in Dom's direction.

"Dom's got to keep on top of the police," Douglas said, "to know which way the investigation is going, anticipate their moves if they start getting close to Owen."

Fred walked over, stood in front of him, threw back his shoulders like he was doing a bad Jimmy Cagney impression.

"You play football?" he asked.

"High school. In Canarsie," Dom said.

"I could tell. By your neck. You were in the ring, too. Right?" Fred said, his tone now chummy, man to man. "Golden Gloves. Right?"

"I had some pro fights, too."

"You win any?"

"All but one."

"You look like a smart guy, Dom. You think you can do two things at once?"

Douglas cleared his throat and spoke.

"Fred, I don't really think . . ."

Fred wheeled on him, getting in Douglas's face, talking low, so the cops still in the house wouldn't hear him.

"Do you think Owen did it?" Fred asked him.

"What?"

"I'm asking you, as my lawyer, as someone who has known Owen most of his life, do you think my son killed this kid?"

"No. No, Fred."

"Owen didn't go into a jealous rage and whack Ben's head with a ten-pound dumbbell?"

"Absolutely not."

"So what's the problem? Let's give Dom a little latitude. See what he can dig up on this guy, on this Rick, the fuck who hit me. Let him just nose around. Find something on him and bring him down. It's out there. It's always out there."

"Okay, Fred," Douglas said, brushing off a leaf that had fallen on his shoulder. "It's your choice."

"Goddamn right it's my choice. And I just made it."

Dom got the distinct feeling he would be dealing more directly with Fred now. That Douglas the lawyer didn't have a clue as to what was really going on.

He smiled and shook Fred's hand, thinking the camera he installed was aimed right at them and would no doubt be recording this historic moment, Fred Gelman shaking hands with Dom DeMoro preserved on surveillance video, if Dom hadn't already snatched the tape and tucked it away to look at later, at his leisure, a little late night entertainment. Better than the movies.

Because unlike the movies, in a good surveillance video you never knew what was going to happen.

They were sitting in Ward's car outside the townhouse. Inside, forensics was working hard, collecting fibers, prints, blood stains. Traces of Bliss would be in there somewhere, too.

The media vans were still parked on Park, reporters hanging out talking to the uniforms. Onlookers stood behind the
barricades, lingering, hoping something might happen, that they
might get interviewed, readying their favorite Holden moment
so they could summon it if a reporter asked them—preparing to
say how sorry they felt, the neighbors not having any idea how
this could have happened, baffled by a death so close to their
front door. And somewhere in the crowd was the goofy kid you
always see in the background, who walks by the camera waving, grinning like a gargoyle, oblivious to any sense of tragedy.
Or maybe the goofy kid understood the deeper significance, that
there was no tragedy, because it wasn't him who got dead.

"You think he did it?" Bliss asked his partner.

"Owen?"

"Yeah."

"Found his friend in bed with his girlfriend and put out his
lights?"

"It's a motive," Bliss said.

"Jealousy."

"Yeah."

"We've seen it before." Then Bliss added, "I was there that
night."

"Where?"

"In the house. The night of the party. I went inside."

"This house?"

"I went to look for Julia. It was 3:30 in the morning. She
was supposed to be home."

"What are you telling me?"

"I went in the house. The door was unlocked. I was looking for Julia." *Lie to your wife if you have to. Your rabbi.* "I went
upstairs."

"What did you see?"

"The kid. In bed."

"Alive?"

"I don't know. I peeked in, saw his feet, closed the door. I wanted to find Julia."

"Was she there?"

"No."

"But she was at the party."

"Just for a few minutes. Early on. Then she left. I didn't realize she was already home."

Ward turned, stared out the window. Bliss knew what he was thinking.

"Whoever has the surveillance tape will know you were there," Ward said. "The whole investigation will be tainted."

"I know."

"It could be bad for you, not saying anything about being at the crime scene. It could be very bad."

Bliss didn't have to respond.

"We need to find the tape," Ward said.

"Yeah."

"And we *really* need to find the girl. Get this thing solved quick."

Bliss nodded. There was nothing more to say.

This case was now as much about him as it was about the dead boy.

"I should go home now," Chantal said. They were on the roof of Malcolm's dad's loft. Malcolm had his arm around her. His dad was taking their picture. "My parents are probably freaking."

"So soon?" Malcolm said, pouting.

Chantal laughed. Just as she did, Malcolm's dad snapped a photo.

Her head was finally clear. She looked at her hand, trying to remember if the blood she saw there earlier was real or just a dream.

"You had fun today?" Malcolm asked.

"Today was one of the best days of my life," Chantal said. "I know that sounds corny, but it was."

Malcolm spread out his arms really wide and she walked into his embrace. She closed her eyes, his long arms held her tightly. His breathing stayed soft and steady, no arousal, no sly hands maneuvering toward her more desirable locales. No, this was just pure hug. He let her go gently. She didn't notice the tear until Malcolm reached up to her cheek and dabbed it with his sleeve.

"What are you going to do next year, after I graduate?" he said. "Who's going to take care of you?"

He kissed her forehead. Then he whispered in her ear.

"My dad thinks you're pretty enough to be a model. But you don't want to do that, do you?"

She shook her head.

"Good. We'll drive you home now," Malcolm asked.

"I can take a cab."

"No. We'll drive you," Malcolm said. "I want to make sure you get home safe."

Clara turned the corner on Lexington Avenue, walking away from the crowd that was gathering in front of the house. Back in the Philippines, she remembered a similar crowd gathering around a small whale that had washed up on the beach. But soon the gulls and herons came to feast on the rotting carcass, and when they needed to relieve themselves, they did it directly on the people watching, perhaps in sympathy for the whale, who maybe they felt deserved to rot in peace.

Clara was glad to be away from the police, afraid they were going to ask her about her green card. She was nearing the subway entrance when she heard her name.

"Clara."

She prayed it wasn't Immigration.

"Clara. Excuse me."

Clara turned, pleased to see the woman was too young and dolled up to be any kind of official. She was marching forward, her hand out for Clara to shake.

"I'm Adelaide," she said when she got close. She was perky and smartly dressed. "I . . . maybe we could talk for a minute. I'm a journalist."

"I don't think so," Clara said. It was late. Clara was tired. She started to turn and walk away.

"Let me buy you a coffee. Tea. Anything. I just want to talk with you about the Gelmans. You *do* work there, don't you?"

Clara stopped, still not saying anything, uneasy about where this would go.

"Maybe you can help me," Adelaide said. "And maybe I can help you."

"How can you help me?" Clara said.

"Well, it depends," the girl said with a suggestive smile.

Clara thought the girl Adelaide had a pretty face. Pretty, but empty. Clara had seen many just like her, sitting in the back row of her classroom, a fashion magazine hidden behind their textbooks. They usually wound up with one of the American servicemen stationed at the base. Sometimes more than one. If

they were lucky, they wouldn't get pregnant and left behind
when the soldier went stateside. Usually they weren't lucky. A
year or so later they would be back in her classroom, the sparkle
gone from their eyes, their baby at home with their mother, trying to finish high school and get a job as a nanny or housekeeper
in America. No Philippine boy would have them now. They
were damaged goods.

Clara decided she should play along with this silly girl, see
where it went.

"Let's get some coffee," Adelaide said.

"No. Just say what you have to say."

"Okay. How does $25,000 sound? For an exclusive story.
The inside scoop on the Gelman household. Who came and
went. How they lived. What they did. Why you think Owen's
friend was killed."

"The friend was killed because he wasn't very nice."

Adelaide looked disappointed.

"That may be true. But there must be more. Did you know
Owen's girlfriend, the one who's missing? Chantal, right? Can
you get me some photos?"

"Photos?"

"There must be some lying around."

"That would be stealing," Clara said.

"No one will know where they came from," she whispered
conspiratorially. "We have freedom of the press in this country."

Clara wanted to ask her: *Who was the twelfth president? What
was Teapot Dome? Who were the Mugwumps?*

"What do you think, Clara? Some photos of Holden and
Owen together. As little kids. Can you do it?"

Of course it would be about Holden, the famous one. If Owen
actually did it, the newspapers would say "Holden's Brother Guilty!"

"Okay, $30,000," Adelaide said, "but that's as high as I'm authorized to go."

Clara thought how in those two seconds of silence she made an extra five thousand dollars, as much money as she took home in three months of housekeeping. Five thousand dollars just by being quiet. That's why everyone wants to come to America.

"Okay," Clara said.

"You'll do it?"

"Yes."

"You have a bank account?"

"No."

"We'll work around it," Adelaide said. She was excited.

"A money order, made out to my mother in the Philippines."

"To your mother?"

"Yes."

"That's precious. You want us to send it directly to her?"

"No. When we're done, I'll take it there myself."

Chantal sat on the couch in her living room. Her father and mother sat across from her in armchairs upholstered in fabric that matched the couch.

Chantal found it curious that her father didn't comfort her mother, hold her hand or pat her on the back. He sat motionless, not saying anything, just shaking his head.

"Why didn't you call?" her mother said through her tears.

"You really should have called," her father said.

Chantal wondered why there weren't any books in her house. Well, there were a few books, best-seller books and some gigantic art books on Michelangelo and Chagall, but nothing like Malcolm's dad's house. His bookcases were packed full and went up to the ceiling. And he didn't take the jackets off like Chantal's mother did, so they would look nicer on the shelves.

"I thought you were dead," her mother said.

"Oh, Mom."

"Why didn't you call, Chantal?" her father said. His voice had an edge to it now. Angry. How was it so many people wound up getting angry at her?

"Where were you?" her mother said, tissues to her nose.

"I was in a church," she said.

"All this time?"

"Yes," she said. Because she didn't want them to know about her driving to Coney Island with Malcolm and his dad in their Impala convertible with the top down. How they got hot dogs and french fries at Nathan's and then went to the boardwalk to eat them as they looked at the ocean. And how each of them had a camera, she and Malcolm and his dad, and how she found things to photograph; like broken signs that meant something different because some of the letters were missing; a toothless woman eating raw clams at a counter on the boardwalk; a baby playing in the sand on the beach; lovers kissing on a bench; an old man fishing off the end of the pier and holding up the bluefish he caught that morning with a smile that seemed ready to burst from his face.

"I was in church, sitting in a pew under a stained glass window with a picture of one of the saints, the one with the arrows through his chest," she said. Because she didn't want to reveal how much she had laughed in the ocean breeze, and how she and Malcolm went on the Wonder Wheel and the bumper cars and failed to knock over the milk bottles so many times that the guy gave them each a stuffed animal out of pity and then they took his picture with his sleeve rolled up to show off his tattoo of a girl in a hula skirt which he could make dance by flexing his muscle. And how they bought souvenirs, snow globes of the parachute jump, a Statue of Liberty pencil sharpener, an Empire State Building that played "New York, New York."

Or about how they gave out money. Malcolm's dad had a thick stack of five-dollar bills and they walked around giving them out to every homeless or sorrowful person they met. And Malcolm's dad would take their picture holding the money, not in a egotistical way, like *here I just made your day you poor slob now smile*, but respectfully, just having them look in the camera, letting whatever feelings they had at the moment play out over their faces. And Chantal remembered each of their faces, feeling a more intimate connection with these total strangers than she did with Owen, with whom she was supposedly in love. With her parents. With anyone she knew. Feeling somehow she was one of these lost souls. And because she touched them, made their lives different, better, without their asking, it made her feel good. Clean.

"I sat in church for so long one of the ministers came over to ask me if everything was all right," she said.

"Where did you sleep?"

"I didn't sleep. I walked through the night," she said. "Just kept walking."

"You walked?"

"Yes."

Because she didn't want to tell them about boiling the lobsters and taking them up on Malcolm's roof and how Malcolm's dad had a whole bag of fortune cookies and they taught her the "between the sheets" game where you read your fortune and then add the words "between the sheets" so it's like "You will meet an old friend . . . between the sheets." Or "You have many hidden talents . . . between the sheets." Or "You will soon make a lot of money . . . between the sheets," and they played for hours and their laughter echoed through the streets and how she was so incredibly happy there on the roof with the two of them, with Malcolm and his dad. Happier than she'd ever been.

"Why didn't you come home?" her mother asked, the tears coming again.

"I don't know," she said, because she didn't want to say *because this doesn't feel like home—my home*.

"Maybe you haven't heard the news," her father said.

"What?"

"It's about Ben Purdy."

"What about him?"

"He's dead. Someone killed him."

She felt her stomach tighten.

"Who did it?"

"We don't know. They found him in Holden Gelman's bed."

"Ben's dead?"

"Yes," her mother said.

"Oh."

Chantal wondered why she wasn't feeling more upset. On the TV, when they showed the kids in those high schools where some tragedy happened, they were always hugging each other and crying in each others arms. But that wasn't happening. Not with her. Not about Ben.

"We need to call the police," her dad said. "We're supposed to tell them if you get back."

"Can't we do that in the morning, Jerry?" her mother said. "It's enough for one night."

Her father nodded. He turned to Chantal. He thinks he's supposed to say something to me, she thought. Something deep and profound, to set me on the right track. He had that look on his face—preparation for depth and profundity. She could sense the thoughts trying to organize themselves in his head. Deep thoughts. Profound thoughts.

"Chantal," he said, his voice with that sound in it, that glaze of something important, that Chantal's behavior was challenging some fundamental law of the universe, how if she continued the future of the cosmos would be jeopardized. She couldn't bear that responsibility. Not tonight.

"Can I go to bed now?" she asked. "I'm really tired."

And without waiting for an answer, she got up and left the room.

Bliss came home, saw the dishes on the counter, knew that they had eaten without him, his plate covered with aluminum foil. He wasn't hungry anyway. He opened a beer. He thought about the bottles scattered around the townhouse after the party. Beer and vodka and the single malt Scotch.

He tried not to think about it, but the panic lodged in his throat, compounded with the new fear, that he had just compromised his and Ward's pension.

Julia came out of the bathroom, her hair wrapped in a towel. Rachel followed, saying something about conditioner.

"Hi, Dad," Julia said.

"I don't want you going to any more parties," he blurted out.

"You mean any more parties at *all*, or just ones like at Owen's?"

"No more parties." He wasn't sure where this was going, but he'd already started it.

"Why?"

"Because," he said. *Because I was there. Because of what I saw.*

"Parties like Owen has, fine," she said, "I hate those parties anyway."

"So why do you go?"

"I don't know."

"She came home," Rachel said. "She didn't like the vibe, so she went home."

Julia started laughing.

"The *vibe*, Mom?"

"You know what I mean."

The two of them giggling now.

"What do you think they do at these parties?" he asked Rachel, getting in her face.

"I know what's going on," she said.

"Do you? Do you really?!" Desperately wanting to say *because I was there, I saw it.* "You think it's like the arts and crafts hut? Huh? You think they're making trivets with tile and grout? Branding their names into leather belts? You think they're playing with *gimp?!*"

"Dad."

"There's beer, there's pot. At the end of the night the empty vodka bottles litter the floor. You think I don't know?"

Julia turned to her mother.

"Mom. Please. Help me out here."

He went on, the image clear in his head.

"Every bed is used, sheets on the floor, blankets twisted together." His voice rising now. "*Every bed!* Even in the parents' room."

"Stop it," Julia shouted.

"Lenny," Rachel said. "Please."

"They take turns. They shower together." *There was blood on his penis. How did it get there?* "They copulate."

Julia ran to her room, slammed the door. Bliss was right after her, wrenching the knob, flinging the door open.

"Don't think I wouldn't come get you," he said. *Julia's father. Hello.* "Don't think I wouldn't come right over to the party, snatch you from wherever you were." *Julia's police.* "Whoever you were with."

"I can't believe this," Julia said, starting to cry. "Don't you trust me? Don't you think I try, every day, don't you think I try so hard not to do that, *any* of that?! Jesus! You think it's easy?"

Bliss didn't say anything,

"Do you, Dad?"

"I . . . no, I don't think it's easy."

"I try so hard. You should give me a little more credit. Now please close my door."

He did.

He stood in the hall, head down. He could feel Rachel staring at him.

He remembered his feelings of jealousy as he lurked through the townhouse before dawn, thinking the *real* Julia was at the party. But maybe he did know the real Julia. Maybe she was right here at home.

"Lenny."

"What?"

"You proud of yourself?"

He didn't answer.

"You happy now?"

"No," he finally said. "I'm trying to be a good cop and a good father. How could I possibly be happy? And if you think Mae Stark is happy, then she's fucking lying to herself. And so are you."

Fred went into the library, got out his cell phone, called Marjorie the flight attendent at her hotel. He woke her up.

"Hey, it's Fred."

"Mnngh," she said. She sounded like a cat.

"I feel like Princess Di," he said. "They're hounding me."

"You poor boy," she said.

"You eat yet? You have dinner?"

"Mmmngh," she said. "I'm knackered."

Knackered. He thought that sounded like an invitation.

"You want some company?" he said. "We could have champagne. We could have strawberries and cream. *Clotted* cream, right? I don't know if our cream has clots, but we can find a way. Then we can knacker together."

"That's nice," she said.

"So?"

"Tomorrow," she said. "I took a pill. It's what we do."

"Who? English people?"

"No, silly. Flight attendants."

"Oh," he said. His felt his dick pressing against his pants, harder than Japanese arithmetic. "You're sure you don't want me to come over?"

"Mmmmnnnggh."

"Okay," he said. "Tomorrow then. And listen, I don't like that hotel you're in. In the morning you move." He gave her the name of someplace more exclusive and discreet and where they had decent Champagne and made French toast with the thick slices of bread the way he liked. "Did you write it down?"

"Mmmm-hmmm."

"You'll like it there. It's better. See you tomorrow."

She hung up the phone.

Fuck fuck fuck fuck fuck.

He could call his secretary, tell her he had important business, couldn't wait until tomorrow.

He tried. He got her machine and hung up.

Well, he was tired anyway.

Fred walked upstairs, past the yellow tape. Death had been behind that tape. A boy had been killed. In his house. His son Owen had let death into Fred's home.

Because of the blood, they would be ripping out another carpet. Then Nedra would call in the interior designer so they could choose a new one. Swatches would be involved. Color samples. His opinion would be sought. It seemed so insignificant now, the color of the rug, the color of the paint, the style of the fucking doorknobs, all the shit Nedra cared so much about when they were "doing" the bedrooms. She showed him catalogues, a whole page of doorknobs, round, oval, silver, brass. What did he think? *Who gives a shit about a fucking doorknob?* he thought. Once he made the mistake of thinking it out loud. Nedra started crying. Because he forgot. This was sex with them. This was their sex. Their intimacy. So he had apologized. He studied the catalogue with keen interest and listened intently as she told him about what the interior designer said, about the difference between nickel and silver finishes and whatever else went into doorknob selection, until she was happy.

Until she came.

2

40

BOB SLOAN

He had to have this kind of catalogue/renovation/doorknob-choosing sex with his wife so he could sleep with Sheena and his secretary and hopefully Marjorie the English flight attendant whose pussy he'd already envisioned—soft as clotted cream.

Nedra was in bed, reading a magazine when he got upstairs. She glanced up. Their eyes met.

"I'm depleted," she said.

He nodded.

"I need to not think about anything."

"Okay."

He wondered if she had taken a pill.

"It's too much."

"Yeah."

He noticed her bare arms, holding the magazine, how taut they were. Wiry, but defined. Muscular. When did that happen?

"I'm just going to read," she said.

"Okay."

He sat down on the bed.

"You're arms are looking pretty strong," he said.

She glanced at them, smiled.

"Oh, thanks," she said.

Sometimes he felt Nedra was on loan from the club. That the club was her real home. She just stopped in here, to change her clothes and grab a bite to eat—literally. Her body existed so she could have something to put on a stationary bike, an exercise mat, a massage table.

He lay down next to her on top of the covers and slipped off his shoes.

"How's your head?" she asked.

"It hurts," he said. Then added quickly, "not from where he hit me, but from when I fell."

She nodded.

Fucking Rick.

He touched her arm, felt the hard muscle.

"I should have had you out there to protect me."

She smiled. A nice smile. Somewhere in there, behind the Nedra of the club, the renovations, the lipo and Botox, the expensive haircuts, the expensive clothes, the diets and vitamins and wheat-grass shakes, the yoga and Pilates, was the girl he had married. Somewhere deep inside there. He wondered if he would ever see her again, hold her hand as he once did, make love to her with all his heart. The way he once did. Nedra, somewhere tucked away.

He sighed and closed his eyes.

He would call Dom tomorrow. Set something up. Get Dom focused on Rick. Just because the guy's son was dead didn't mean he could go around hurting people.

Dom took off his shirt, picked up the twenty-pound weights, and did three sets of curls with each arm. Then he worked his triceps for a while. He got down on the carpet, held a weight to his chest, and did his hundred sit-ups. Then he turned over and did fifty push-ups. When he was done, he lay back on the broadloom and tried not to think about the shimmering chandelier of shit dangling above him, lit up with the name of Felix Hernandez, hanging by a thin wire, waiting to come crashing down on his head.

He had to hope this thing with the rich kid getting dead would keep everyone occupied, that it went on for a while, the papers playing it up. Keeping people's minds off Felix.

Dom got up and showered. He popped open a beer and lay on his bed and thought about how glad he was not to be a cop anymore, not having to do everything by the book. He liked being a free agent, playing both sides, always on his toes. Like what Fred was asking him to do. You didn't get to fuck with people that way as a cop; at least you weren't supposed to.

He wanted to see the novelist, Mae, thinking how she'd be a welcome change from the gum-chewing community college girls he was used to. Girls whose dads were all cops or firemen and whose older brothers were cops or firemen and whose one hope in life was to marry a cop or a fireman and give birth to baby boys who would grow up to become cops or firemen and baby girls who would sleep with cops and firemen indiscriminately for several years before finally settling down and marrying one.

Mae clearly had class. He'd track down her number. Then call her up and tell her how he'd be moving to Manhattan soon. He'd have her over to his new place, open a nice bottle of wine, not one of those squat bottles of shitty Chianti wrapped in straw like they served in Tommy DeTolo's, but a *nice* wine. French. They'd sit on the terrace and watch the sunset sipping French wine. He'd need some glasses. The ones with the stems.

Dom popped in the Gelman surveillance video, sat back, and started running through it, jotting down some notes.

8:18—The housekeeper leaves.

8:30—The victim arrives, before everyone else, making a face at the camera, knowing it was there. Smart kid. A nose for security. Too bad he's dead.

9:23—Guests start coming, a steady stream until 11:14.

12:52—A large group leaves, must all have to get home at the same time.

1:24—Another large group, followed by a few stragglers.

2:27—A boy leaves with a girl, the girl having trouble walking. He carries her down the steps.

Then nothing, the patch of streetlight on the front stoop.

Then a man walking up the front steps, trying the front door, turning the handle and walking in. *Turning the handle and walking in!* Forty thousand dollars' worth of security and someone waltzes right in off the street. A large man. Familiar.

After rewinding the tape several times, Dom was sure it was Lenny Bliss going into the house, turning the handle and going into the Gelmans' house at 3:12 and then coming out twenty-two minutes later.

Lenny Bliss was in the house around the time of the murder. For twenty-two minutes.

Dom stopped the tape.

What did you do in there, Detective? Were you looking for someone? A boy, perhaps? A boy who subsequently had his head smashed in by someone strong enough to do it?

Dom wasn't sure how, but he sensed this turn of events was going to work in his favor.

He sat back in his chair and smiled.

On his toes. Dom was always on his toes.

Detective Bliss was there, that night, in the house around the time of the murder. And Dom had him on tape.

Gotcha.

TUESDAY

Bliss lay in the bathtub, his eyes closed. He was thinking about Julia, his daughter, being talked about by the boys in school, the same way he and his friends had done. In the hallway, by their lockers, watching as Julia walked by, talking in deep, hushed tones, assessing his daughter's tits, her ass. Rating her. Imagining how she would look naked, what it would be like to have her.

He sat up, arms raised, fists clenched, ready to pummel the shit out of them, but succeeding only in sending a wave of water over the side of the tub, where it collected near the corner of the bathroom.

Shit.

He stood up and grabbed a towel and dropped it on the puddle to soak up the water. The last thing he needed was his downstairs neighbor's ceiling leaking, like the time Cori was doing some kind of science experiment in the bathroom sink.

He sat down slowly in the tub. Bliss knew a judge who could probably get him one of those house arrest collars, the ones they use to keep someone from leaving town. He could have it set for Julia's bedroom, so he would know if she went out. He wondered if they came in assorted colors, to go with different outfits, in case Julia didn't warm to the idea right away.

He tried to relax. Breathe into the stretch. Be in the present.

He pulled his leg toward Lotus. It moved more easily. Maybe because he was in the bath. Maybe because he was so pissed off. He wondered if too much stress was the same as no stress. Sometimes opposites worked that way. He almost had his leg in place when his butt slipped and he slid down and his nose filled with suds and warm water.

Once again the floor was soaked, though not as badly.

He settled back into his tub position, used his toe to turn the faucet to add more hot water. There was some yoga in that, he thought. It was his own pose. Toe Turning Faucet.

His thoughts drifted back to his daughter.

Even if she hadn't stayed long at Owen's party, there would be other parties. Give her time. Or worse, she would meet some sensitive, thoughtful guy with European parents who would take her to a Truffaut double feature, and after that for herbal tea, and then back to his apartment, which was empty because his parents were in Milan, at La Scala for the opening of the opera season. And soon he would be making his moves. Putting *Kind of Blue* on the CD player and making his well-practiced Euro moves.

He'd have to have a talk with her. More calmly this time. Just the two of them. A father-daughter talk. And if that didn't work, a cop-daughter talk. Sort this out. Then maybe Bliss could avoid dangling some high school boy out a tenth floor window until, weeping and drooling with fear, he promised never to touch Julia or any other girl again for the rest of his life.

He got out of the tub, to get ready for work. He had to go back to Ben's house, to talk with Mr. and Mrs. Purdy again.

But he could deal with their grief and pain. Give me a murder, he thought. A triple homicide, any kind of dead body, because Lord knows it was a lot easier than being a parent.

*   *   *

The detectives were back. Rick let them in. Bliss spoke softly to him, sounding paternal. Comforting.

"How are you feeling, Mr. Purdy?" he asked.

"All right," Rick said.

"No more outbursts, I hope."

"I don't know what got into me. I've never done anything like that before."

He felt Ellen stiffen, knew she was thinking *now*, when it was too late, he was taking control. How many times had she wanted him to raise his voice, shouting at Ben the way he did in the street last night at Fred. Getting angry. Climbing out of his suitcase and shouting at his son *No. I don't want you to do that!*

"We need to look in Ben's room," Bliss said. "Is that okay?"

Rick led them down the hall. A funny little procession. Rick, the two detectives, and Ellen. The door was locked. Rick didn't have the key.

"Do you mind if we force it open?" Bliss asked.

So polite, Rick thought. *Nonjudgmental.* That Rick couldn't unlock his son's room was evidence neither of Rick's weakness nor of his pitiful impersonation of a father. It was just a minor inconvenience. Something to be overcome.

But he knew Ellen wanted so badly to tell the detectives it was Rick's fault. *He's* the one who allowed this to happen. Not having a key to Ben's room was just the tip of the iceberg. *You have no idea, detectives, how bad it got. No consequences! No repercussions!* She wanted them to know that Rick was the one who really killed their son. *Never mind opening the door, never mind the clues. Arrest him! Arrest my husband! The one who works for my father.*

"Mr. Purdy?"

"Huh?"

Bliss gestured to the locked door.

"Oh. Do whatever you have to," Rick said.

The other cop lifted his huge foot and kicked the door. Not using his shoulder the way Rick had always imagined, but his foot. That made more sense. The wood splintered. One more kick and it opened.

That's all it took.

Of course Ben wasn't in there now, so it was easier.

The detectives went inside. Rick hovered by the door, Ellen near him.

"Maybe it's better if you don't watch this," Bliss said.

"It's okay," Ellen said.

Bliss got down on his hands and knees and looked under the bed. The bed stood where Ben's crib once was. Rick remembered when they bought the crib. He and Ellen had picked it out together, spending hours in the baby store, Ellen with her belly about to burst. They were both so excited, eager to be parents, Ellen wanting so much to be a mother.

They had gone to several stores to find exactly the right crib, a mobile to hang above it, and cushioned bumpers to go around it, to keep their boy from bumping his head (they knew from the whattayacallit, the X-ray thing, that it was a boy). And they bought a monitor so they could hear his cries from the next room if he got hurt. And safety plugs for the sockets and the locks for the drawers. All so he wouldn't get hurt.

Making his room safe so Ben would never get hurt. Childproofing, they called it. So there was less risk. So nothing bad could happen to their son.

The detectives surveyed the space, taking it in, like a couple thinking about buying the apartment. Rick and Ellen had done the same thing years ago, in this exact room, with Ellen's mother, walking around what the agent said would be a perfect baby's room. A perfect room for a perfect baby. And Ellen and her mother were mapping things out—the crib would go here, the changing table here, the rocking chair, where Ellen would sit while nursing, would go here. His mother-in-law with them because Ellen's parents were providing the down payment for the apartment, were buying all the baby furniture. Luggage paying for everything.

"He had his own phone line?" Bliss asked.

His own line. Yes, Ben had his own line. Rick called him once, late at night. Rick sitting in the kitchen, thinking about Ben, how he hadn't spoken to him, *really* spoken to his son in what seemed like months. Had no idea what was going on in Ben's life. Like Ben was far away. And then it struck Rick—what do you do when people are far away? You call them. So he called his son, and the phone rang in his son's room not ten feet away from where Rick sat. Ben didn't answer. Apparently Ben wasn't home, even though it was 10:30 on a school night. *Consequences! Repercussions!* So Rick left a message on his son's answering machine. *Hi Ben, it's Dad.* Rick asked how he was, what he'd been up to. Then Rick remembered saying nothing, trying to say *I miss you* but the words not coming, his mouth dry. Then he had hung up and quickly had an image of Ben playing the message and laughing, not hearing any of his father's pain and sorrow. Playing it for his friends and laughing.

"Mr. Purdy?"

Just laughing.

"Mr. Purdy?"

"Yes."

"His own line?"

"Yes."

Bliss made a note of the number. He hit *69 and listened, jotting down what Rick assumed was the number of Ben's last incoming call. Then Bliss called someone, the precinct maybe, and told them to pull the phone records.

The other detective, Ward, was searching the closet, feeling the sleeves of the sport jackets, checking their pockets, tapping the floorboards, opening drawers, feeling inside. They worked together without speaking, so proficient. Partners.

"Are you looking for clues?" Ellen asked him.

"Yes," the detective said.

"So am I," she said, turning to Rick with disgust.

Good, Rick thought. Maybe now they'll get it. A taste of it. Pure Ellen. They would understand how he felt.

"Your son keep a diary?" the detective asked.

"My son had no feelings, detective," Ellen said. "So he had no use for a diary. I'm sorry."

Excellent. Keep it up, Ellen.

"You sure you want to watch this, Mrs. Purdy?" Bliss asked her. He was on his knees behind Ben's bed, his arms between the mattress and the box spring, feeling for something. "We can call you if we need to ask . . ."

"No," Ellen said, interrupting her. "I want to be here when you find some clues. Maybe I'll discover something about my son, what he was like. What he dreamt about. His secrets."

Rick felt Ellen's eyes burning into him. But the detectives displayed no pity for her, the woman who had to live with a husband who let her down every day. Who sold *luggage!* Who worked for her *father!* The detectives simply went about their business.

But Ellen wasn't finished yet.

Ellen always had more.

"Do you have children?" she asked Detective Ward.

"No," Ward said.

"You're lucky," Ellen said. "When you have a child you become vulnerable to the greatest pain a person can possibly feel. I've been thinking about this. Putting this together."

"Yes."

"If your husband dies, or your parents, there is always sadness. But if your child dies . . . if your child . . . I once thought when I was pregnant, I was carrying a little life inside me, a precious little life. Now I realize what I really had was a death growing in my belly."

"Mrs. Purdy," Ward said, "I really think it would be better if . . ."

Ellen interrupted him.

"Maybe you have a young nephew or a niece . . ."

"Ma'am . . ."

"Because I was going to say, if you saw anything in there, in the room while you were searching it, saw anything you think some child might get some use out of, might bring them a little happiness, then you should feel free to take it. Once you've dusted it for prints, of course."

Bliss looked at Ward, who shrugged his shoulders. If the wife wants to stay, let her. They resumed the search.

"Got something," Bliss said.

He pulled his hand from underneath the mattress. It was holding some kind of videotape. He put it in a plastic bag, then wrote something on the bag, perhaps: *found under Ben's mattress—father had no idea.*

"Got something here, too," Ward said. He held the drawer with Ben's underwear. Taped to the outer side of the back of the drawer was a baggie containing a small amount of white powder. The detectives didn't seem very excited.

"You know anything about this, Mr. Purdy?" the detective asked.

This started Ellen laughing.

"Him?" she said, turning to him with bitter disdain, hatred. "Know *anything?*" Her voice, incredulous. "About our son?"

Then more laughing. They waited for her to stop. She didn't. Her laughter turned to sobbing.

Bliss turned to Rick, seeming genuinely mad at him for not taking care of his wife.

But Rick couldn't be bothered with that right now. He had something else on his mind. Rick wanted to ask the detectives if they knew where he could buy a gun. They'll know, he thought. They deal with this kind of thing all the time. People buying guns.

So, detective, tell me, where do you get one?

And how much do they cost?

And could you take me?

Maybe later today, if you guys aren't too busy, no more murders to investigate, do you think perhaps we could all go together and find me a gun?

They were in the back of an appliance store on the West Side, owned by a guy Ward knew who wouldn't say anything about the two detectives borrowing a camera to play back a videotape.

Bliss and Ward stared at the image on the small screen of the camera, the front stoop of the Gelman house—empty. The Gelman backyard, empty.

Bliss thought for a moment that this could be the tape, but once again he was disappointed. The clock in the bottom corner said 10:02 A.M. The date was last month.

The tape showed Fred Gelman, arriving, keys in hand, at the front stoop of his house and unlocking the door. With him was a woman. She looked younger than Fred. Cut to the backyard. Cut back to Fred, turning to the woman, eyebrows raised salaciously, à la Groucho, and opening the door. Cut to the backyard, cut to the front stoop, empty now, Fred and the woman inside.

Like father, like son.

Ward fast-forwarded the tape, caught the fleeting image of Fred and the woman leaving about two hours later.

Then nothing. Then the housekeeper coming home with groceries.

Bliss turned away.

"This isn't the right tape," he said.

"Guess Fred forgot he had surveillance installed," Ward said. "People who live in glass houses shouldn't bring their secretaries home."

"So who has the tape from the night of the party?" Bliss said.

"If it was Douglas the lawyer, he'd have said something by now."

"Maybe he's saving it," Bliss said. "He might soon be reading about himself in the *Daily News*—'Hero Dad, Killer Cop?'"

"Anyone at the party could have snatched the tape," Ward said.

"Maybe the perp took it," Bliss said.

"Or maybe it was never there," Ward said. "Maybe the tape of *Backyard Rapture* starring Owen and Chantal was supposed to be in the machine and no one replaced it. That's the scenario we'll go with. Let Douglas try to prove something else."

They could both lose their shields for this. Or worse.

"Seeing Owen getting serviced is going to make Douglas wish the surveillance never existed," Bliss said.

What if it had been Julia, he thought, on the tape, on the bench next to the smirking boy, reaching into his pants, touching him? It was her best friend, after all. The same age. So close. What would he do?

"That night," he said to his partner, "I panicked. I had this vision something was wrong. She'd never missed her curfew before. Never not called."

Just don't come home dead, Lenny. I don't want to be working your case tomorrow.

"It's okay, partner."

"No. Listen. I was so sure something was wrong. I could see it so clearly."

"She's your daughter."

"My father never went looking for me," Bliss said. "I guess I don't want to be like him."

"Few of us do," Ward said.

Fred heard girls shrieking outside his house, and knew his son Holden had arrived from Hollywood.

He opened the front door, saw Holden waving to the crowd from the top of the stoop. Next to Holden, Fred's flaky brother-in-law Arnie, carrying both his and Holden's bags. All the cameras were aimed at them. Reporters were shouting questions, shoving their microphones forward, hoping for an answer, begging for a few words from his son, as if he were a saint, someone holy who could save them from pain and pestilence, instead of just a horny, empty-headed, fourteen-year-old actor who had spent so much time in front of the television cameras that he probably didn't know how to do long division.

"Get in the house," Fred said.

Holden waved once more, eliciting another round of screaming. Fred grabbed his son by the arm and yanked him inside. Then he shut the door.

"Dad," Holden said.

"It's enough," Fred said.

Then the doorbell rang.

"Who the fuck is that?" Fred asked.

Holden went to open the door.

"Don't," Fred said.

"It's Uncle Arnie, Dad," Holden said. "You locked him out."

Holden opened the door and Fred's brother-in-law struggled in, banging the suitcases on the table in the foyer, almost knocking over the bowl of Venetian glass fruit they had to take the special boat to get on the island near Venice, not the island *everyone* goes to, but another island, a smaller one, a *special* island that Nedra's friend had already gone to to get *her* glass fruit, standing sweating like a pig by the furnaces so Nedra could watch them blow the glass fruit and the glass bowl to put them in, the same glass fruit and bowl they saw in a store the next day near San Marco for the same price only without spending the four hundred bucks to charter a boat.

Hey, as long as it made her happy.

"Dad," Holden said. He spread his arms wide and gave Fred a hug. For a second Fred feared Holden was going to kiss him on both cheeks. He wanted see Sheena. He wanted to be with Marjorie the flight attendant. "You okay, Dad?"

"Yeah."

"Where's Mom?"

"At the club."

"I thought Arnie called her, to say when we were coming."

"She's at the club," he repeated. "She'll be back soon. She's spinning her Pilates or something."

Owen came downstairs.

"Hey, Holden," he said.

"Hey, Big Bro," Holden said, which was what he said in his sitcom to his sitcom brother.

Holden hugged him, too.

"Sorry about your friend," Holden said.

Shit, Fred thought. I should have said that.

Then Holden clapped his hands excitedly.

"Hey, I want to check out Dad on the news. I didn't get to see the fight yet."

"It's on CNN," Owen said.

"Whoa! National coverage," Holden said. "Way to go, Pop!"

Before Fred could say anything, Holden had sprinted to the library. Fred followed, arriving in time to see himself on TV getting the shit kicked out of him on the national news.

Fuck fuck fuck fuck fuck.

Fred watched in disgust as he got smacked in the nose, kneed, punched, and kicked.

"Ouch," Holden said.

They had two different angles, one of which they slowed down, so everyone could, in the words of the broadcaster, appreciate the unprovoked savagery of the attack. They would probably play the footage over and over for weeks, like the Rodney King beating.

Fred wanted a Scotch, but it was too early. They showed yet another angle. Here Fred was greeting Rick, the dead boy's father, who was smiling broadly. At least everyone would see clearly how Fred had been sucker punched. Though looking at it now, Fred could easily see the anger in Rick's eyes.

"Way to kick back, Dad," Holden said, commenting on Fred's spastic attempts to keep Rick away when he was on the ground. "I used to do that when Owen was pummeling me. It must be in the genes."

They laughed—Holden and Owen and Arnie.

Fred turned away from the television. He thought about Dom, the boxer, the ex-cop. Dom wouldn't have been lying curled up in a miserable ball on the street kicking like a spastic six-year-old. No. Dom would have ducked, slipped the punch, and then countered with some kind of combination. Dom would not have lost his composure. Dom would have stayed on his feet, grabbed Rick by the balls and squeezed them until tears poured from Rick's eyes and he passed out. That's what Dom would have done, what Fred *should* have done, what they should be showing on the national news, that you don't fuck with Fred Gelman. But Fred had panicked. He had punched like a pussy. He had kicked like a girl. And a nation was watching.

Dom was going to fuck Rick up. Dom would do for Fred what Fred couldn't do for himself—get Rick's testicles between his brutish, boxer fingers and clamp down tight.

"C'mon, Dad," Holden said, "lighten up."

"The kid's right, Fred," Arnie added. The fawning little prick. Fred couldn't believe this dipshit dick-in-the-air was taking care of his son. The guy still had a ponytail, for Chrissake. Fred wanted to get the kitchen shears and lop it off. Mincing spineless little toady.

"Just want you to know, Arnie," Fred said, "it won't be long before Holden will be living on his own, then I'm cutting off your stipend and you can try working again for a living. Toothpaste. Right, Arnie? Isn't that what you used to do? Commercials for toothpaste? Close-ups of Close Up? And how many takes to get the little bit at the end curled up just right, that perfect crest of Crest? A hundred and twenty? A hundred and twenty takes of fucking toothpaste being squeezed on a toothbrush! Mr. Toothpaste. Isn't that what they called you in the biz? Huh? Huh Arnie? Huh, Mr. Toothpaste? So shut the fuck up."

Arnie hung his head like a little kid. Fred had no pity.

"And as long as you're in my house, Mr. Toothpaste, get rid of that ponytail. Now go to your room, and don't come out until you cut it off."

"I won't be talked to like that," Arnie said, but he was already easing his way out the door.

Jesus, things were totally out of control. Fred hit the remote and turned off the TV. Unison groans of protest issued forth from his progeny.

"Dad!"

"It's not healthy to watch your father getting beat up," he told them.

"Sorry, Dad," Owen said, hanging his head. "It's all my fault."

"Yeah, well, you should have thought of that before . . ." And he was about to say, *before you whacked your friend over the head.* Jesus, how could he think that? How could he believe his own son was guilty? Wasn't there something which prevented those thoughts from occurring? Some parental instinct insuring that, no matter what happened, Fred would always believe his son to be innocent? But Fred knew he had the uncanny ability to override any parental instincts, spending their birthdays closing deals instead of helping blow out the candles, sleeping through Holden's school plays, coming late for little league. Any parental instincts he had left were now just broken and rotting stumps.

"I gotta go lie down," Fred said. "My head is throbbing."

He went down the hall to his bathroom.

Fred dug out his cell phone and called Sheena, waking her up. He told her to get on the next plane and come see him. He'd booked her into a suite at a posh little hotel on Madison. Then he called Marjorie, just to touch base. Maybe she had seen the news and would take pity on him, invite him over, but she wasn't in her room. She was probably moving to the new hotel. The same one he just told Sheena to go to. That would be convenient.

Then he called Douglas and, after threatening to fire him and find a new lawyer, got Dom's number. He wanted to talk with the ex-boxer directly. He turned on the television, saw himself again, on the pavement, being kicked in slow motion. Rick wasn't even in jail, wasn't being held, his grief excusing his violence, mitigating it. In the top corner of the screen they showed a photo of Holden, almost as if he were looking down at his own father and watching as he got the shit kicked out of him.

He called Dom, left a message on the boxer's machine concerning Rick and what he wanted done.

The message was short and sweet.

It hadn't working out quite the way he'd planned. Beating up that man, the father, wasn't enough. Rick needed a gun. So he had gotten into his Saab and driven up to Harlem.

They were supposed to have guns in Harlem. He heard about it in the news, read about it seemingly every day in the papers. The problem of too many guns on the street. Well, he'd been driving for an hour already, he'd been looking in the street, he didn't see any guns or anyone who looked like they might sell him a gun. Maybe it was too early in the day. Or something. But all he could think was that someone was doing some serious false advertising.

He turned onto 123rd and Lenox. He was trying to figure out why the street was lined with trees, why the brownstones had flower boxes in the windows. A man was sweeping the sidewalk. Sweeping! What was the deal here? This was supposed to be Harlem—burned-out buildings, people living in empty lots under lean-tos made from scavenged pallets. He drives up to Harlem to get himself a gun and instead he finds a page out of *House & Garden*. Where were the crackheads? Where were the young thugs, the pockets of their leather jackets filled with semiautomatic weapons instead of slingshots? The young boys carrying .22s instead of baseball gloves? He figured that once he was above 125th Street they'd be selling Saturday night specials at stands on the corner like hot dogs, from blankets spread on the sidewalk, in the grocery right next to the milk and orange juice. He could get the bullets from candy dispensers instead of gum or M&Ms. Or they'd give them as change instead of pennies.

One lousy gun was all he wanted.

But there were no gun stands, no vendors. This wasn't any way to run a business. No salespeople on the floor? A customer waiting, a customer cruising in a white Saab and no one trying to help him? This was a joke. What was going on? He wanted service. He wanted to speak to someone.

Where was the manager?

He turned south and drove slowly around Marcus Garvey Park. Parks were good. Kids with malicious intentions hung out in parks, waiting for someone who wanted to buy a gun to pull up to the curb. He cruised slowly around the perimeter, staring at everyone he passed, getting curious looks in return. (Curious, but not suspicious.) Maybe they thought he was a cop. Maybe they thought he was a pimp looking for some new talent, a real estate agent looking for cheap property, a slumlord checking on his buildings. He drove by an old lady pushing a shopping cart filled with laundry and thought she must have pistols folded in her towels, bullets in the washcloths. He drove past a guy in splattered overalls carrying a gallon of house paint in each hand. He surely had a couple of .22s in each can. Why wasn't he selling? Why wasn't anyone open for business today? It wasn't Sunday. He read every day about some heinous crime committed by someone with an illegal handgun. Where were they?

Jesus Christ, where were all the guns when you needed one?

The newscasters made it seem like any twelve-year-old who wanted one could buy a gun. Well, maybe Rick needed to find himself a twelve-year-old to buy one *for* him.

His son had been murdered. He should get some kind of dispensation. A coupon good for one gun at any street corner in Harlem. He was entitled to whatever he wanted.

My son was murdered! I just want a gun! I'm entitled!

He banged on the horn, pummeled the horn, the Saab bleating his pain to the world.

In a far corner of the park he saw some boys hanging out, looking his way, attracted by the horn. They were in their early twenties. That was good. Early twenties, black kids. A few even had their hair in cornrows like Latrell Sprewell. That suggested anger. Antisocial hatred. Now he was getting somewhere.

He pulled up to the curb near where they stood and rolled down his window. The young men stared at him through hooded eyes. Rick waved to one of them, beckoning him to the car. They didn't move. No one moved. What was going on? A white guy in a Saab wants something, you'd think they would jump at the chance. It was only then that he realized he should probably be a little bit nervous, being alone in Harlem. But he wasn't. There was nothing to be scared about, because the bigger fear, that he wouldn't avenge his son's death, that he would do nothing, that he would live the rest of his life seen by Ellen as the man who did nothing, *that* fear eclipsed any other.

Finally one of the kids sauntered over to the car. Rick could see tattoos on his arm, earrings dangling from both ears.

"You 5-0?" the kid asked.

"No. I'm Rick," Rick said. "I want to buy a gun."

"A gun."

"Yeah."

"Here? Now?"

"I have cash."

The kid raised his eyebrows.

"Cash is cool," he said. He scrutinized Rick, then the car, searching for clues which only he understood. He looked around, down the street, up to the rooftops.

"Let me see some ID," he said.

Rick showed him his driver's license. The kid examined it carefully.

"You *are* Rick," the kid said.

"I told you," Rick said.

"Pleasure to meet you, Rick," the kid said, pronouncing it very properly, his imitation of a white guy. "How are you this fine day?"

"What about the gun?" Rick asked.

The kid thought for a moment, then leaned down and spoke in a soft voice, his lips quite close to Rick's ear.

"I tell you what," the kid said. "For two hundred dollars I can sell you some loaves of bread. Now if there happens to be something else inside that shopping bag with the bread that I didn't notice, well I guess that would be just a lucky accident."

The kid smiled. Bright white straight teeth. A radiant smile. Rick smiled back. He wanted Ellen to see him, the way he was taking control, making something happen.

"I could use some loaves of bread," Rick said. "About two hundred dollars worth would be fine."

"Let me talk to some of my boys," the kid said. "Be back here in fifteen minutes."

"Okay."

"Oh, and by the way, Rick, you prefer Wonder or Pepperidge Farm?"

Chantal was on the couch, her mom on one side, her dad on the other. She held her favorite stuffed animal in her arms. Across from her sat the woman detective. Garcia. She spoke with a slight accent. She was youngish and wore a bit too much makeup. She made a big deal about pulling the armchair close to the couch, like they were in cahoots together, the girls against the boys, maybe. While Garcia was dragging the chair over, the gray jacket she wore over the matching skirt shifted slightly and Chantal could see she had a gun on her hip.

The other detective, Ward, stood near the window, away from them, but not too far away. Listening. Mr. Bliss, Julia's father, was apparently waiting outside.

Garcia wanted to know what she remembered about the party.

She described coming into the townhouse, seeing Ben in the fur coat.

"Did Ben say anything to you then?" Garcia asked. "When he was dressed in the coat?"

"No," she said. "Nothing special."

Come into my furry lair. My furry lair.

"Did he seem worried? Preoccupied?"

"Not really."

Let me kiss the ring.

"Nothing out of the ordinary?"

"No."

I love you, Chantal.

But after that, the party was kind of a blur. She recalled dancing with Malcolm, but the rest of it wasn't there, in her head, the way her memories usually were.

"Did you have a lot to drink?" Garcia asked.

"No," Chantal said. Then to her parents, "Really. I'm not just saying that. But I remember feeling really weird."

Detective Ward then came forward and whispered something in Garcia's ear. Garcia nodded.

"How many drinks did you have?"

"One, I think," she said.

"Did you make it yourself?"

She tried to remember. At his parties, Owen kept everything in the kitchen. She didn't remember going into the kitchen.

"I don't know."

"So someone might have made the drink for you."

"I guess."

"What do you usually drink at parties?"

"Vodka and orange juice," she said. She heard her mother catch her breath.

"It's possible it was drugged," Garcia said. "If you really only had one drink. Some GBH was found in Ben's room."

"What's that?" her father said, all indignant.

"It's a date rape drug," Garcia said. "It may explain why Chantal can't remember much."

"Someone drugged her?" her father shouted. He clenched his fist in anger. She tried to remember other times she'd seen her father as angry as this.

"When did you go upstairs to the bedroom?" Garcia asked. She tried to think.

"I can't remember."

But she did remember the boy who scared her.

"Billy Dix," she said. "You need to find him. And his friend, too."

"Who's his friend?" Garcia asked.

"I don't know. But he was scary. He doesn't go to my school."

"T-Bone?" Ward said, looking at his notebook. "Was that his name?"

"Maybe," Chantal said.

Ward wrote something down, then closed his notebook.

"How did you get to Malcolm's house?" Garcia asked.

"Malcolm took me," Chantal said. "That's what he told me. We did the Hustle."

"At his house?"

"No. At the party."

"Why did Malcolm take you to his house?" Garcia asked.

"He said he thought it might be better if I woke up at his house instead of mine."

"Why?"

She looked at her parents, didn't say anything. Her mother sniffled.

"Malcolm takes care of me," she said. "I felt sick. I needed to sleep. Besides . . ."

"What?"

"My parents weren't home. They were still in the Hamptons."

Her mother flashed an angry look at her father, then started crying in earnest. Chantal was surprised she had lasted this long. She waited for her father to comfort her mother. He didn't move.

"Why didn't you call home, Chantal?" her mother said, her voice shaking. "Why didn't you call? I was so . . . I was . . ."

"I'm sorry," Chantal said, not sure what else she could say.

"Why?" her mother said.

"I was in Coney Island."

"You said you were in a church." Her father's voice was stern. He puffed up his face to go with it.

"I was having fun," she said. "With Malcolm and his dad."

"You should have contacted us. It was irresponsible. Very."

Her father sounded like he had memorized some passage from an outdated parenting book.

Fortunately Detective Garcia got things back on track.

"Did you have your clothes on when Malcolm found you?" Ward asked.

"I guess so," she said. "I don't remember taking them off, but it seems I did."

Her mother raised her face from her hands. She stopped crying.

"Did Malcolm say anything to you about Ben being dead?"

She flashed to the blood on her hand. The blood she thought she saw. That was there, then not there. She decided not to mention it. Maybe it was a dream.

"We were busy all day. His dad doesn't own a TV."

"So Malcolm didn't say whether Ben was alive or dead when he took you from his bed."

"Whose bed?" Chantal asked. Garcia wasn't making sense.

"The bed in Holden's room. Where you were. Where Ben was sleeping. Where he was found dead."

"I was in *Owen's* room," she said. "I was with Owen. It was his birthday."

I love you, Chantal.

Chantal felt confused, felt sick, a darkness was moving through her, it was hard to see, to hear.

"A strand of blond hair was found on Holden's bed. There was blood on the sheets, on Ben's penis," Garcia said. "I have to ask you, Chantal. Did you . . . ?"

And Garcia stopped, because there must have been something on Chantal's face, some expression that stopped her.

Not Owen's room? Not Owen's bed?

She hadn't gone to Owen's bed. *I love you, Chantal.* That voice in her head. Owen didn't talk to her softly like that, had never said those words to her. *I love you, Chantal.* It wasn't Owen's voice at all. *Let me kiss the ring, Chantal.* It was Ben's voice. *Let me kiss the ring. You know I love you, Chantal. You know I love you.*

And then Chantal jerked forward as if she was hit by a sharp blow to her stomach and she wanted to vomit everything out of her, her organs, her lungs, her vagina, vomit it all out. Because she disgusted herself, her body disgusted her, was her enemy now, and she wasn't sure she could continue to live with the vile filth that was everywhere beneath her skin.

Bliss sat in the car outside Chantal's building. Chantal used to come over to their house all the time. She'd go directly into Julia's room and close the door. He never knew what they did, only that there was a lot of laughing.

Once he had driven out to Chantal's house in the Hamptons. It was the beginning of the summer. Julia had been invited for a few days and Bliss had agreed to pick her up. The house was on the ocean. The father gave him a lengthy tour, offered him a Cuban cigar, then made a joke about how he shouldn't admit to having them, Bliss being a cop and all. He asked Bliss if he'd brought his tennis racket, they could play a set on the guy's court. Or maybe his golf clubs, they could run to the club, play a quick nine holes. Bliss remembered wanting to take out his gun, *yeah, I got my clubs*, and then shoot one of the hyperthyroid goldfish swimming in the fake stream that snaked through his front lawn. *Hole in one*.

A media van was parked nearby, the cameraman out on the sidewalk, his lens aimed at the front door of Chantal's build-ing, hoping to get a glimpse of her coming out. Bliss remembered her being a pretty girl. Maybe the national exposure could re-sult in something, a part on Holden's show. Real-life girlfriend of the star's real-life brother playing his sitcom girlfriend. Why not? *Vanity Fair* could make a story out of it.

He took out his cell phone, dialed a number. Since Garcia was helping them on this case, he thought he'd lend a hand with Felix.

"Hello."

Bliss remembered voice, the accent.

"Andrej."

"Who is this?"

"Detective Bliss. We talked a few months ago. About Felix."

Silence, except for Andrej's breathing.

"I am thinking you will call," Andrej said. "I am thinking you will come to building, ask same old questions."

"You have any new answers, Andrej?"

"No," Andrej said, "but English is better. I am giving same answers, but having more words."

"I'll look forward to it, Andrej."

"Nothing is changing," Andrej said. "You are needing to find other person. Person who killed Felix."

Bliss had a strong suspicion Andrej was right.

"We'll talk anyway, Andrej," Bliss said. "For old time's sake. We'll catch up."

"Felix Floats," Andrej said.

"Yeah," Bliss said. "Right back into our hearts."

Rick pulled up at the same spot by the park. He turned off the car, closed his eyes.

Rick once had a girlfriend in college. The two of them had been so close, so in love. He could be standing in a crowd on the other side of the quad and she would see Rick and she would smile, singling him out from everyone else, walk to him alone from among all the others, and they would embrace. Only Rick was allowed into her embrace.

But then something happened. He never knew what. She grew bored or restless or was just the kind of person that could fall out of love as quickly as she fell in. He never knew. But literally in one night, it was over. No explanation. She had loved him, now she didn't love him any more.

She was walking with another boy. Rick wanted to reach out and take her hand, to hold her, but he couldn't. She wasn't there for him anymore. He was unwelcome. It had been, but now it wasn't anymore.

It was over.

He didn't understand. He couldn't wrap his mind around it. To touch her now would be a violation. She would recoil, cry out, call campus security, run away. They were strangers.

It was the same with Ben.

It also seemed to happen overnight. Ben was once his son. Rick could throw an arm around Ben's shoulder and Ben would look up with admiration, with love. Ben would see his father in a crowd and smile.

Then, one day, they were strangers—nothing between them but emptiness. His son was gone.

Rick opened his eyes. He looked around but didn't see the black kid he had made the deal with. He leaned back against the headrest and closed his eyes. He was a white guy in a white Saab in the middle of Harlem waiting to buy a gun. He didn't care if anyone saw him. He didn't care if thieves and junkies hiding on roofs or in trees or behind curtains had zeroed in on him like amateur astronomers on a comet. Let them come. His son was dead.

He spoke in a soft whisper, as if in prayer.

Let them come.

I'm not afraid.

I know, Ellen, you think I should have been tougher. Limits! Repercussions! I know, I know. But his strength frightened me. You never saw that, never cared to see that. Repercussions! Consequences!

I know! I was the father, but I was envious. I wanted to ask him: How do you do it, Ben? How do you get what you want?

There was a light rapping on his window. Rick turned his head. The black kid stood next to the Saab, holding a paper shopping bag.

Maybe now it's my turn.

"I forgot to ask if you wanted paper or plastic," the kid said, smiling.

"Paper's good," Rick said.

The familiar Wonder Bread polka dots peeked out the top.

"Here's the bread you asked for," the kid said.

He tipped the bag and parted the loaves so Rick could see a package wrapped in newspaper at the bottom of the bag.

"Two hundred and twenty dollars' worth of Wonder Bread," the kid said, smiling. "Enriched. It's good for you."

"I thought we said two hundred," Rick said.

"You need something to put in your sandwich, don't you?" the kid said, and opened his hand slightly to reveal the dull brass finish of some bullets. The kid smiled again.

Rick counted out eleven twenties, folded them up, and slipped them to the kid. He then took the shopping bag through the window and placed it on the passenger seat. He felt something hard and heavy on the bottom. The kid handed him the bullets.

"Don't pop anyone I know," he said, and then walked away. Rick noticed a light, jaunty spring to his step.

He pulled away from the park and drove west on 125th Street until he came to the river. He pulled into a makeshift parking area just before the entrance ramp to the Henry Hudson Parkway. Beyond the concrete barriers, two men were fishing. They turned, checked out the car, then returned to their lines.

Rick reached into the shopping bag and found the package. He ripped off the newspaper and was delighted to find that he was now the proud owner of a piece of rusted pipe attached by masking tape to a block of wood. Well, at least he had some bullets. He heard his wife laughing.

Go ahead. But the point is, I didn't back down! I went through with it! It could easily have been a gun in there with the bread. So laugh all you want. I don't give a shit.

He threw the bread and the pipe in the back seat, put his car in gear, and tore off down the Henry Hudson. He wasn't exactly sure where to go, but he figured criminals had guns so all Rick had to do was find himself a criminal. The irony wasn't lost on him that if his son Ben were there, he would probably know just what to do.

But Rick didn't have time to waste on irony.

Fred sat back in his limo, relieved to have escaped the phalanx of reporters keeping vigil outside his house, aiming their cameras and telephoto lenses at him, shouting *How's your head, Fred? You going to press charges, Fred? Fred, turn this way so we can get a shot of your eye!* He wanted to shout something back, but he didn't have the energy that morning. But he did roll down his tinted window just enough to give them all the finger as he drove by.

Holden was napping. Owen was in his room going over stuff with Douglas. Fred had two hours before he had to be at Douglas's office, when Owen would be talking to the detectives. Marjorie the flight attendant was waiting for him at her new hotel, the one Fred was paying for. He needed to go there, to see her. To get away.

Fucking Ben Purdy, fucking everything up.

Then it occurred to Fred that maybe he was being followed. That some intrepid rookie reporter eager to impress his boss might be tailing him. He whipped around and stared out the back window—a meat delivery truck, three taxis, and a Town Car like his. The reporter could be in one of the taxis, having jumped in as Fred left his street, shouting to the driver, "Follow that limo." Would a driver do that, actually follow someone, or was that only in the movies?

He called the hotel and asked Marjorie if she wouldn't mind ordering room service, since breakfast in the restaurant might be tricky, what with these media piranhas around him.

"You poor dahling," she purred, her English accent exciting him. "Whatever's best for you."

Just like a flight attendant to be so accommodating. Eating in the room would work out better anyway, since he couldn't be late for Owen's interview with the police.

"How do you like the new hotel?"

"The tub," she said, "is substantial. Quite big enough for two."

"Run the water," he said. He hung up.

He wondered if Owen would confess. He felt a wave of remorse for his older son. He called his secretary and told her to make a reservation at Smith & Wollensky for dinner. For three. He wanted to be with his boys. They'd have some champagne, get a little drunk, shoot the shit. It had been a long time since they were together, the three Gelman men.

He looked out the back window and was sure the same cab was still there. He remembered the numbers. Shit.

"Drop me off at the next corner—Fifth and 58th!" he told his driver. The driver started edging to the curb. "No, the left side!"

He would jump out, run into F.A.O. Schwarz, sprint through the store, exit on Madison Avenue, and hop back in the limo. Then he'd head to Marjorie's hotel.

"Go down 58th and pick me up around the corner on Madison."

"What time, sir?"

"Now! Right now!"

"Drop you off and pick you up?"

"Yeah! What're you, fucking deaf? Where's my usual driver, anyway?"

"Off today, sir," the driver said. *Just my luck*, Fred thought.

He jumped out of the car and sprinted across the small plaza in front of F.A.O. Schwarz, almost running over some guy dressed like one of the guards at Buckingham Palace. It only made him want to see Marjorie that much more. Christ, his eye was throbbing. He'd have to ask Marjorie for some aspirin.

As he ran through the store, he bumped into some whining five-year-old and knocked the practically life-size stuffed orangutan out of her arms. It dawned on him that he ought to bring Marjorie a present. He picked up the orangutan and headed with it to the cashier in the back, ignoring the cries of protest in French from the mother and the piercing Gallic wails of her kid. Fucking tourists.

He stormed to the front of the line.

"My kid's in the hospital," he said by way of explanation to the people whose place he usurped. He shoved a charge card at the black woman at the cash register, marveling at her nails as she rang up the sale. They were painted like carnival tents and jutted out from the ends of her fingers at an inhuman length, like she'd been part of some medical experiment that had run amok. She had to force her fingertips skyward to touch the keys of the register. When did this start happening, he wondered. This nail thing.

"Can you hurry, please?" Fred said. She gave him the evil eye. Fred hoped she wasn't going to use her lurid nails to put some kind of hoodoo spell on him.

He signed the slip and ripped the receipt from her fingers, hoping he didn't get a nail for his troubles as well. Grabbing the orangutan, he stormed toward the exit, whacking some kid in the back with the monkey's head as he went.

"Watch where you're going," the mother said.

Fred turned to her, met her eyes with his coldest stare.

"My son's about to be taken off life support," Fred said, his voice low and level, his faux anguish in check. "And we don't know whether he's going to live or die. Your kid may be crying, but at least he can feel pain. At least he can feel *something!* You should feel *lucky!* You should feel *blessed!*"

Fred saw his limo pull to the curb and he raced out of the store. He didn't know what Marjorie would do with the orangutan, but whatever it was, he hoped she'd let him watch.

Jerry's lips were locked on Jen's aureole and his tongue was orbiting her nipple with the manic insistence of a dog chasing its tail. Their daughter had been missing for two days. She had been at the scene of a murder. They had just been visited by the police. For all they knew, Chantal could be a *suspect.* And now Jerry wanted some action. In the middle of the day, no less. She should be with her daughter, Jen thought. She should be with Chantal.

But when Jerry wanted some action . . .

Once, when Jen asked him why he could have sex so easily but he couldn't talk to her about things that were important to him, Jerry told her it was because he communicated better through sex than with words. So Jen lay back and listened intently now to Jerry's lips and hands while he sucked and pawed at her, trying to find the message he was so earnestly communicating. Her nipple was in his mouth. Her *right* nipple, not the left. Was that part of the message? Then kissing her neck and ear—her neck first, *then* her ear—was that a clue? In World War II they used Navajos to send secret messages and the Germans never broke the code. The Germans would never break Jerry's code either.

Jerry maneuvered her hand to his groin. Maybe there was something written there in Braille. Some message embossed on his cock like the cover of a cheap paperback.

She decided this wasn't communication. This was just Jerry getting his rocks off. He wasn't saying shit.

Jerry moved on top of her and started in with his "oh Gods." How many times had she heard Jerry's "oh Gods," the first one filled with surprise, almost shock? Surprise at what, she wondered? It's exactly the same every time. What could possibly be surprising? Then the others, more brazen, building in intensity and speed. This segued into the "oh babys," traveling in pairs, afraid to be alone, maybe.

Around the third set of "oh babys," Jen decided get a divorce and go back to school and do something useful with her life.

But then Jen was startled by another voice—a fragile, frightened voice—Chantal.

Was she really there, or was it a dream?

"Mom," the voice said.

Jen was sure she was dreaming. Because if Chantal was really talking, Jerry would have stopped moaning and humping. Wouldn't he?

"Mom?"

Jen decided to answer anyway, to get the voice out of her head.

"Yes," she whispered.

"Mom," the voice said, "when Dad's done, could you come into my room? I think I'm pregnant."

Then the final "oh baby" came and Jen turned her head just in time to catch a glimpse of her daughter, eyes wide with fear, leaving the room.

Bliss and Ward sat on one side of the dark mahogany table, Owen and Douglas Lipper on the other. The tape recorder was between them. Douglas's secretary had put matching place mats under the tape recorder and microphones so they wouldn't scratch the wood. It was clear Douglas was used to his clients being deposed.

"I'd like to wait until Owen's father arrives, if you don't mind," Douglas said.

"Fine," Bliss said.

He took a drink of water. He knew Douglas and the boy had gone over everything beforehand. He'd even been in depositions where the lawyer's lips were moving silently in sync with the client.

"The father's coming soon?" Ward asked.

"Yes," Douglas said, though the boy's expression displayed some doubt.

They sat in silence. Bliss observed the boy. The slightest twist of fate and it could have been Julia who had been going out with him. She drops her textbook, they both bend down together to pick it up, their eyes meet, and all at once, polka dots and moonbeams and it's Julia who has fallen in love.

He hoped (no, prayed) Owen was not her type. There was an emptiness about him. Not as a result of his present circumstances, but a basic, essential emptiness Bliss noticed in many of the kids. Faces filled with vacuity, bursting with barrenness. As if daily life held nothing for them. All that mattered was something phenomenal: sex, drugs, sports, WWE, a rock concert, a rave, something to bring them to life. They weren't jaded, because that implied excess, overindulgence. It was something more casual, a part of them. Being alive was not enough, it seemed. The day was something to be used up, to be filled as quickly as possible—like the basketball regular season—so they could get to the playoffs. Because that's all that counted.

It's all about the present, the yoga teacher said. But the present was absent for these children.

He wondered what Julia's type was. Whether she would be seduced by the kind of overly dramatic reading of "Prufrock" he used to give in college, his New York tough-guy accent lending a distinctive, earthy tone to the verse—*Let us go den, you and I / When duh evening is spread out against duh sky.* Or would Julia see through that ploy? It was all so precarious, that high school world. You're always one step away from trouble—one friend of a friend, one older brother, is all it takes, someone who hears about a party and shows up and someone winds up dead.

"We need to start," Ward said. "The boy is here. Counsel is here. No reason we shouldn't begin."

"I really wanted to wait for Fred," Douglas said.

Owen chuckled.

"He's probably busy screwing his secretary," Owen said.

Bliss caught Ward's eye, thinking about the surveillance tape. Ben had probably been holding on to it for safekeeping.

"If it was *Holden*, he'd be here," Owen said. "But it's just me. So we might as well get started."

"Fine," Douglas said.

Ward turned on the tape recorder and entered the date, time, and appropriate names. Douglas poured some water into Owen's glass. He patted the boy's arm and told him to answer truthfully, that he had nothing to hide. Bliss had no doubt Douglas would interrupt any of Owen's answers that might sound the least bit incriminating. And probably some others as well, just to mess with Bliss's head.

"Go ahead, detectives," Douglas said, with just a hint of condescension, as if he and Owen had more important things they could be doing.

"Who's Billy Dix?" Ward asked.

"Some guy Ben knew. I never liked him."

"And his friend T-Bone?"

"I don't know," Owen said. "Ben bought drugs from him. From Billy Dix."

"A lot?"

"I don't know."

"He was your best friend."

Douglas jumped in.

"That does not preclude knowledge of Ben's private affairs," Douglas said.

"Was Ben dealing?" Bliss asked.

"Detective," Douglas said.

Bliss turned off the tape recorder.

"Off the record," he said.

"Then it's hypothetical," Douglas said.

"Hypothetically, Owen," Bliss said, "if your friend Ben was hypothetically dealing, do you think Billy Dix might have been his hypothetical supplier?"

"Yeah," Owen said. "Hypothetically."

Bliss switched the recorder back on.

"Back to Chantal," Bliss said. "She never came up to see you that night?"

"No."

"So what did you do?"

"I fell asleep."

"You fell asleep?"

"I guess I had too much to drink. And we smoked some pot. That puts me out sometimes."

"Your big night and you fell asleep?"

"Hey, I had my big night already, detective," Owen said. "Several times, in fact. This was just my big night with Chantal."

"But you never saw her."

"No."

"Never had intercourse with her."

"No."

"But it's possible she could have had intercourse that night. With someone else, of course."

"What did Chantal say?" Owen asked, angry now.

"Take some water, Owen," Douglas said.

"I'm not thirsty," Owen said. Then to Bliss, pressing. "What did she say?"

"Take some water anyway," Douglas said, putting the glass in Owen's face, in front of his mouth, trying to keep the boy calm, or at least from talking.

Bliss pushed.

"Chantal could have been with Ben, for instance. Speaking hypothetically again," Bliss said. "That's possible, right? After you fell asleep, the two of them could have had intercourse in your brother's bed? Maybe that's why she never showed up to see you, Owen? To give you your birthday present. Whattaya think?"

Bliss saw Douglas's hand gripping Owen's arm, trying to keep the boy cool.

"We found a long strand of curly blond hair on Ben's pillow," Bliss said. "We found blood on his penis."

"Detective!"

But Douglas was too late. Owen was clearly thinking about his best friend and his girlfriend being together. Bliss watched him. Everyone was watching him. Owen didn't seem to care. He was chewing his lower lip.

What Bliss had to decide was whether he was getting angry now for the first time, or whether he had already expressed that same anger two nights ago in an act of jealousy and violence and whacked his best friend over the head.

"And what about the dumbbell?" Bliss added. "Do you know how that got in your room?"

Then Owen stood up, his large chest heaving. Douglas stood up, too. A head shorter, peering up at the boy, reaching up to his shoulders, trying to get him back in the chair.

"Owen?"

Bliss kept at it.

"The dumbbell, Owen. The ten-pound dumbbell under your bed. With Ben's blood on it. How did it get there?"

Owen opened his mouth, but no words came. Then tears started pouring from his eyes, dripping down his face and his mouth moved silently like a great fish out of water. His body shook.

He was lost to them for the moment. And with Douglas there, glowering in his righteousness, Bliss thought it might be a long while before they get him back.

It was about a year ago. Nedra had finished her shower at the club and was drying off as she passed the large mirror at the end the row of sinks. She had walked by that mirror after her shower practically every day for the last three years, seeing the women in various stages of dress and undress, never thinking twice about it. But that day, for some reason, she turned and really looked in the mirror.

And one woman in particular caught her eye and captivated Nedra; her arms were sinuous and beautifully toned, her shoulders were broad and her neck long, the muscles there sublimely present; and her legs, which stretched out elegantly from under the towel, were perfectly shaped, strong and lean and gallant. And this woman's skin, still wet from the shower, glistened with vitality and allure. And though she knew it was indecorous, perhaps intrusive, Nedra stopped in the middle of the locker room and stared at the woman's reflection. She simply couldn't contain the feelings racing through her body, feelings she hadn't known were inside her. She smiled, the woman smiled back, and suddenly Nedra's face was transfixed with a joy and delight she had never experienced before. It had only taken a glance, but in that moment, Nedra's whole life changed, because that woman in the mirror, who boldly returned her gaze, who smiled just as broadly, was herself.

She was giddy. She owned this taut and powerful body. She had made it. She had never done anything so profoundly perfect in her life, something that gave her so much pride, that others might envy. Her body was a finely honed instrument she had built in the last three years. It was all hers.

So Nedra stayed close to her club. Felt safe there. Protected. It really was like a club, the kind you had as a kid, when you devised special codes to talk with the members, secret signs and calls. Away from the club, things could go wrong. There was uncertainty. Lack of direction. But inside the club, she was safe. They knew her, respected her, understood what was required to make her body strong and taut. Fred only saw her as fat, looking at her body with contempt, seeing only her faults. But here in the club they challenged her and pushed her. Then they soothed her and stroked her.

They loved her.

It was early. She knew Holden would be coming home soon, was maybe there already, but she wasn't ready to see him yet. She needed to get on her bike and spin it all away, lose herself in the music and the rhythm and the exertion. Lose herself for hours as she rode and rode, eyes closed, legs pumping, her breath an entity all its own. And though she never actually moved, each turn of the wheel took her farther away, deeper into the safety of the club, where no one could touch her, no one could judge her. She could spin it away.

Spin it away.

Spin it all away.

Jen was in the office of Neel Keller, Esq. She wanted a divorce, she told him. She wanted to leave her husband and take her daughter Chantal and live somewhere together by themselves and when could they get started and how long would it take.

Neel Keller, Esq. wasn't sure. He wanted to know about the house in the Hamptons—was it on the beach, how big was the pool, did they own a boat. Jen said she didn't care about the money. Keller wanted to know if the tennis court was clay or hardtop.

"I want a divorce," Jen said. "The fastest way possible."

Keller sighed and opened a leather-bound notebook. He clicked his pen deliberately, as though he was a spy sending a signal to the rest of the spies.

He asked Jen if Jerry ever hit her.

"No."

Did he hit their daughter?

"That's ridiculous."

Had he sexually abused their daughter?

"Oh my God, no."

Was Jerry was having an affair? Did she suspect him of having an affair? Was he gay? Did they have sex?

"Yes."

He asked if Jerry liked rough sex; weird, demanding, brutal sex? Did he need her to put her hands around his neck in order to achieve orgasm? Was there any mention of other couples? Rodents?

Jen shook her head. She was starting to feel queasy.

Did he gamble? Drink to excess? Take drugs? Did he humiliate her in public? In private? Did he take pleasure in her failures? Did he steal money from her?

"No, no, no no NO!"

Moments later, Jen was crying. Her head pressed against the lapel of Neel Keller, Esq.'s Hugo Boss suit. He held her with trepidation with one arm while he picked up the phone with the other and called in his secretary, who immediately came in the office.

"Feel free to sustain your lamentation, Jen," he told her, "but I will want someone present to witness the exact nature of our physical contact. I will continue to offer a reasonable degree of tactile comfort, but in order to do so I will need you sign a document affirming that I did not initiate said physical contact either directly or through innuendo, metaphor, or tone of voice."

The secretary held out a typed form and a pen. On the bottom of the form was a line with an X next to it where Jen was supposed to sign.

Later, Jen was with the secretary in the ladies' room, splashing water on her face.

"You should probably get some counseling," she said. "Maybe couples therapy."

She handed Jen a card.

"This woman is excellent," the secretary said. "Tell her Gloria from Neel Keller's office recommended you."

"I just want a divorce," Jen said.

The secretary studied her face in the mirror, touched up her makeup, ran lip gloss swiftly and expertly over her lips. She puckered them and smiled, pleased with the results. She held the lip gloss out to Jen.

"Try it?" she asked. "It's a good color for you."

Jen left the office, wondering if she just had the bad luck of finding the one divorce lawyer in New York with a conscience or whether the next one would say the same thing.

The report from the lab said there were several prints on the dumbbell. Most were Owen's, matching the prints Bliss got from the glass.

But the lab also positively identified another print belonging to Marcello Fuchs, known to his friends as T-Bone. T-Bone's prints were on file because he had one prior, a fare violation, and probably a much longer sheet sealed away by juvie.

And while the print belonged to T-Bone, T-Bone, from what Owen said, belonged to Billy Dix. Bliss thought it might be a good idea to talk to them, find out what they did at the party, if maybe T-Bone got carried away with his exercises.

Being the middle of the day, they were seeking out T-Bone Fuchs at his school, though Bliss was not optimistic about finding him there.

"You never know," Ward said. "Maybe they're serving something good for lunch."

"Good name," Bliss said. "T-Bone."

"Colorful," Ward said. "I wonder if he plays the blues."

They arrived at Paul Laurence Dunbar High School and double-parked.

"Dunbar's a *real* poet," Ward said. "Not self-indulgent, like whatsisname."

"Eliot."

"Dunbar's poems rhyme. He was the first to write in Negro dialect. I wonder how many of the students here know who he is."

The guard at the front door of the school was waving excitedly at them.

"He know us, partner?" Ward asked.

"Maybe he thinks we're trying to park here," Bliss said. He flashed his shield at the guard. The guard waved again.

The school was set back from the street. They walked down the broken concrete path and up the steps to where the guard stood. They showed him their shields.

"Detectives," he said, apparently surprised not by their being there, but at their rank. "Okay. Whatever. Second floor, third door on the left."

Bliss nodded, wondering what was going on. The front door was propped open by an institutional-size can of peas that had been filled with sand. Several cigarette butts were stuck there, like a little flowerpot filled with the stunted sprouts of strange, deformed plants. You had to take your flora where you could get it in New York.

They walked into the building. The staircase was boxed in with wire mesh, to keep kids from falling over the railing. The banister flopped in Bliss's hand. It had been attached to the wall with a thick coil of duct tape. The tape had come loose.

Bliss had gone to a school like this, though there weren't bars on the windows when he was in high school. The paint wasn't peeling from the walls.

"Reminds me of Riker's," Bliss said.

"Riker's is in better shape," Ward said. "I could have made three shivs just with the loose pieces of metal and tape that I've passed on this staircase."

They opened the door on the second floor. The hallway seemed to stretch on endlessly in either direction, a metaphor, perhaps, for the students' state of mind. To their left, a small crowd was gathered outside one of the classrooms. A woman turned, and as soon as she saw them, gestured wildly.

Bliss looked at his partner. They hadn't alerted the school they were coming.

"Getovah heah!" the woman shouted.

They gotovah there.

Inside the classroom, a large black girl had someone in a headlock who Bliss thought at first was another girl, but turned out to be a much smaller boy. Eyeglasses, which Bliss assumed belonged to the boy, lay on the floor, the temples twisted, one lens separated from the frames. The room was empty of students. They were in the hall, shouting stuff into the room, encouraging Lloyda, the girl, to jam the knife she was pointing at the boy's face into his eye.

"Fuck Karim up!" someone shouted. "Pussy white boy."

Karim, Bliss observed, was far from white.

Bliss now realized this was the situation the guard thought they'd come to address. Two detectives. No wonder he was surprised.

They pushed through the crowd of kids, who were in no hurry to let them through, bristling when Bliss put his hand on their shoulders to get them out of the way.

Once inside the classroom, Bliss could see that the girl Lloyda wanted it to be over. That the encouragement, the ovation she would no doubt receive if she went through with it, was not enough motivation for Lloyda to put her knife deep into the eye of Karim. Her expression said she wanted it to be over. The violent urge had passed. It was about pride now. How she would look. The boy's fate resting now on whether Lloyda could walk away from the situation without feeling too humiliated.

Enter Ward.

"Lloyda," he said.

"Get out of my grill," she said without looking up.

Bliss heard sirens, the real cops arriving.

The girl heard the sirens, too.

"The police are coming," Ward said.

"So who are you?"

"I'm your only hope," he said.

She raised her head and looked at him now, standing before her in his full majesty, powerful, all-knowing, his regal black skin, his head held high, tribal king and shaman both.

"I'm head of the School Task Force," Ward said, his voice low and calm.

"Huh," Lloyda said.

He showed her his badge. "It's a secret agency. I deal with situations just like this. They call me before the uniform cops. You understand, Lloyda? I am your one chance."

"Stick him, Lloyda!"

"Secret School what?" Lloyda asked.

"Task Force."

"Fuck that Oreo up!"

The sirens stopped.

"When the uniform cops get here, they take over," Ward said. "I walk away. I leave you with them. They can do with you what they want. But until they get to the scene, I'm in charge. You hear me, Lloyda? The cops will probably think you're wrong here. Are you? Are you bad here, Lloyda?"

"No."

"That's right. The situation's bad, but you're not bad."

"He called me stupid."

"That's not nice."

Karim was making squeaky sounds of pain and panic.

"Because he has glasses he thinks he's smart," she said.

Bliss heard the clap of the cops' shoes in the hallway. He took out his shield, to buy Ward a few more minutes.

"He's going to apologize now," Ward said. "I can make him do that. Say it, Karim."

"I'm stupid."

"Louder."

"I'm stupid!"

"Now drop the knife, Lloyda!"

Lloyda dropped the knife.

Ward walked over and before Lloyda could open her mouth he wrenched the girl's thick arm from Karim's throat and twisted it around her back.

"That hurts!"

"Lloyda," he said, "who was Paul Laurence Dunbar?"

"Huh?"

"Paul Laurence Dunbar. Who was he?"

"How should I know?" she said. "The guy who built the school."

Ward was silent as he walked Lloyda through the crowd of students, into the arms of the uniforms.

"Let her go," someone shouted. "She didn't do nuthin'."

When Lloyda saw the uniforms, she started shouting at Ward, about the Task Force, his promises. But Ward's face was fixed hard, inpenetrable.

The uniforms had the cuffs on her fast. Her shouting escalated, her curses uglier as she disappeared down the Up staircase.

The teacher was comforting Karim. Bliss and Ward walked over to them. Ward picked up Karim's glasses, handed them to the boy.

"*I know why the caged bird sings,*" Karim said.

Ward looked at him for a moment, then reached out and hugged Karim, pulled him close to his chest.

"*Ah, me,*" said Ward. "*Ah, me.*"

They stayed that way for a minute. Some of the kids in the hall laughed behind their hands while others didn't even bother to hide it. Then Ward let Karim go.

The students started filing back into the class. The vice principal escorted Karim out of the room. Bliss and Ward went with him.

"We need to speak to a couple of kids," Bliss said.

"Who?"

"Billy Dix and his friend Marcello."

"T-Bone."

"Yes."

"That was their class," the vice principal said. "Where you just were."

They turned, went back to the room. The teacher reported that Billy Dix and Marcello had been there before the incident, but had not returned. Bliss heard more snickering from the back of the class.

The guard was stubbing out a cigarette as they left. He didn't say anything. The uniforms had Lloyda in the car and were talking things over with a balding, harried man who must have been the principal. He made a gesture with his arm, as if to say *I don't give a shit, just get her out of here.* The window on the police car rolled up and the car pulled away. The principal lit up a cigarette, took a deep drag, and slowly blew out the smoke. He took a few more tokes, walking, head down, past Bliss and Ward. He stooped to shove half-smoked cigarette into the can of sand before disappearing into the school.

"Let's get out of here," Ward said,

They drove off.

When they stopped at a light, Ward turned to him.

"That private school, the one where Ben went," Ben said. "That a good school?"

"Not bad," Bliss said.

"It seems to me with Ben's sudden demise, they must have an opening."

"That's true," Bliss said. "What are you thinking?"

"About Karim," Ward said. "The Oreo knew why the caged bird sings."

"Cheerio," Fred said, waltzing into his lawyer's office, feeling buoyant.

"You're very late," Douglas said. Fred thought he sounded like some peevish old lady who had hired him for yardwork and not someone who was beholden to Fred Gelman Real Estate Inc. for tens of thousands of dollars in revenue every year.

"Where's Owen?" Fred asked.

"In the bathroom."

"You mean, the loo?"

Fred was positively giddy after his morning with Marjorie. She had such incredible posture. He made her do the seat belt fastening demonstration naked, which had them both rolling hysterically on the floor. She said she'd never be able to do it again without laughing. He was going to see her in London in a week. She loved the orangutan.

"How'd Owen do?" Fred asked.

"He did fine," Douglas said. "I only wish he hadn't given the detectives the suggestion that he could easily slip into a jealous rage and whack his friend over the head."

"He's got my temper," Fred said.

"And your lack of discretion," Douglas said. "Geraldo called. Personally. He wants you on his show."

"Geraldo still has a show?"

"To tell your side of the story," Douglas said.

"There is no story," Fred said. "Have you heard from Dom? He have any luck with that thing he's working on?"

Douglas scowled.

"Why don't you bring Owen into the business now, Fred?" he said. "Why waste his time in high school and college? He's going to work for you eventually anyway. He's never going to get any smarter. He'll just get a bunch of girls pregnant, get arrested for drunk driving, wreck all the cars you give him, pay kids to write his papers, get caught in a whorehouse when he should be studying for finals."

"Is that your advice, as my lawyer?"

"Yes."

"I'll keep it in mind. So what about Dom?"

"Nothing yet."

'He didn't check in?"

"No."

"Well, keep him on it."

"Dom was hoping you could help him out with an apartment in Manhattan."

"He gets some electrodes attached to the testicles of that prick Rick and I'll give him a fucking penthouse."

"You shouldn't make promises you know you won't keep," Douglas said.

"Hey, what can I say," Fred said, opening his palms in a gesture of beneficence, "I'm in real estate."

Just then Owen walked in.

"Hey, buddy," Fred said. "Sorry I couldn't be there. Heard it went well."

Owen mumbled something that Fred couldn't make out, but it didn't matter. There was nothing to worry about.

"We're going to Smith & Wollensky tonight," he told Owen, keeping things upbeat. "You, me, and Holden. Just the guys. Boys night out. Get some mammoth steaks. A few beers. Whattaya say?"

"The cops think I did it."

Douglas stepped in, on this right away.

"No. No no no," he said. "It went fine. They have nothing."

"They think I did it because Ben had sex with my girlfriend and I got really mad and hit him with the dumbbell."

Owen blubbering now, his words spewing out of him like vomit.

"The police think I got really mad and h-hit him over and over and over because he was, was su-supposed to be my friend."

"I'm sure they don't really think that," Fred said, looking over at Douglas, letting Douglas know he wasn't happy, that Douglas wasn't doing a very good job.

His son's head was pressed against Fred's shirt and he could feel the warm wetness of his tears against his skin.

"It's okay, Owen," Douglas said.

I should be saying that, Fred thought. *Would* have, if Douglas hadn't jumped in, with that superior tone, like Fred would be nowhere, would be sleeping out on the *street* in some kind of *box* if it wasn't for *Douglas*.

"Yeah, it's okay, Owen," Fred said, patting his son's shoulder as he glared at Douglas, the self-centered asshole, suddenly now the big expert on consoling children. "C'mon," he said, "stop crying now. Everything's okay."

"It's n-not. It's not okay."

Then more tears, and all Fred could do was stand there feeling the dampness spread over his shirt. Jesus. "Hey," he said, "how 'bout we go get those steaks right now? For lunch."

"C-can it just be, just be you and me?" he asked, wiping away his tears.

"Whattaya mean?" Fred said, trying to be jolly.

"Does Holden have to come?"

"We gotta have Holden," he said, laughing big low yuks, trying to lighten things up. "Wouldn't be boys' night out if Holden wasn't there."

Fred slapped his son on the back—a big, fatherly slap. Douglas couldn't do that. Douglas could give Owen a slap on the back, but it couldn't be a *fatherly* slap. Only Fred could do that.

"Just the Gelman boys," Fred said. "It'll be fun."

Owen pulled away, turned, and looked at him with a face that was hard, that was no longer sniffling, that was no longer the face of a boy.

"Yeah, lots of fun," Owen said, wiping his eyes with his sleeve so that all trace of tears was gone. "Nothing like a murder in the house to bring a family together."

Rick knew they hung around the meatpacking district. He pulled off the West Side Highway onto 14th Street and there they were, standing on the corners of the cobblestone streets, leaning against the loading docks where, every morning, sides of steer and lamb were pushed out of the delivery trucks and into the packing houses to be cut into steaks and chops.

But there was also another kind of meat for sale in the meatpacking district.

They stared at Rick as he drove by, pressing their lips together in exaggerated kisses, letting their tongues roll provocatively over their teeth. They wore incredibly short skirts and black, knee-high vinyl boots—just like in the movies. They looked seductive, sexy—at least from twenty feet away. He wasn't sure what they would look like from up close. They kind of crouched as he drove by, trying to make eye contact through the car window, their faces contorted in prurient smiles.

They wanted him. Each one wanted him more than anyone had ever wanted him before. He could open up the passenger door and, for twenty bucks or maybe fifty, he could have more warmth and comfort, more hugs, more intimacy in five minutes than he'd had in the last five years of his marriage.

But he didn't want that. Rick wanted something else.

The first two Rick talked to were no help at all. He let them get into the car before asking them if they knew where he could get a gun.

"Get real," Simone, the first one, said.

"Go back to New Jersey," the second one, Clarissa, said.

He gave them twenty dollars anyway and thanked them.

The third was Jasmine.

He sat demurely across from Rick, hands in his lap, his short skirt revealing taut, thin legs. His blond wig was long and full. He had medium-sized breasts that he showed off to their best advantage in a low-cut leopard-patterned shirt. But the heavy makeup couldn't hide his sallow complexion and the pain around the edges of his eyes. Rick also noticed that Jasmine's red polished nails had been picked at, the polish scraped away in patches as though vandals had been digging there, looking for something buried. Rick liked Jasmine for that.

Jasmine nestled into the passenger seat, rubbed his cheek against its back.

"Leather," he purred, his tongue protruding between his teeth when he said the "L." "Mmmmmm," he moaned. "Corinthian."

Jasmine puckered his lips and coquettishly blew Rick a kiss. Then he told Rick to drive a few blocks away.

"We need a little privacy," Jasmine said. "Don't you think?"

Rick didn't move.

"What do you want more than anything right now?" Rick asked, his voice sounding different, stronger, the words coming from a place he didn't recognize.

Jasmine brought his hand delicately to his mouth and tilted his head.

"To make you happy, lover."

"You're not going to touch me."

"That's what they all say," Jasmine whispered. "At least in the beginning."

"I'm serious. Now be honest. What do you want?"

"Okay. I'll play along," Jasmine said, his voice now more matter-of-fact, as if he was getting ready to call a PTA meeting to order. "Since you insist on honesty, if honesty is what turns you on, I'll tell you. What I really *truly* want, this very moment, is money." Then the flirtatious smile came back. "Happy?"

"How about a hundred dollars?"

"Ooooh," Jasmine said, letting his eyes wander down to Rick's crotch. "I hope we're talking *big* bills." Jasmine pulled back a strand of the shimmering synthetic gold hair that had fallen in front of his face. "So tell me, what does a girl have to *do* for this hundred dollars?"

"Find me a gun. With bullets. Just set me up with someone. I'll give you the hundred."

How am I doing, Ben?

Jasmine licked his lips, didn't speak.

"Okay, *two* hundred dollars," Rick said.

"You a cop?" he asked.

"No. I'm Rick. I just need a gun."

Jasmine stared at him. Then almost like magic, like a special effect, his face transformed and the mask of the lewd seductress gave way to reveal a tired, sad young man.

"Take a left at the corner and keep driving," his voice deeper, the sultriness gone. "I'll tell you when to stop."

Rick pulled away from the curb and followed the directions.

"By the way, Jasmine," Rick said, "you think you can use a few loaves of Wonder Bread?"

Jasmine immediately perked up, as if cameras were rolling, as if the director said "action." He turned to Rick, sparkling, the pose in place, once again all allure and seduction.

"Wonder Bread?" Jasmine said, slowly licking his lush, ruby lips. "Well now, what *did* you have in mind?"

Now *what's he doing*, Dom said to himself. First the shopping escapade in Harlem, whatever that was about (Wonder Bread?), and now the transvestites. Dom leaned across the front seat, got Rick in the telescopic, and shot a roll of film. Hooker leaning over, arms resting on the lowered window. Hooker listening. Hooker looking around. Hooker getting in the Saab. Hooker and Rick talking. Saab driving away.

He started up the Caddy and got back on Rick's tail.

This was the third one Rick had picked up in the last half hour. Dom wondered what was wrong with the first two. Was he casting a film? Maybe he didn't like the way they did their hair. Or the smell of their perfume. Or maybe they were pre-op and that freaked him out. Or maybe they weren't, and that was worse.

How did they do that operation? Dom wondered. Make a pussy. He shivered at the thought. Was it something they just inserted, ordered from a catalogue and it came overnight packed in dry ice, shrink-wrapped from PussyTech or SnatchCo? And then what? Did the doctor just make a slit and shove the pussy in? And were there better pussies? Different models? Tighter or shinier or with thicker lips? And what kind of doctor would *do* a pussy implant?

How was work, Honey?

Oh fine, I installed a couple of new pussies today.

And what happened to the guy's dick and nuts? At some point it had to be cut off. You couldn't get rid of it with weed killer or shrink it like a plantar wart. Someone had to take a knife or a scissors or a cleaver and slice it away. Was there a guy who just did that, like the executioner? Did he wear a hood? Maybe it was a woman. Maybe they auctioned it off, a premium on a box of cake mix. Ten proofs of purchase and you get a coupon good for cutting off one dick. Bitter wives, jilted girlfriends from around the world would line up, bring their own bread knives. Dull ones. Rusty. Have their picture taken with it, holding it up, like proud fishermen.

And then, once it was cut off, what did they do with it? He had a vision of the doctor stepping on the lever of one of those pop-up garbage cans and tossing in the handful of dick, where it landed with a dull, sickening splat, flopping on to the pile of other severed dicks. Then counting down, like kids do in their backyards, the final seconds of the game, trying to hit the winning bucket as time runs out—5-4-3-2-1—before popping in the nuts, one at a time, just before the buzzer went off.

The thought of it made Dom feel clammy and his face contorted like he was smelling really bad milk and he instinctively reached for his groin, making sure everything was still in place, protecting it.

Then his cell phone rang.

He checked caller ID. Blocked. It might be Fred Gelman, he thought. Checking in on his progress regarding Rick. He liked dealing directly with Fred. Then he could talk to him about the apartment. Douglas probably didn't even mention it last time.

So he answered.

"Hello."

"Dom?"

It wasn't Fred. It was a woman.

"Yeah."

"It's Mae Stark."

It took him a second, then it flashed.

"Hey, how are you?"

"Good."

"How's the book?"

"Coming along."

"Guess what I'm doing?" he said.

"What?"

"Surveillance. Tailing a guy."

"Cool."

"He just picked up a transvestite in the meatpacking district, now they're driving somewhere."

"To do what?"

"Use your imagination," he said.

She laughed.

"Hey," he said, "if you were here now you could use the camera. It's not easy taking pictures and driving at the same time."

"That's tempting."

"It could be for your book," he said. "Research."

Dom had to goose it to get through a light to keep up with the Saab.

"So how about it?"

"What?"

"You want to join me? There's plenty of room in the front seat."

"What's he doing now?" she asked, avoiding the invitation.

"Not much," Dom said. "Just driving around with a transvestite in the car."

"Is she cute?"

"Hard to say. Personally I don't understand the attraction. Either you go with a woman or a man, but this in-between stuff? Anyway, for me, three holes are better than two."

There was silence on the line. Dom was afraid he might have said something offensive. She quickly allayed his fears.

"Great line," she said.

She must have been writing it down in her notebook. The nitty-gritty. Dom was full of it. The grittiest nitty around.

Dom focused on Rick. The Saab was easy to tail, but traffic was thin in this part of the city and it would be harder to be discreet. And the hookers kept leering at him, coming up to the window whenever he stopped at the corner.

"Who are you following?" she asked.

"Can't say," Dom said. "Confidential."

"He do anything bad?"

"Not yet. Just curious. Wait," he said. "The guy just stopped."

"What's he doing?"

"I said wait." Dom put the phone down on the seat.

He drove past the Saab, averting his head, and pulled up a few cars in front. Dom adjusted his side mirror and watched the hooker get out and ring one of the bells at a ratty six-floor walk-up across the street. He spoke into the intercom, then signaled for Rick to come. Rick got out of the car.

"Dom."

He heard the tinny sound of her voice coming from the phone. He picked it up.

"Hold on," he said. "They're going inside. This is when I coulda used you. I gotta put the phone down again." He picked up the camera and got a few shots of Rick crossing the street, looking around nervously, and then walking into the building.

"Was that the camera, the whirring sound?"

"Yeah."

"What size lens you have?

"Mine's big," he said.

"Don't be infantile, Dom," she said. "I'm trying to get all the details right. The details are the most important part of a book."

"It's 800 mm," he lied. He only had 200 mm because that's what the kid he bought it from had been able to steal, but he wanted the 800 mm—the white one, like the photographers had at football games. "The motor gives me ten shots per second. It's almost like a movie."

"Mmmm-hmmm," she said.

He could hear her breathing as she wrote. He liked her breathing.

"What are you doing now?" she asked.

"Sitting," Dom said. "A lot of what a cop does involves sitting."

A parking spot opened up down the street and Dom pulled in. He adjusted his side mirror so he could see the front of the building.

"Back when I was a cop," he said into the phone, "I worked Vice for a while. I used to hang around here, mostly at night, playing cat and mouse with the 'girls.' It wasn't much of a game."

"How come?"

"It's hard to move quick in spike heels," he said, "especially on cobblestones. A few of these guys were probably athletes in high school. In sneakers they'd outrun me. Now they have tits bigger than my grandmother's."

"It's sad, I guess."

"You don't think that way as a cop," he said. "If your cop thinks that way, he'd be wrong."

"My cop's a she.'"

"Well, maybe it's different, then," he said. "I don't know how a woman cop would feel. Soft and wet, I guess."

"Dom," she said, scolding him.

"Sorry. Hey, I should be here for a while. Usually an appointment is for an hour. You could grab a cab and pop over. I could tell you stories. Details. Nitty and gritty."

"Another time, maybe," she said. "But can I call you?"

"Sure," he said. "But I'm more authentic in the flesh."

"I'll keep that in mind, Dom," she said. Then she hung up.

She was something. Smart. He wasn't used to that. The women he knew couldn't walk and chew gum at the same time. Actually, they *could* walk and chew gum, but unfortunately that was the thing they were most proud of.

Dom got out of the car and casually made his way to the Saab, like he was admiring it. If Mae were there, they could have pretended they were a couple thinking about buying one.

Oh, Honey, it's just what we need. It's us. Whattaya say, Dom?

There were several loaves of Wonder Bread in the back seat, some newspaper, and a piece of pipe taped to some wood in the shape of a gun.

He went back to the Caddy and got inside.

Wonder Bread.

Somehow the bread, the newspaper, and the pipe in the shape of a gun all fit together. He just wasn't sure how. Dom went over his cases as a cop, trying to think if this resembled anything he'd worked on before. Wonder Bread and a pipe kind of shaped like a gun a kid would make to play a game with.

He checked the mirror. No movement from the door. Rick was still in the apartment, doing God knows what.

Rick was on the ropes. Dom could feel it. Rick was ready to go down. Dom had to make it look that he was the one to do it, the one responsible for putting Rick down for the count. Then Fred would be indebted to him, get Dom the apartment. With a terrace. So he could sit outside and have drinks with Mae.

He closed his eyes for a minute. He patted the pocket inside his jacket. The videotape was still there. Detective Bliss enters, twenty-two minutes go by, Detective Bliss leaves.

What did you do in those twenty-two minutes, Detective Bliss?

Or, more to the point, what could you prove you *didn't* do?

Dom smiled. He wasn't quite sure yet how it was going to play out with the tape. But he figured something would present itself. You have an edge on a guy, you know something he doesn't know you know, you have to use it, take the advantage, and then knock the guy through the ropes and out of the ring.

* * *

Rick followed Jasmine up to the fifth floor. The smell lingering in the hall was a pungent mixture of incense and urine. There was a window at the end of the hallway that was painted over in green and cast a sickly pallor over the walls and floor. A bicycle was chained to a rusting radiator. It was missing its seat, both tires, the gears, and the chain. A bicycle skeleton, its flesh ravaged, as if by ravenous ants. It reminded Rick of how in Westerns they always had those cow skulls in the desert, a signal that bad things would happen if you went any farther.

Bring them on, Rick thought. *Bring them all on*.

Rick was ready.

The door was unlocked. Jasmine pushed it open.

"After you," he said.

Rick hesitated.

"Don't worry," Jasmine purred. "Harriet won't bite. Or, at least she won't bite hard." And he gave a girlish giggle.

Rick walked in the apartment. It was decorated like an old fashioned New Orleans whorehouse. Floor lamps with fringed shades cast a lurid reddish light on walls covered with striped wallpaper. Heavy red velvet curtains cascaded in front of the windows. There was an overstuffed Victorian couch on one wall done in the same red velvet. And against the other wall was a divan on which lounged a large, bald man in a silk dressing gown. In his red gloved hand he held a black cigarette holder on which was pinioned a smoldering cigarette, the thick smoke drifting straight up in a dense, narrow stream. His other hand rested on his chest, a ring sporting a bulbous stone arranged elegantly over his gloved index finger.

"*Se llama Rick*," Jasmine said. "*Tiene dinero. Quiere una pistola.*"

Harriet nodded, then cast a lazy eye on Rick.

"Rick," Harriet said, rolling the "r," letting the word drip off his lips like warm fudge. "Rhymes with lick."

Harriet laughed like an old woman who had just won at bingo.

"What about the gun?" Rick said. "I'd like to get out of here before I get a rash."

Harriet looked deeply hurt, as if Rick had just snubbed the Ritz cracker canapés he had worked so hard to prepare.

"And why, Rick, should I sell you, of all people, a gun?" Harriet asked.

"I'm a friend of Jasmine's. I'm a really nice guy. And my son was murdered recently."

Harriet shook his head. "Tsk, tsk, tsk. You should be more discreet, Rick," Harriet said. "You should remain anonymous. Just plain Rick. If I choose to endow you with one of my rods, I want my conscience to be clear. I won't be pleased to read in the periodicals stories of vengeance orchestrated with what was once part of my arsenal. I want to be able to sleep at night. You understand, I hope."

"Sell me a gun because I've got two hundred dollars in twenties. And because you'll never see or hear from me again."

Harriet raised his eyebrows.

"Aren't you the fickle one. How does Jasmine feel about that?"

Jasmine hung his head and turned to the wall, a delicate flower.

"I'm not sure," he said. "We haven't known each other that long."

"It doesn't take too long to get to know someone. Oscar Wilde said he knew more about a person after meeting him for ten minutes than that person knew about himself."

This was a strange kind of game, Rick thought. At once both perverted and sublimely elegant. More interesting than selling luggage.

He softened, sensing this was a better approach.

"I feel Jasmine needs more from me than I am able to give right now," Rick said.

"That's too bad," Harriet said, "because I am thinking I have no pressing need for such a paltry taste as two hundred dollars. But what I *do* need is for Jasmine to be happy. Can't you see how sullen she is?"

Rick nodded.

"No. *Really* look at her," Harriet commanded.

Rick looked, saw Jasmine, the leopard top he wore now showing its age, not fitting him properly, something there, some subtle slope of the shoulders or shape of the hips that didn't let the clothes hang quite right, that belied Jasmine's true gender. The wig exuding a sheen Rick didn't see in the street, an unnatural gloss. Jasmine's feet were not dainty, his chin too strong. No posturing or pouting could undo it. Rick suddenly felt so sorry for this man, undone by these tiny details. Not like Rick, who could hide everything, who could spend years in luggage without anyone knowing how much he despised it, every new model, every improvement in retractable handles and wheel bearings and synthetic leathers and latches. But he understood that sense of being completely trapped inside his skin. Because Rick was trapped inside his life, inside a locked bag, banging to get out, locked inside and screaming silently to get out.

He bit his nail.

"Don't do that," Harriet said.

He stopped. He looked at Jasmine and smiled
Jasmine hesitantly smiled back.

"Good," Harriet said. "Now, R-r-r-ick, this is like one of those fairy tales you read in school. I am the queen and Jasmine is my daughter, the princess. But Jasmine is unhappy. She has not laughed in years. I have sent word throughout the kingdom that anyone who can make the princess laugh will get whatever they wish for. In your case, I assume that would be a heater for the price you offered."

"What kind?"

"A nine-millimeter Baretta with a spare clip," Harriet said.

"Is that good?" Rick asked.

"It's a beautiful thing," Harriet purred. "Now, R-r-rick, are you willing to give it a try?"

"And what would make princess happy?"

"Oh, that would be cheating. Besides, I'm not sure myself. As you know, it's not easy being a princess."

Rick nodded, surprised at the way he accepted all this, the ease he felt here.

"I guess I'll have to use my imagination," Rick said.

"That's what it's there for," Harriet replied, and a Cheshire-cat grin spread across his face with salacious abandon. Rick sensed that Harriet's mouth had been in places he could never possibly imagine.

Rick turned to Jasmine, walked over to where he stood, still curled against the wall. He put his hand on the man's shoulder, felt a hard edge of bone through the thin material of his shirt, felt Jasmine shudder at his touch. Rick ran his finger up Jasmine's neck, along the distinct line where the thick pancake base left off and his bleached, pallid skin began, like a border between two countries on a map, two countries at war with each other. He could see the veins in Jasmine's neck, a cluster of craters under his cheekbone (the palimpsest of teenage acne) now only partially hidden by the almond-hued powder, the scarlet lipstick outlined with dark pencil, the tiny stubble of a mustache that had sprouted insidiously since his morning shave, giving him, Rick thought, no end of heartache.

Jasmine gradually warmed to Rick's touch and eased away from the wall. He turned and Rick faced him now, a helpless creature, trapped in some tremulous world where nothing was solid, nothing held together.

"Hi," Jasmine said in a high, soft, timorous voice, like it was his first day at a new school.

"Come here," Rick said.

Jasmine walked into his embrace. Rick held him close, stroking his hair, which felt crudely synthetic. They stayed that way for several minutes, Rick feeling Jasmine's breath growing softer, deeper, happier. He wasn't sure what to do next. Harriet must have sensed his indecision.

"As Queen, I really shouldn't be abetting you like this," she said. "But you're trying so hard, R-r-rick, I just can't help myself."

Harriet reached behind one of her satin pillows and pulled out a remote control. He aimed it across the room, to an unseen stereo, and a moment later lush violins filled the loft, muted trumpets, a harp, the drummer on brushes, then a soft, sultry voice singing above the strings.

"Jeri Southern," Harriet said with a touch of reverence. "The forgotten angel of song."

Harriet leaned back and closed his eyes.

Jeri Southern sang in her wistful contralto, her voice rising gently above the lush strings.

Be still, my haunted heart.

Rick knew what to do now. He took Jasmine's hand and curled his fingers around it. He placed his other hand at Jasmine's

back, and together they moved slowly about the room, dancing gently to the music. Rick had not danced in years, resisting
Ellen's requests at weddings and parties until she finally stopped
asking. But here he moved freely, with ease and lightness.

The song stopped, but they stayed together a few minutes
longer. Rick rubbed his face against Jasmine's crudely rouged
cheek and thought about his son, Ben. His dead son Ben, who
never seemed to have a weakness, but now was dead, who
moved through his life without courtesy, without care, while
Rick fled from conflict, never sent food back, even if the chicken
was pink or the fish burned to a crisp, for fear of . . . always
for fear of. Rick clung tightly to Jasmine, his cheek against the
stiff hair, and thought about his defiant son who constantly
reminded Rick of his own weakness. How many times he hated
his son, a dark hatred that emerged when Rick saw Ben's swag-
ger, the amoral curl of his lip. Hatred because the boy left no
entrance for Rick, no possibility of connection. He wanted to
slap Ben. No, he wanted to hold his son's head in a sink full of
water, his neck bucking as the air started to burn and burst from
his lungs, then let him up just long enough to breathe, then
shove him down again, using all his weight to keep his son's
face submerged until Ben weakened, until he gave in, until he
promised to start over, start over from when he was just a baby
and they would find a way to make it work, for them to be
together and then they would hold each other tight, both desperate never to let go.

Father and son.

But that wouldn't happen now, because Ben was dead and
Rick was dancing with a sad transvestite.

Look at me, Ben. I'm like you now.

I don't give a shit.

He kissed Jasmine gently on the cheek and released him. He turned to Harriet, about to ask for the gun, and saw it was already being offered him, dangling nimbly from one of Harriet's gloved fingers like the last petal left on a rose. He took the money out of his pocket and held it out. Harriet eased it from his fingers and slipped it in down the neck of her gown.

Rick took the gun. It was a lot heavier than the rusted pipe. The metal was smooth and cold, the lines elegant and fierce.

"Thanks," he said.

"No, Rick," Harriet said. "Thank you."

Rick smiled at Jasmine, thought of blowing him a kiss, but decided that would be patronizing. Instead he gave him one short wave of his hand.

"Take care of yourself," Rick said.

"You, too," Jasmine replied. Then made a gesture, putting his hand behind him as if he were tucking in his shirt.

"Oh," Rick said, and slipped the gun under his belt in the small of his back where it was neatly covered by his sports jacket.

"Go get 'em, tiger," Harriet said.

Rick nodded slowly, then left, closing the door gently behind him.

Dom was on his cell phone calling his friend at the precinct. He was trying to find out what was happening with the Felix case.

"Bliss is supposed to be working it," the friend said, "but now he's also got this kid, you know, Holden's brother, whatever his name is."

"Owen."

"Whatever. Anyway, so I think Garcia is working Felix now. . . . That's right, honey, I'll be home at six."

"Huh?"

"You want me to pick up anything at the store?"

"What's . . ."

"Listen, Sweetie, put on that little red number I like, so when I get home we can. . . . Okay, sorry, someone was walking by. Anyway, you know Garcia, right?"

"No."

"They use her whenever they have to interview a woman. Rape victims, domestic abuse, etc. They use Garcia because *she's* a woman, too. Get it? You know, for purposes of sensitivity."

"So Bliss is off the case."

"Far as I know."

"And no action yet on Felix, right? No leads?"

"Not that I've heard," his friend said. "Why you interested?"

"I'm seeing this woman," Dom said. "She's a writer."

"The Screamers?"

"No."

"Then what?"

"Books. She went to *college*. She writes books from scratch. She's curious. About Felix. The details. That's the most important part of a book, you know. The details."

"You boffing her?"

"What do you think?"

"And she's really a writer?"

"Yeah."

"Books?"

"Yeah."

"Not bad for a dumb-ass left tackle from Canarsie."

"I'm moving to the city soon," Dom said. "A one-bedroom. With a terrace."

"A terrace?"

"Yeah."

Dom caught sight of Rick in the mirror finally coming out of the building. Dom's trained eye picked up the slight bulge at Rick's back, just above the waist. Jesus Christ, the guy was packing. What's next?

"Gotta go," Dom said. "Guy I'm tailing is on the move."

Dom started up the Caddy and pulled out behind Rick.

Wonder Bread, newspaper, some pipe and a piece of wood shaped like a gun, and a real gun.

He wondered what Mae would think. It might interest her as a writer. Because between the black kids in Harlem, the toy gun, the Wonder Bread bags, the transvestite, and the real gun, Dom figured whatever Rick was up to would make one hell of a novel.

Bliss drove downtown, to Rivington Street. Garcia wanted his help with Felix. Two days on the case was already enough, she said. He knew how she felt. Fucking Felix. Bliss had to remind himself that every human being had a little piece of the divine spirit in them. Even a man who cheated at dominoes and beat up his wife and then, dead, somehow managed to wiggle himself free from the ropes that held him to the bottom of the river and float up and rot right in Bliss's face.

"What did I ever do to you?" Bliss asked no one in particular.

The Lower East Side had changed, even since he'd last worked the Felix case. Gentrification was edging closer to completion. Rows of what had once been destitute, five-floor walk-ups were now coveted pieces of real estate. You had to know someone to rent here, you had to have big bucks to buy.

Dumbbell apartments, they called them when they were first built, because the floor plan looked like a dumbbell. How many immigrant families went to sleep at night on Rivington Street, their one collective dream to someday be able to move out of their wretched apartment on this crowded, noisy, rat-infested street where it was sweltering hot in summer and deadly cold in winter. Get enough in the bank to move to Sunnyside or Utopia Parkway or Riverdale. *Anywhere* but Rivington Street. And now, in one of those great New York ironies, young people were clamoring to find an apartment there. A Starbucks would probably be opening soon. If there wasn't one already.

Felix's building now had new windows, the façade was cleaned up, new security buzzers on the front door. Tree branches peeked over the top ledge, indicating that someone had already done some landscaping on the roof.

Garcia wanted Bliss to talk to the building's super, Andrej. She liked Andrej for something, she told Bliss. She wasn't sure what. But Andrej wasn't being forthcoming. Maybe he had something against her, Garcia being both a cop and a woman. Bliss wasn't surprised. He remembered Andrej from the last time they talked.

Bliss walked to the basement apartment, rang the bell. The door was answered by a hulking man with thick arms, fists the size of bocci balls, ragged blond hair like he had cut it himself, in the dark, with dull scissors, drunk when he did it. This was Andrej, the super.

"Hello, Andrej," Bliss said.

Andrej didn't answer. Only looked Bliss up and down with disdain.

"No apartment," Andrej said. "Two hundred dollars getting name on waiting list." Bliss said nothing. Andrej started to close the door. Bliss put his foot out to stop it. Behind Andrej was an old woman at the stove, stirring a pot. The smell of stewing cabbage and meat and prunes wafted toward him.

Andrej tried again to shut the door.

"Remove kindly foot," Andrej said.

This is how it starts, Bliss thought.

"Your English has gotten better, Andrej," Bliss said.

Andrej studied him, like a predator, wondering which part of Bliss he might eat first.

"Police," Andrej said.

The old woman said something in Polish. Andrej answered, then turned back to Bliss.

"Is about Felix," Andrej said.

"Yes."

"I am telling you on phone," Andrej said. "Is same now. Nothing new."

"I wish that were the case, Andrej," Bliss said. "Believe me. But it's not the same. Felix floated up. He missed you, Andrej. He has something he wants to whisper in your ear. I have his lips in my pocket."

Andrej was trying to make sense of out what Bliss was saying. So was Bliss. There was nothing to make sense *of.* There was only Felix's rotten, river-soaked corpse—silent, immutable, dead.

It was a stupid case. He hated Andrej for being part of it, for answering the door. He hated Felix for floating up, for buying a belt with his fucking initials on it. He hated whoever sank Felix under the East River for using shitty rope or tying loose knots. He knew it was not good to have these feelings. That once they started, they would rot out your core and you couldn't work Homicide anymore.

Fucking Felix.

"Tell me you remember something, Andrej," Bliss said, his foot still wedged in the door. "Tell me you remember tying the cinder block to Felix's feet and dumping him in the river. It all came back to you. I need you to tell me that now."

"I am giving what I know," Andrej said.

"Confess," Bliss said. He got down on his knees, his hands clenched together, begging. "Please."

Andrej looked down with disbelief. He was large. He'd been hit before, was used to pain, welcomed pain. The man had to be surprised.

Bliss stayed on his knees.

"Pretty please." he said. He looked upward, to Andrej's puzzled face. As he did, Bliss slowly moved his hands forward and ever so gently looped his index and middle fingers under the bottom of Andrej's pants.

"Why can't you confess?" Bliss said in a small voice. "It would help me out a lot."

Andrej turned to the woman, said something in Polish. The old woman said something back and laughed and stirred the pot. While Andrej's head was turned, Bliss tightened his hold on Andrej's pants and yanked with all his strength, pulling up with one sudden, ferocious movement, lifting Andrej's feet off the floor. Andrej let out a cry of alarm as he fell back, his shoulders and head slamming into the floor. Bliss was on him fast, driving his knee into the man's gut as he got his cuffs out, found one arm and secured the wrist.

"Turn over," Bliss shouted into his face, pushing him on to his stomach so he could get the other cuff in place.

Bliss sensed movement, turned in time to see the old woman coming toward him holding the pot, frayed pads folded over the handles, steam rising from the boiling soup. The woman was shuffling forward, impossibly slowly, like in some kind of wacky comedy, but the soup was hot enough to do serious damage. Her face was set with deep anger. Not only was someone hurting her son, but she was being forced to sacrifice a whole pot of borscht.

Bliss pulled out his gun, pointed it at her head.

She didn't stop. Maybe she knew they wouldn't shoot her. Maybe behind her pot she felt invincible. Maybe policemen had pointed guns at her many times before. Whatever the reason, she kept coming forward, her hands tight around the handles, steam clouding her face like a demon. Death by borscht, Bliss thought.

He shoved his gun into her son's neck.

Everything froze. Andrej moaned softly.

"Tell her to put the pot back on the stove," Bliss said to him.

Andrej mumbled something in Polish. The woman growled, made a gesture toward Bliss with the pot. Andrej shouted. She turned, shuffled back to the stove, put the pot on the flame. Keeping it hot. Just in case.

"Turn over," Bliss said.

Andrej snorted some curse in Polish as Bliss cuffed the other wrist. He grabbed the chain between the cuffs and stood up. He placed his foot in the small of Andrej's back and put pressure on his arms, pulling them up, bending them the wrong way, just enough to put a strain on the shoulder sockets. Andrej cried out in pain. The old woman simmered by the stove, slowly stirring her pot, her face strongly suggesting she wished Bliss were in it.

"I have green card," Andrej shouted.

"This isn't about a green card," Bliss said. "You're going to jail whether you have a green card or not."

"Green card," the old woman said.

"Quiet," Andrej said to her.

"You got a lawyer?" Bliss asked him.

"Why?"

"Because one of those old guys from the building ID'd you. He told me how you tortured those old people. Then you killed Felix, to get him out of the building."

Bliss yanked back on Andrej's arms, forcing him to howl in pain.

Bliss didn't care.

"Then you killed Felix," he said.

"No."

"Dumped him in the river. Who's your mother going to cook for if you go to jail, Andrej? Huh?"

Bliss waited. The borscht boiled. The old woman started singing a song in Polish.

"That's it, Andrej. You had your chance. You killed Felix. Let's go."

Andrej squirmed on his belly, shouting now.

"Was him!"

"Who?" Bliss said, bending close to Andrej's face. "Tell me Andrej, it'll all be over."

"He is paying us cash."

"His name."

Bliss sensed it was on its way.

"He was cop," Andrej said. "Used to be cop. Is all I know. Cop with thick neck. Strong. He beats me in arm wrestle once."

Bliss leaned in close to Andrej, talking right into his ear.

"You saw him kill Felix?"

"No," Andrej said. "But he does it."

"You help dump Felix in the river?"

"No!"

"What was his name?"

"Was motherfucking cop," Andrej said. "Like you."

"Not like me. No one is a cop like me. What was his name?"

"Only know first name."

"What was it?"

"Dum," Andrej said.

"Dum?"

"Is what we call him."

"Dom?" Bliss asked.

"Yeah," Andrej said. "Dum."

Once he heard the name, Bliss was relieved. He didn't have to worry about the use of unnecessary force with Andrej, about violating Andrej's rights. Because with Dom involved, the case was no longer about procedure or rights or taking statements. It was now about blowing up a transverse, twisting some track and hoping for a derailment, but above all, Bliss was sharply aware he was now directly in the path of a mean and very powerful train.

Rick had his gun.

He did whatever was necessary to get it.

Whatever was necessary.

He wanted to see that prick in stereo equipment, the one who sold him and Ben the cassette deck. When they got it home, Ben realized he wanted the *dual* cassette deck, so they went to return the one they bought, only the guy wouldn't take it back because Rick didn't have the original packaging. He had the box, but not the Styrofoam—you need the Styrofoam, the salesman said, a reedy kid with a toothy grin that was fixed on his face even as he knew he was screwing you over. It isn't considered original packaging unless it has the Styrofoam, he said. I have the *box*, Rick said, but he knew there was defeat in his voice, and the salesman could easily see there was no real fight in Rick. Ben could see it, too. And indeed, he made a few more whimpers of protest, but soon Ben was picking out another cassette player, the dual kind, and Rick was putting it on his charge.

He wanted that lying, grinning, pimply prick of a salesmen in front of him now. Smile at *this!* as Rick held the gun on him, pointed it right at his head, right at his teeth. Here's your original packaging! Here's your fucking Styrofoam! He'd turn to Ben. Whattaya say, Ben? Should we do him or let him go? And Ben would look at Rick his father with something like admiration and pride.

Do him or let him go?

Look at me now, Ben.

Please, look at me now!

Ward was already sitting at the bar in the Subway Café when Bliss walked in. Next to him, a large man, burly in his Yankees jacket, a gun strapped to his hip. This man turned when Ward did and Bliss saw the eyes of a veteran cop—eyes unfazed by anything they would ever see again. His hand, when Bliss shook it, was rough and hard.

This was Sergeant Billy Dix Sr.

"Thanks for seeing me, Bliss," he said.

Bliss nodded. They left the bar and took one of the tables. The banquets were dented from the weight of several decades' worth of people who sat in the Subway Café because they didn't want to be home, didn't want to be at work, didn't want to be walking around New York with no prospects, didn't want to be anywhere, really, so they stayed in one of the booths of the Subway Café, adding their weight to the already deep dents in the Naugahyde, the one mark they were leaving on the world, hoping, perhaps, that some day the seat might swallow them up.

Billy Dix drank half his beer in several large gulps, then put it down on the table. He stared into the glass. From his moribund expression, Bliss guessed that Billy Dix was thinking that this, like most of the glasses in his life, was much more likely to be half empty than half full. Billy wasn't ready to say anything yet. Bliss gave him time. It was Dix's call.

"Fucking B. J.," Dix said at last. B. J. standing for Billy Jr., Bliss figured. Then Billy Sr. laughed. One of those laughs you do to keep from doing something else. "Being the son of a cop you'd think he could keep his nose clean. But no."

Bliss didn't necessarily see any real correlation there. If nuns could have kids, he figured a certain percentage would wind up corrupt—working on Wall Street, say, or in telemarketing, calling people at dinnertime to offer them another credit card to put them further in debt. So why should every cop's kid be expected to turn out like Opie?

"He's messed up plenty," Billy Dix said, "the drugs and whatnot. Every kid is into drugs, now. You know what I'm saying?"

"His friend's prints were found on the murder weapon."

"T-Bone," Dix said. "*I* should have shot that little prick. He steals my beer."

"Good name, though," Ward said. "T-Bone."

"My beer from *my* refrigerator. His father's worth millions. Flowers. Calls himself Maurice. Flowers by Maurice. Weddings at the Plaza and shit. Thirty thousand for flowers by Maurice and his kid is stealing my beer."

"What's he doing in public school?"

"Got kicked out of too many private schools," Billy said. "Father wanted to teach him a lesson. Should have sent him to boarding school. Instead he screws around with my son. With Billy Jr. You gotta be so careful who your kid's friends are."

Bliss nodded, understanding.

"I have a daughter," Bliss said.

"Then you *know*," Billy Dix said.

Dix took a moment with his beer, staring down into it like Narcissus into the pool, seeing not his beauty, but a radiant sadness.

"T-Bone's prints," Billy Dix said. "That's all you have at this juncture?"

"Yeah."

"So nothing that points directly at my son."

"Just that he was there," Bliss said. "And Owen, the kid whose house it was, said Ben owed your son some money."

"For drugs?"

Bliss didn't want to, but he nodded yes. He could see Billy's eyes flash. Cops always reserved a place in their hearts for some extra bit of pain and remorse, saved like a bottle of fine Champagne, to be opened on occasions like these.

"You know, I go to this apartment a couple of weeks ago to look for a kid named Rakim—no offense, Ward, but what is it with these black names, like word scramblers before you figure them out—anyway, we like Rakim for kicking the shit out of another kid. Kid who got the shit kicked out of him is retarded—can you say that anymore?—anyway, he was—retarded. So when I get there, to Rakim's house, it's just his little brother playing video games. Seven-thirty in the evening. No dinner on the table. I'm looking for Rakim, I say. He shrugs his shoulders. I ask if his mother's around. No. I ask if his father's around. No. Does he know where they are? No, he hasn't seen them in a couple of days. And I think, of course this kid's older brother is going to kick some retard in the head—his parents are never around. The younger brother will probably turn out similar. And then I realize I'm doing the same thing with *my* kid. How can I fool myself like that, thinking just because I *know* it, that I understand it up here," he pointed to his head, "that it will turn out any different. *I'm* never around. I'm always dealing with other people's shit, trying to solve *their* crises, and I totally ignore my own house."

He finished his beer and stood up.

"You can't do nothing. I know that. It's a homicide," Billy Dix said. "I'll talk to him myself. I'll find out what went on."

Bliss saw the man's fists clenching tightly, imagined what kind of conversation would transpire when Billy Sr. got home.

"I've been meaning to have a little talk with Billy Jr. anyway," Billy Sr. said. "A little father-son talk." He went to some deep place for a few minutes. When he came back, he didn't seem any happier. "I'll get back to you with the truth," he said. "Whatever the truth is, whether it's the truth I want to hear or not, I'll get back to you with it."

"What do you think, partner?" Bliss asked Ward after Billy Dix Sr. had left. "You like Billy Dix Jr.? You like T-Bone?"

Ward shook his head.

"I'm still liking Owen," Ward said.

"You got a motive?"

"Yeah. Love. Ben was in love."

"With Owen's girlfriend."

"Yeah. He drugs Owen, like he did Chantal. Then he waits until Owen falls asleep and Chantal gets woozy."

"Then what happened?"

"Ben has sex with Chantal. The lab report confirmed it. Owen wakes up. Ben starts bragging. So Owen waits for *him* to go to sleep and, his heart full of malice and revenge, whacks him with the trophy."

"How's he wake up if he's taken the drug?"

"Maybe he only had a little of it. Maybe Chantal's spirit came to him in a dream and woke him up. 'Help me, Owen. The Big Bad Wolf has got me.' I don't know."

"And what's he do with the trophy?" Bliss asked.

"He throws it away."

"We checked the garbage."

"He buries it out back."

"We looked. No signs of digging."

"He hides it in the house."

"We were all over the house."

"So he walks farther away. He walks ten blocks away. He puts it in the garbage there."

"Owen wouldn't do that," Bliss said. "He's lazy. He's not used to throwing things out, cleaning up his own mess. He's probably never cleaned up anything in his life. Anyway, why does he dispose of the trophy and not the dumbbell?"

"Too heavy."

"But I'm thinking the anger Owen displayed finding out Ben slept with his girlfriend, I'm thinking that was genuine."

"Meaning he didn't know about it that night," Ward said.

"Meaning that night Owen would not have been jealous enough to whack his friend because he didn't know about Ben and Chantal until we told him."

"If we had the surveillance tape," Ward said, "we might know when Billy Dix and T-Bone left the party. Or if Owen left with the trophy, to dispose of it. Or if someone else came into the house that night, someone we don't even know. Lieutenant says if we found the surveillance tape we might learn a lot of things."

"Too many things," Bliss said.

"By the way," Ward said. "You'll never guess who oversaw the installation of the Gelmans' surveillance."

"Who?"

"None other than Mr. Personality himself—Dom DeMoro," Ward said.

"He could have taken it that morning," Bliss said. "When we all showed up."

"He knew where to look."

"You think we have grounds for a warrant to search Dom's apartment?" Bliss said.

"We'd need a motive," Ward said. "A reason why he would have taken it. You got one?"

No, Bliss didn't have one. But he felt certain he now knew where the missing videotape was. Suddenly Dom DeMoro, with whom Bliss had never exchanged more than a dozen words before this week, was at the center of his universe.

When Adelaide called and said she had the check, Clara suggested they meet at a little bakery on Third Avenue just north of 96th Street. Clara didn't want to run into the Missus or any of her friends. She knew the oversize cupcakes in the window with the shiny white frosting and bright red cherries in the center would scare away the fancy ladies the way farmers back home

would hang the skin of a fox they caught on a fence as a warning to the other foxes.

Clara ordered some tea and dunked the tea bag in only twice
because she liked it weak with lots of sugar, the way she'd been
drinking it since she was a child. She told herself not to, but Clara
couldn't stop thinking about the money. Thirty thousand dollars
would buy a small house for her family, maybe with an extra room
to rent out. Holding the check would be like holding the house.
A house, just for talking. Because the Gelmans were rich and the
son, Holden, was famous, money floated in the water around them
like the guts of the fish cleaned by the fisherman on the way back
to the dock, floating in the Gelmans' wake for whichever birds
were lucky enough to be around.

She never once thought she deserved this money, even if
she did work hard and put up with so much humiliation. Clara
knew no one got things simply because they deserved them.
Her grandfather taught her that on his boat. You could do
everything right, work for days without sleep on the unforgiv-
ing sea through heat and rain, and you could still come home
with an empty hold. But another man in another boat, a man
who arranged for his daughter to do favors for a local policeman in exchange not for money, but for blasting caps, *that* man,
her grandfather said, could go out in the water, drop in the
blasting cap, and then wait leisurely for the low thud of the
explosion, like dull thunder, and the erupting mound of water
and spray that followed, like something a child could make in
a bathtub with a bucket. And though they didn't deserve it,
that man and his brothers could dip their sleeve nets over the
side of the boat and fill their hold completely with fish stunned
dead by the blast, setting aside several choice fish for his daughter to cook for the policeman's dinner. All this while another

brother stood poised on deck with a rifle to keep greedy, self-ish men like her grandfather away.

Her grandfather could come later if he wanted, hours later, to see if any more fish floated up, fish that hadn't been killed immediately by the explosion but lingered near death for a time, swimming slowly, like old drunken men, until their gills gave out and they turned belly up and watched their cold, dark, silent world disappear as they floated helplessly up to the surface. But her grandfather had too much pride or felt too much pity for these fish, so he let them be, even though he might have deserved them.

Adelaide arrived, dressed smartly in a dark green suit, carrying a briefcase. The silly face was now harder, more focused, more self-assured. She sat across from Clara and placed a small tape recorder on the table.

She switched it on.

"Let's talk about the Gelman family," Adelaide said. And a very evil smile crept across her sweet young face, which made Clara uncomfortable, but she assumed some kind of devilish force would eventually present itself when so much money was involved.

Bliss lay on the couch in his living room, sipping a beer. The latest installment of the adventures of Mae Stark were propped in his lap. Rachel sat across from him, nervously waiting as he read them.

"I don't know why you need my approval for this," he said.

"Maybe I don't," she said. "Maybe it's not about approval. Maybe it's something else."

"My expertise."

"Possibly. Though I may not need that so much any more."

"You found another cop?"

"Stop being such a dope and read."

Mae watched Jimmy T. in her side mirror. She'd been tailing him for the past five hours. Now she was sitting and waiting. So much of what a cop did involved sitting. They didn't train you for this, Mae thought. Her gut hurt from cramps. She had to pee. She had to change her Tampax.

Bliss looked at her, incredulous.

"I know what you just read," she said, sitting back, smug. "But that's what a *woman* would think about after five hours."

"I get it."

"But you don't like it."

"It's just . . ." He knew any rejoinder was hopeless

Rachel lambasted him anyway. "If Mae was pissed that she'd eaten the last donut or her pack of cigarettes was empty or she finished the last of the pint of whiskey she kept in the glove compartment, then it would be fine. Right?"

"It would be better," he said.

"I can't help it if Mae is a real woman," Rachel said.

"She *should* have a bottle in the glove compartment," Bliss said. "That would make her more interesting. A tragic flaw."

"What's yours?" she asked.

"Consciousness," he said.

"Besides that."

"Nothing," he said, sipping his beer. "I have no other flaws."

"Keep reading."

But Bliss sensed the idea of Mae having a drinking problem had captivated Rachel the novelist. Maybe he'd get a mention for it in the acknowledgments.

It had been fifty-five minutes since Jimmy T. had gone inside with the hooker. If he was paying for an hour, he'd be out soon. Mae's back was starting to hurt. She adjusted her position. She didn't like sitting in one place for so long. She thought about when she was in labor, lying in bed for twelve hours until she was fully dilated. This was worse, although now, at least, she didn't have to suffer through her husband's cloying attempts to be funny.

Again with the husband, Bliss thought.

She kept her eye on the mirror, waiting for Jimmy T. to emerge. It reminded Mae of the plane ride she'd taken recently where she had her own personal movie screen. The in-flight movie today was The Adventures of Jimmy T. *The hooker Jimmy had picked up looked good. He was the third one he had talked to. Jimmy T. hadn't approved of the first two for some reason. But third seemed to suit his fancy. He was quite alluring.*

"You keep saying 'he' when you talk about the hooker," Bliss said.

"That's because it's a transvestite," Rachel said proudly.

Shit. He should have picked that up.

He had bigger tits than her grandmother. And he was certainly a lot sexier. His legs were long and smooth and slim. He must work out, Mae thought. And the skirt he wore barely covered his svelte butt. Mae wouldn't have had the balls to wear a skirt that short. But then again, maybe you needed balls to wear a skirt that short.

"Where'd you come up with all this?" Bliss asked.

"I made it up," she said. "Isn't that what you told me writers were supposed to do?"

"Yeah, but . . ."

"But what?"

He knew she was goading him on, waiting for him to say something about how she should be more ladylike, more discreet.

"It's great," he said.

"You mean that or you just saying that to appease me?"

"Both," he said.

"Good answer."

She got up and kissed him on the lips, a soft, wet, open kiss.

"When are you coming to bed?" she asked.

"In a little while."

"Don't be long," she said.

She snatched the pages out his hands and fairly skipped back to her room.

He put on some music and headed back to the couch. Monk's curious piano quietly filled the room. Then Coltrane's tenor. Monk and Trane, just the three quartet sides, which he programmed to repeat several times for the next hour. These three tunes, about fifteen minutes of music, were the only studio recordings of the legendary Monk quartet that played the Five Spot for more than a year in the late fifties, before Trane left to play with Miles. For Bliss they were perfection, embodying the entire history of jazz, incorporating all that had come before, anticipating everything that would come after. Music that was funny and joyous and full of longing and mystery that never failed to transport him.

And there was one more thing about these sides that intrigued Bliss. They were among the last recordings made by Monk's bass player, Wilbur Ware. Not long after this, at a gig in the Village, Wilbur went outside to smoke a cigarette between sets and never came back. Disappeared off the face of the earth, his bass still resting on the bandstand, his music unplayed. Where did Wilbur go?

Where would Bliss go, he wondered, if he just walked away? Work for his father-in-law? Oversee Anton's corporate security, supervising a bunch of dissolute ex-cops in flashy suits, running background checks, making sure everyone who worked for his father-in-law's firm was who they said they were?

But that wasn't the answer.

It was something else, some other solution. Washing dishes in some remote diner. Bagging groceries. Pumping gas, like Burt Lancaster in *The Killers*. Until one day his past showed up to reclaim him, which it most certainly would, if Dom DeMoro really had the surveillance tape. His past would be there so quickly it wouldn't even have a chance to get out of the present.

He listened to Monk's quirky chords and skewed phrasing, which perfectly complimented Coltrane's virtuoso inward searching. He listened hard, trying to forget about his own predicament, about Ben's murder and Felix floating up; about how he had hurt Andrej today, about how he seemed prepared to shoot Andrej if the old woman came any closer with her pot of soup; about Billy Dix Sr. and the pain he was feeling because of his son.

Bliss did not feel very centered, did not feel much in harmony. He tried to breathe into the stretch, but he was being pulled in too many directions. He was thinking that the three yoga sessions would not be nearly enough. That the Downward Facing Dog was facing down on him, baring its teeth and growling.

He stood up and shook his head. He turned off the music. In a few minutes he would say good night to Julia, would go into Cori's room and kiss her cheek while she slept, tuck her in, knowing that love was maybe all that was holding him together.

Then he would go into his bedroom and close the door and make love with his wife and try to lose himself. Lose himself completely.

He would have to tell Rachel about that, the "losing himself completely" thing. So Mae could do it, too. Otherwise Mae might not make it to the sequel.

Dom's phone rang. Not his cell, but his regular phone. He hadn't given anyone that number for months. Maybe it was his mother. He picked it up.

"Dum?"

He knew who it was.

"Policeman put gun to my head."

"Okay," Dom said. He hung up. He knew the rest of the story. He called his friend in the precinct. The friend said he'd find out what he could.

Dom got out his weights and worked his arms and abs. Then he stretched and went for a run. He took the first three miles at a quick pace, slowed for the last three.

His cell rang around the fifth mile. He stopped and answered it. It was his friend from the precinct saying Detective Garcia was still working the Felix case, but that Bliss was helping out, stirring things up.

Dom thanked his friend and hung up. He resumed running. He needed a plan. He had to work out a plan. This fight was becoming someone else's story.

Dom stopped at a phone booth and called Rick.

"Who's this?"

"Someone who wants to help you, Rick."

"Why should I talk to you?"

"So you can tell me about the Wonder Bread," Dom said. "The pipe taped to the block of wood I figured out. And the piece you bought from the transvestite, that you carried stuck in your pants under your jacket, I worked that out, too. But the loaves of Wonder Bread, now that, my friend, has me stumped."

"What do you want?"

"I want to tell you you've got the wrong guy, Rick. Owen didn't kill your son. Forget Owen. Forget Fred."

"Then who?"

"It was the cop," Dom said.

"A cop?"

"He went to the party that night and crushed Ben's skull. Crushed the skull of your son."

"How do you know this?"

"I've got it on tape," Dom said. "I'll show it to you. Clear as day. It was the cop. You can see for yourself."

"I want to do that."

"Of course you do," Dom said. "You can't let this go un- punished. And it will be up to you, Rick. Believe me. No way they'll let a cop go down for this."

"What's his name?" Rick asked. "I want to be able to say his name."

"All in due time," Dom said.

"I need to see the tape."

"Tomorrow."

"The funeral's tomorrow."

"Then right after the funeral." The plan was taking shape. It was a weird plan, but it was *his*. *That* was the important part. Dom was back to fighting his fight.

The recorded voice on the pay phone alerted him that his time was almost up.

"Tomorrow, Rick," Dom said. "At the funeral. I'll find you. We'll set up a time. It will all happen tomorrow. And by the way, if you have any questions about how to use your new gun, like how to load it, where to aim to make sure when you shoot it someone gets killed, I'll be happy to answer them."

He hung up the phone. He wondered if Fred Gelman would be at the funeral. He needed to ask him about the apartment in Manhattan right away. Because the way Dom had things planned out, it was all going to happen in the next round.

WEDNESDAY

The morning news was still playing the tape of the Mister getting beaten up in front of the house, scurrying across the road on his back like a crab, kicking like a little baby, ripping his suit (which he threw away but which Clara rescued from the garbage, thinking she could easily mend the few tears and give it to her grandfather). Clara tried not to smile as she watched the Mister get beaten up.

She put on her coat and headed out the door to the health food store. The Missus had vitamins and exotic-sounding herbal supplements that needed to be picked up. She took them three times a day, the Missus holding the pills with reverence, closing her eyes before she swallowed them, as if she was praying. They were supposed to put her body in a state of balance. The Missus explained it once to Clara. The stress of daily life put her *out* of balance, and the vitamins and herbs helped put her back *in* balance. Clara wanted to say that maybe if the Missus cooked a meal or washed even a single dish or made her own bed in the morning, then just maybe she might not *feel* so out of balance.

Just before she got to Lexington Avenue she heard footsteps, moving quickly, clearly getting closer. She stopped and turned.

It was a tall young man, neatly dressed. His white, polished teeth glistened unnaturally as he smiled, as if lit from a tiny row

of lights discretely hidden behind his lips. Children used to approach her this way before class when they'd forgotten their
homework.

"You're . . ." His hand made little revolutions as he tried
to remember what he wanted to say. He scowled and quickly
checked his notebook. "You're Clara," he said.

"Yes," she said.

"I'm Roger. I'm a journalist." He unfurled his teeth again
for her.

He named a magazine Clara had never heard of.

"What do you want?" Clara asked.

"You work for the Gelmans, Clara, am I right?"

"Yes."

"I was wondering if you wanted to tell your story."

"Why would anyone want to hear my story?" she asked
innocently.

"Oh you'd be surprised," he said in an unctuous singsong
voice, like she was a child, like he was going to tell her a fairy
tale and tuck her into bed. "And believe it or not, Clara, my
magazine would actually be willing to give you a little something
for your perspective."

"Thirty thousand," Clara said, her voice all business. And
suddenly Roger was all business, too, the boyish innocence
clearly just an act.

"But only for an exclusive," he said.

"I want half in front," Clara said.

"You mean *up* front.'"

"Yes. Before I tell you what I know."

"I don't want the same pallid shit everyone already knows.
I need buzz. Can you do that, Clara? Can you service me? Can
you give me buzz?"

* * *

Rick put on his suit for the funeral as soon as he woke up. He put his gun in his side jacket pocket, but he could easily see its silhouette through the material. He switched it to the inside breast pocket, but then there was a large bulge by his shoulder exactly where a gun would be. So he wedged it in his pants in the small of his back like he did when he first got it and tightened his belt. The metal was cold against his skin. He wanted it with him, all day, all the time, right through the funeral—the gun, his pacifier.

He had purpose now. He could go to the funeral knowing he had a future, that he was not buried in the coffin along with his son.

It was rage when he went after Owen's father. Now he was fueled with a kind of clarity. Rick felt light, moving easily, like a machine, like something riding on rails. It was an amazing feeling. Some people live this way all the time, he thought. With this kind of ease, moving smoothly from point to point on glistening rails laid out before them, directing them, moving them forward (people who rode on rails carried luggage!). And now Rick was getting a taste of it. Finally.

Maybe this was the future Rick, the *real* Rick.

He was going to see the video of the person—the cop—who killed his son. The man on the phone said so. Promised him. The man on the phone knew everything.

He buttoned his jacket, shifted his shoulders so his jacket hung properly. He turned to the side. The gun didn't show.

He faced the mirror again. He felt good. He felt like he could sell a dozen sets of luggage.

Right after he was married, his father-in-law put him to work in one of the stores, so Rick could get a sense of the retail operation, to get a feel for the leather, a grasp of the clasps, a hold on the handles. Luggage humor.

Hah hah.

"I'm going to start you on the floor," his father-in-law said, "but don't worry. That's just the beginning."

His father-in-law told him to always refer to the merchandise as "luggage." Never "a suitcase." Never "a bag."

"'Suitcase' is singular. One. A suitcase. The word 'luggage' is plural. It suggests a family. A larger need. A way of life. If you need a suitcase, you can buy one and be done with it. But a need for luggage can never be satisfied. There is always more to get."

Suitcase. Luggage. It didn't matter. Rick was a pitiful salesman. Despondent. He pasted a smile on his face, but even that didn't last more than a few days. It didn't take long for word to reach his father-in-law. After the first week Rick was called into the office.

"You have to believe in the merchandise," his father-in-law told him, getting out from behind his desk, putting a hand on his son-in-law's shoulder. "You don't have children yet, but when you do you'll think of them, each of them, as the most wonderful child ever placed on earth. You won't see their flaws. (Hah!) It's the same with luggage. Each matching set is like one of your children. Your progeny. You need to brag about them, Rick. You need to make the customer swell with an intense feeling of joy that they are buying this luggage, joy that flows from you."

But when Rick returned to the store he was just as miserable. He could offer the customers no advice.

Are these good? the customers asked. *Durable? Will this fit in the overhead rack? Do I need all six pieces?*

It's *luggage*, he said. (What else *could* he say?) You should be happy you have some place to go.

Then he'd furtively pick at his nails and his eyes would wander to some far away place and the customers would slowly edge their way out the door.

That's when he was moved to the front office, so he wouldn't spread his misery and weakness around the store anymore.

But now Rick had his son's strength, could feel his son's resolve keeping him focused.

And he had the gun.

He could be an ace salesman now. He could take on the world.

You don't need a suitcase. You need *luggage*. And I know the *perfect* set for you. Exactly what you need. I love this luggage. I love this luggage like I love my son. But I want *you* to have it. A perfect stranger. So take it. No need to pay.

Just take the luggage and get out of the store. Pack it up. Go to the airport. Get on your plane.

Just leave the store.

NOW!

I've got to close up.

There's something I need to do.

Something I absolutely *have* to do.

Then, together with his wife, Rick took the elevator down to the lobby and got into the waiting black limo to drive to the cemetery so he could watch the funeral of his son.

They were waiting for Bliss on the bench in the front lobby of the precinct. The three of them—Billy Dix Sr. and Jr. and one Marcello "T-Bone" Fuchs.

Dix Sr. stood up.

"The boys have something they need to tell you," he said. "There a place we can go?"

Bliss found an empty interview room. Ward was at the funeral, watching what transpired, if anyone unexpected showed up. Someone connected with the murder. It sometimes happened at funerals. It was unlikely to happen today.

They went in, taking seats around the table. The two men and the two boys, like they were getting ready for some kind of family dinner.

Billy Jr. resembled his father. If he stayed out of jail, he'd probably become a cop. He already had the look.

His friend T-Bone was a big kid with formidable arms. Yet his skin was curiously smooth, almost babyish, skin that belonged on the face of a Sicilian schoolgirl. His lips were disarmingly red. T-Bone reminded Bliss of Sal Mineo, only taller.

Both boys looked sheepishly at the table. Billy Dix Sr. must have had them alone for a few minutes. But that was no guarantee they would now be telling the truth.

"We came to see you in school the other day, Billy," Bliss said. "But you skipped out."

Billy Jr. nodded.

"We had to go on a field trip."

"Billy!" his father said.

"Sorry," Billy Jr. said.

"So why'd you leave when my partner and I showed up?"

"We just panicked," Billy Jr. said.

"What were you afraid of?"

Billy didn't say anything. He stared at the table, scratched his cheek, stared at the table some more. Bliss tried the friend.

"T-Bone?"

T-Bone didn't have much to say, either. He rubbed his arm. As he did, the sleeve of his T-shirt lifted and Bliss could see part of a tattoo. A pointed tail. Maybe part of a dragon. A devil. T-Bone unconsciously flexed his biceps, or maybe the muscle did it by itself, a mind of its own—perhaps the only mind T-Bone had.

They continued to sit. No one speaking. Just breathing. Then Billy Sr. stood up, lifted his chair, and slammed it into the floor. He did it again. Then one more time until the wood splintered and the legs separated from the seat.

This seemed to encourage Billy Jr. to reach into his pocket. When he pulled out his hand, a necklace was dangling between his fingers. He placed it on the table along with some earrings. A gold ring also dropped out. It rolled on the table in ever-decreasing circles until it fluttered and finally came to rest. The jewelry glittered, even in the dull light of the interview room.

"Is that everything?" Bliss said.

Billy Sr., grim-faced, standing because his chair was now kindling, reached behind him. Bliss feared Billy Sr. was about to get out his piece and blow his kid's head off. Instead he took out his wallet. He pulled out a handful of bills and flipped them on the table. About a dozen twenties.

"He also found three hundred bucks," Billy Sr. said, "which he spent. He and T-Bone. His friend. His best fucking friend."

T-Bone didn't like that remark.

"Hey," T-Bone said, but that's all he was able to get out before Billy Sr. shut him up with a hard slap to the back of T-Bone's head.

"Shut the fuck up, Marcello," Billy Sr. said.

T-Bone did as he was told.

Bliss gathered the jewelry and cash together. The Gelmans hadn't mentioned anything about stolen jewelry. He and Ward would try to find a way to make the theft go away—say they busted a fence and the jewels just turned up. He wouldn't say anything about the cash, somehow finding a way to get it back in Billy Sr.'s wallet.

"Let me see what we can do," Bliss said.

"No!" Billy Sr. said. "I want them to go down for this. Both of them."

Billy Jr. turned ashen.

"Dad," he said, plaintively, sounding suddenly like a little kid.

"I want them booked. They'll make a statement. Both of them. Get some paper. Get them each a pen!"

Billy Sr.'s voice started to crack. Tears were forming in his eyes, his face wrenched with pain.

"Dad," Billy Jr. said.

"It's too late for that," Billy Sr. said.

T-Bone's eyes were darting wildly in his head. He was just beginning to understand what was happening.

"But Mr. Dix . . ."

T-Bone covered his head as Billy Sr. drew back his fist. But the blow never came.

"Dix!" Bliss shouted.

Billy Sr. turned away, walked to the wall, stood there clenching and unclenching his fists.

"We can't book them now," Bliss said. "There's been no report of a theft. The Gelmans have to identify it."

"They say they did it," Billy Sr. said.

"We need to wait," Bliss said. "A day or two."

Give Billy Sr. a chance to think this through. Meanwhile, they still had the issue of Ben's getting dead. Just because these two robbed the place, didn't mean they hadn't killed Ben, too.

Bliss cleared his throat.

"T-Bone."

"Yeah?"

"Your prints were on a dumbbell in Owen's house."

"I see some weights, I have to pick them up," T-Bone said.

"Did you leave it where you found it?"

"Yeah."

"Where?"

"In the bedroom."

"Whose?"

"I don't know," he said.

"Owen's?"

"I don't *know*," T-Bone said. "It had Batman on the bedspread. That's all I remember."

Holden's room, Bliss thought. Which meant he hadn't left it under Owen's bed, where Bliss found it. He seemed to be telling the truth. Which meant another dead end.

Rubber Soul, as Ward liked to say. "Nowhere Man."

There was more silence.

"What should we do now?" Billy Dix Jr. asked.

"You should go," Bliss said. "Just stay somewhere where we can find you."

"You won't have to worry about that," Billy Dix Sr. said.

They all stood up.

"Wait," T-Bone said, "I got something else." T-Bone reached in his pocket and pulled out an inch-thick stack of baseball cards held together with a rubber band.

"I took these, too," T-Bone said. "There was a Mark McGwire card on top. I like him. Big Mac."

Bliss had the feeling that Maurice of Flowers by Maurice would be reconsidering his decision about not sending young Marcello off to boarding school. That he and Mrs. Fuchs would probably be in the car tomorrow, driving to Connecticut to look them over, checkbook in hand, T-Bone's suitcases already packed and in the trunk.

Rick stared at the coffin containing his son and thought how this funeral was not just for Ben, but for himself, too. He was burying part of himself in there. He held his wife's hand. It felt limp and cold—dead—another door closed to him forever. But Rick wasn't upset. He thought of Jasmine.

I took care of you, didn't I, Jasmine? I didn't hesitate.

I did what I had to do.

He had made love with Ellen last night in a way he never had before. Recklessly. Practically forcing himself on her, grabbing her mouth between his fingers, forcing her to kiss him, her husband, the man he knew she blamed for the death of her son. Then he took her from behind, not stopping until he'd had his fill, not stopping even when he heard her start to cry.

He wanted to tell Jasmine about it. He imagined Jasmine's coy smile, impressed. Harriet's knowing look, that Rick had finally discovered something they'd probably learned long ago.

Rick looked around at the people at the funeral, gathered solemnly around the grave. His in-laws, his relatives, friends he'd known for years, whom he'd gone to high school with. Teary-eyed. Sniffling quietly as the minister spoke. But they had no meaning for Rick. No history. Like the girl in college, like his son Ben, he had turned away, left them behind. They were not part of his life anymore.

The only one who mattered was the voice on the phone, the one who spoke to him last night. The voice of the man who understood what he had to do.

The coffin was slowly lowered into the grave. Ellen was crying freely now. His mother-in-law held her. But Rick was thinking he would not miss the part of himself that was in the coffin, being buried along with Ben.

Then it struck him that the coffin was like a big piece of luggage, and that *that* part of his life was being buried, too.

It was all fitting into place.

He felt strong.

He put his finger to his mouth, bit off a nub of flesh at the corner of his thumb.

He felt joyous, but made sure he wasn't smiling.

That certainly wouldn't look right at a funeral.

Bliss sat alone in the interview room with a strong premonition that T-Bone had done his share of bad things, but killing Ben Purdy wasn't one of them. He and Billy Dix found some money and jewelry, which would cancel Ben's debt, at least partially. Certainly enough to allay the feeling that they needed to kill him. Besides, T-Bone was too dumb to be a good liar. Bliss meant that, of course, had anyone asked him, in the nicest possible way.

So once again there were only two likely suspects—Owen and, if the surveillance tape ever played in local theaters, himself.

Garcia came in.

"How's it going with Felix?" Bliss asked.

Garcia had done her hair differently, put some blond streaks in it. It didn't help to lighten her demeanor, however.

"I went to the nursing home, showed Dom's picture to one of the old men who used to live in Felix's building," Garcia said. "The poor guy's in diapers. He couldn't ID Felix. If I showed the guy a picture of himself, he probably couldn't ID that, either. Who told Felix to come up from the deep, anyway? It's much better in the water. Didn't he see *Little Fucking Mermaid?*"

"I like the highlights in your hair, Garcia," Bliss said. "Like brush strokes."

Garcia didn't exactly smile, but she made it clear that she wasn't *not* smiling.

"The Polish super," she said, "you remember him?"

Bliss nodded.

"He's got a cousin. Also a Polish super. He recognized Dom right away. 'Dum,' he said. Just like his cousin. Then he thought maybe it wasn't such a good idea, his remembering Dom right away like that. Then he got all hinky and said he didn't recognize Dom at all. That it wasn't Dom. 'Nut Dum.' Then he forgot he knew how to speak English."

"Funny how that happens," Bliss said.

"But I like Dom for Felix," Garcia said.

"Dom's a likable guy."

"Though I don't see why he needed to *kill* Felix to get him to move out of the building. Now that I've gotten to know Felix, I'm thinking for fifty bucks you could get him to do just about anything. *Malhombre.*"

"Andrej and his cousin aren't going to be much help anyway," Bliss said. "We've got no leverage. Nothing we can trade.

We need Dom to make a statement. *I killed Felix.* Show us the knots he used to tie him to the cement block."

Garcia didn't say anything. She sensed Bliss was right.

"Fucking Felix," she said, finally.

"My sentiments exactly," Bliss said. He checked his watch. He was expecting another kid to show up. To talk to about the party. He was due there soon.

When he looked up, Bliss saw him, the tall, wiry frame of Malcolm Marcoux, resplendent in a lime green suit, looking like he was auditioning to work behind Gladys Knight as one of the Pips. The pants to the suit were just a tad short, allowing a full view of his boots, which were black with a square toe and a buckle, like the ones the Puritans wore. His hair was parted in a neat, straight line.

"Malcolm Marcoux," Bliss said.

The boy bowed slightly from the waist.

"At your service, Detective."

Dom drove the limo under the shade of a large tree. The cemetery parking guy had wanted him somewhere else, but Dom liked the look of this tree. He liked the shade. He didn't want the front seat to be a hundred degrees later.

He got out, adjusted his shades, then went to open the back door for Owen. That's when he saw Ward strolling toward him through the gravestones—a large, black specter. Ward's stride was relaxed, his arms hanging loose, but Dom sensed this was anything but a casual, chance encounter.

"*Kemosabe*," Dom said.

"Dom," Ward said.

"I have to stay with the kid," Dom said, gesturing to Owen who was focused on his Game Boy. "Because of the father the other day. Exploding like that. The threat of more violence."

"I understand," Ward said, his voice calm and even. "I just have to ask you a couple of questions."

"Go ahead, Dom," Owen said. "I'll wait here." He pulled the car door closed.

Ward must have seen that, Dom thought, the kid giving me directions like that. It didn't look good.

"The surveillance tape from the Gelmans," Ward said. "From the night of the party. It's missing."

"Uh-huh."

"You installed the camera, right, Dom?"

"Yeah. Me and another guy. Gave me technical assistance."

"You know anything about the missing tape?"

"No," Dom said.

"But you knew where to find it."

"Of course."

He's worried about his partner, Dom thought. Which means he knows about Bliss being in the house that night. (Twenty-two minutes. What did you do, Detective Bliss?) Ward is covering up. He's complicit, breaking the law for his partner. Which means he's vulnerable. They're *both* vulnerable.

The only reason Bliss isn't a suspect is because the tape hasn't surfaced. And I have the tape.

Every fight tells a story.

"Sorry," he said. "I wish I could help you."

"You'll alert us, should something come up," Ward said. "You're aware we got this Felix thing working, too."

"Felix?"

"You know. 'Felix Floats.'"

Dom shook his head.

"Doesn't mean anything to me," he said.

"You never know what you might suddenly remember," Ward said.

Dom knew Ward wanted to hit him, wanted to land a haymaker to Dom's jaw and end it right now. But the bell had rung.

Sorry, Ward. Can't throw any punches after the bell. All you can do is go back to your corner and wait.

Dom smiled.

"By the way," Dom said, "there's this writer says she knows your partner. Her name is Mae. Tall. Black hair. Any chance you happen to know her number?"

Chantal sat in her room. Her dad was at work. Her mom was at some appointment. Avis was shopping. She didn't mind being alone. She was happy not to have to talk about recent events. Her mother wanted to talk about it every second now. Like she suddenly realized Chantal was alive.

It occurred to her the funeral was about to start. Ben's funeral. She couldn't say she was glad he was dead. That didn't feel right. But she was really glad she would never have to see him again.

She picked up Crime and Punishment, the book they were reading in English. Raskolnikov had just hit the lady over the head with the axe, crushing her skull. Her teacher wanted them to think about why he did it, what drove him to do the deed. Was it that Raskolnikov wanted to play God? Did he just want to see what it was like to take a life? How much guilt did he feel? How much remorse?

She wasn't sure about the answer, but she knew she'd better come up with something. Mr. Glassman had an annoying way of making you think, even if you didn't want to.

Then the phone rang. Not the real phone, but the one from the lobby. The doorman said Holden was on his way up to see her. He had a heavy Hispanic accent, so she made him repeat the name.

There was no mistaking it the second time.

"Holden," the doorman said. "He say you ess-pecting him."

She went to school with Holden for a few years before he left for Hollywood. He was nice enough, didn't tease her like some of the boys. But why was he coming to see her? What was *that* about?

He arrived with flowers, a bouquet too large for him to carry, so he had the guy from the florist with him.

"Your room still down the hall?" he said, already moving that way, the guy from the florist trailing dutifully behind him.

Holden carried a wicker basket.

"I thought we'd have a picnic," he said. "I hope you don't mind."

She remembered Holden had come over for a play date one time. They had played Lego together. This didn't seem to be about Lego.

He directed the flower guy to set the bouquet on her window sill. Just told him to do it. Didn't say please or anything. Holden put down the picnic basket, took a thick wad of bills out of his pocket, and handed the delivery guy ten dollars.

"For your troubles, my good man," Holden said, acting suave. Chantal had the eerie feeling it was a line he had once said on his show, that maybe *everything* Holden said was lines from his show. The delivery guy nodded effusively.

"*Muchas gracias,*" he said.

"*Adios,*" Holden said, patting the guy on the back. "*Amigo mio.*"

Holden opened the basket and took out a blanket. It was brand new, still with the tag on it. The plates had stickers on them, too. The silverware was wrapped in a box.

"I figured you needed some cheering up," he said, "so I came by. Your knight in shining armor. Let down your golden tresses." He put on his endearing smile and paused, maybe for the canned laughter. "I'm here to rescue you."

"Did you say that in a show?" she asked.

"Yeah," he said, "but that doeasn't mean I don't mean it now."

The food arrived a few minutes later. Delivered from a nearby gourmet shop. Platters of smoked salmon, pastries, exotic cheeses with thick, crusty rinds, breads of every shape and size.

"They kept giving me stuff," Holden said. "The chef posed for a picture with me. To put on the wall."

He arranged everything on the rug.

"You know what this is?" he asked, showing her a tin with a pretty decoration on top.

"Caviar?"

"Beluga. The best."

He twisted open the top to reveal the glistening black eggs. She was immediately hit by the smell, like the ocean. Fishy, but fresh and clean.

"Some people get all fancy with chopped egg and sour cream, but I like it straight."

He slipped a spoon into the glistening blackness of the caviar and handed it to her. Then he filled up a spoon for himself.

"I just eat it?" she asked.

"You never had caviar?" His mouth dropped open in mock disbelief. "That's all we eat in Hollywood."

"That's not true," Chantal said.

"It's Hollywood true," Holden replied, slipping the spoon between his lips.

Chantal was still holding hers. She brushed her tongue against it. It tasted salty.

"Go ahead," he said.

"What does 'Hollywood true' mean?"

"That if enough people believe something, it becomes true. Like Tinkerbell."

She smiled and put the caviar in her mouth. She liked the texture, the way the eggs felt against her tongue. She wasn't sure it was worth the two hundred dollars Holden said the container cost, but it was definitely different.

"You're incredibly beautiful," he said.

"Thank you."

"No. I mean it. In Hollywood there are tons of girls who are supposed to be beautiful and when you look at them, I mean, they have a lot going for them, they're in shape and everything, but it's like they made a deal with someone to get it—their look. But you're just beautiful. Just, like, on your own."

She didn't say anything. She wondered what this was about, why the attention, the lavish gifts. Had he heard something about her, from his brother? Heard she was easy? That for caviar and flowers he could get something in return?

Dostoyevsky knew the answer. She felt sure of it. Somewhere in *Crime and Punishment* was the answer to why people acted this way, what drove them to try to see what they could get away with, what they could take, how much pain they could heap on others, how much punishment they could carry around with them before they broke.

"Hey Chantal, you got any music?" Holden asked. "A little samba? Some bossa nova?" He kicked off his loafers and leaned back, making himself at home. "'Girl from Ipanema,' maybe?"

Dostoyevsky understood, the scary darkness that lurked beneath the surface. The hidden meanings. She was sure of it. She just had to read the book enough times and it would become clear to her, too.

Dom liked a good funeral. He stood between Owen and Douglas, feeling big in his shades and black suit, hands clasped below his belt, watching, studying the crowd, the different ways people dealt with death. A funeral was the flip side of a fight, where, from the ring, he could see the frenzied excitement on the faces in the crowd, desperate for blood and pain. But when an old fighter dies, in his memory, before a fight, they ring the bell. Ten times. They count him out. Down for the big count. And the crowd is quiet, saddened by the loss, but also thinking about their own mortality. It was surprisingly easy to get laid after a funeral. He wished Mae were here.

But Dom was thinking about his own mortality, too. Fucking Felix. Ward had been there to let Dom know they were getting closer to him, that Felix's waterlogged finger was pointing right at him. It was almost like Ward was offering some kind of deal— the tape for Felix.

But Dom had something in mind.

Dom had Rick.

He looked across the grave and saw him, expressionless, eyes unblinking, looking down. No tears. He had a finger in his mouth and was nibbling at a nail. Guy should have had a snack before he came over. Dom tried to see if Rick was packing, but he was turned the wrong way.

"You keeping an eye on him?" Douglas whispered.

"I got him," Dom said.

Dom was also supposed to watch Rick, in case he had another outburst. Some plainclothes cops were also in the crowd, probably for the same reason. But Douglas didn't need to worry. Dom knew what was going on in Rick's head.

Dom hoped the funeral didn't last too long. He had a lot to do.

He felt his phone vibrating in his jacket pocket as the minister finished up his speech over the grave. He'd check the message later. Then Owen started to walk away.

"Where are you going?" Douglas whispered.

"I was just going to . . . I wanted to . . ." He gestured toward the Gelmans.

"Stay here," Douglas said.

"Can't I . . . ?"

Douglas gave Dom a look.

"No," Dom whispered, discreetly putting his hand against Owen's chest.

"Then I'm leaving," Owen said.

He turned and, before Dom could grab him, started walking fast away from the funeral.

They caught up to him about fifty yards away.

"You can't leave," Douglas said. "It doesn't look good. Your best friend is dead. You should be at the funeral. You should mourn."

Owen looked at him, must have seen something in Douglas that amused him, and started laughing.

"You're a monkey on a string, Douglas."

"I know what's best," Douglas said.

"Fuck you, Douglas," Owen said, "Fuck my father and fuck you. I'm going to see my girlfriend. And if Dom won't take me, I'll get a cab."

"When I found Chantal, her pants were on," Malcolm said, "but they were unzipped. Also, her shirt was off."

"She wasn't wearing a shirt?" Bliss asked incredulously.

"No."

Bliss played with this idea in his head, caught Malcolm looking at him, seeming to know what he was thinking.

"Is that common at parties," Bliss asked, "girls in various states of undress?"

"Oh, you know," Malcolm said. "A little more than *Beach Blanket Bingo*, a little less than *Eyes Wide Shut*."

Bliss laughed, telling himself he was making the witness feel at ease, but really thinking the kid was funny.

"So Chantal was just wandering around the party without a shirt?" Bliss asked.

"She wasn't *wandering*," Malcolm said, disdain creeping into voice. "Chantal wouldn't *wander* around the party without her shirt. She was upstairs. In the hallway. She looked lost."

"Drunk?"

"Maybe," he said. "But not gaily. Not devil-may-care. More solemn. Anyway, the party was already over."

"It was over, but you were still there?"

"I lost track of the time," he said. "I was in the library. The Gelmans have an amazing collection of books. I'm not sure the Gelmans have read any of them, but I like to. It's one of the reasons I go to Owen's parties. They have several *Books of Hours*—not the originals, of course, though they could probably afford them, but very fine reproductions. Also, they have all the books by Lynd Ward."

"Who's he?" Bliss asked.

"He made these novels in woodcuts. All pictures, no words. They tell a story."

"Like a comic book?"

"More subtle than that. The drawings are dark and haunting. The stories are about the theme of the individual versus the cruel capitalist society. Lots about right and wrong. Vengeance. Selling your soul."

"How did you get Chantal's shirt on?" Bliss asked.

"One arm at a time," Malcolm said.

Bliss smiled again.

"And then you walked Chantal home?" he asked.

"We went to my dad's house. I thought it might be better if Chantal didn't wake up at home. Her parents were in the Hamptons. I didn't think she should be alone. I carried her, at least as far as the taxi. The stairs were the hard part. Or, actually, getting her out the front door was hardest."

He'd rescued her, what Bliss was planning to do if he found Julia.

"Did she say anything?"

"Once she was in my arms she fell back asleep," he said. "That happens to me a lot. Women either want to dance with me or fall asleep on my shoulder." He sighed. "Ah, the lonely life of a *boulevardier*."

"So she never said anything, about what might have happened?"

"Only when I was tucking her into bed later. She looked up at me with her Catherine Deneuve eyes and said very softly 'my hero.'"

"Where was her shirt?" Bliss asked. "She wasn't carrying it with her, was she?"

"No."

"So where was it?" Bliss was trying to make this casual, waiting to see how Malcolm answered, how much credence there was to this story.

"On the floor in the bedroom," Malcolm said after a moment's reflection. Was he remembering or making it up? "She must have taken it off there."

"Did you notice Ben in the bed?"

"He was sleeping. Wait. Did you say *Ben?*"

"She had intercourse with Ben Purdy that night," Bliss said. "Presumably before he was murdered."

"It wasn't Owen?"

"No."

Malcolm considered this for a moment.

"Not Owen," he said.

Bliss watched him. What did he really know? In the future, they'd probably have some kind of electronic device that would access a person's memory, project it on a screen. Then none of this questioning would be necessary. There would be no lying. No one would be able to lie ever again. But for now, Bliss could know only what Malcolm told him, could only wonder what it was Malcolm was leaving out.

"Well," he said, "who*ever* it was that was asleep under the Batman bedspread, I didn't want to wake them. I just tiptoed in and tiptoed out."

Malcolm smiled, leaned back in his chair, and crossed his legs.

"Did you notice anything out of the ordinary at all?"

"Beside the fact that Chantal was wandering around with her pants unzipped and her shirt off?" Malcolm said.

"Yes."

"Well, actually, I did notice there was a fair amount of blood on her hand."

"Blood."

"Yes."

"On her hand?"

"Yes."

"Anywhere else?"

"No."

"Chantal didn't mention that."

"I washed it off the next morning," Malcolm said. "After she got up to vomit. So she might not remember."

"Was there any kind of cut there?"

"No."

"Weren't you curious where the blood came from?"

"I guess," Malcolm said, "but I figured blood can come from all kinds of places, many of which I am not as yet intimate with, detective. And perhaps never will be."

Bliss had to assume the blood came from Ben, that Ben was already dead when Malcolm found Chantal. It also could be a good alibi if they found any of Ben's blood on Malcolm.

"Anything else, Detective?" Malcolm asked, his voice gentle and demure. "I'd like to be as helpful as possible."

Was this eagerness on purpose? Was this Malcolm's way of suggesting that there was no way someone so delicate, someone attuned to the finer things in life, who knew more about the books in the Gelmans' library than the Gelmans did, no way could this person brutally smash in Ben Purdy's head, first with a baseball trophy, then with a ten-pound dumbbell?

Clara took the check Adelaide gave her, the second half of her money, and put it in her pocket. Later she would add to it the check Roger would give her.

She waited until Adelaide had the recorder on, then told more stories, of overheard conversations, of things found in drawers, of women who came by in the late morning, while Owen was at school and the Missus was at the club and only Mr. Gelman was at home. She showed the photographs she snagged from the bottom of the photo box—Holden in his Little League baseball uniform, Holden as an Indian in the school Thanksgiving pageant, Holden dressed as a cowboy for Halloween. There was also a picture of Owen. He was dressed as a vampire, which struck Clara as somehow more than appropriate.

She had more photos that she was saving for Roger.

Clara described in detail what she found the morning after the party, the mess, the stains, the design made out of olives on the coffee table, but as she spoke, her mind drifted to the house, the one she would buy, her own house, how she and her children and her grandfather would all have breakfast together before they went to school and she went to teach and her grandfather went to the couch where he could rest, if he wanted to, for as long as he liked.

The detective seemed stumped for a moment, temporarily without questions.

"I'm afraid I've kept you from the funeral," the detective said.

"I supposed I could have said something if I wanted to go," Malcolm replied.

"How did you feel when you heard Ben had died?"

Malcolm sensed the detective was trying to catch him off guard. But Malcolm was always on guard. If he ever dared let anything show, the ridicule, the humiliation would have been unbearable. He heard something, it seemed, almost every day, walking past a group of boys, clustered together like conspirators. A whispered insult and then the low chuckling that followed, that held them together, the *real* reason they went to a fancy, private school—*not* to discover allusions in *The Odyssey* or how Western expansion has shaped the American character. No, they went to find fellow chucklers. And together they would chuckle themselves right down to Wall Street or some law firm, clustered together and chuckling for the rest of their lives, chuckling about the new secretary, about Knicks tickets they procured, Cuban cigars, a deal, another deal, or the faggot in the office. It wouldn't change. Yahoos. Jockhoos. Chuckle chuckle. It would never change.

The detective would have to work a lot harder to catch Malcolm. He was considerably more practiced in keeping things hidden than they could ever possibly imagine.

"I had mixed emotions when I heard Ben had died," he said. It was better not to try to hide his feelings.

"Did you know him well?"

"It's a small school."

"Did you like him?"

"Not my type," Malcolm said

"I meant as a person."

"No."

"Not really."

"So when he died, you weren't really that upset."

"Well, I was shocked that someone was killed at a party that I was at. *That's* a little bit disconcerting." Malcolm took a sip of the water. "What does your daughter think about it all?"

"Much the same as you, I imagine."

"You haven't talked to her?"

"Of course I have," Bliss said, an edge to his voice. They were dancing, he and the detective. Doin' da Bump. Malcolm guessed Bliss was not a very good dancer. But he sensed it would be better not to step on the detective's toes.

They sat quietly for a moment.

"You think it might happen again?" the detective asked.

"No," Malcolm said, maybe too quickly. He had to be careful not to protest too much. "I don't think so."

"So you don't think whoever smashed in Ben's head will do it again?" Bliss asked, looking right at him, letting Malcolm know he was on to him, that he would never get away with it.

"I haven't a clue as to how that person thinks," Malcolm said, his composure back. "So I wouldn't even hazard a guess."

"So you believe this was just about someone getting even with Ben," Bliss said. "Something only the two of them knew about."

"That would make sense to me," Malcolm said.

"How much sense?"

"Oh, quite a bit, I would imagine. Otherwise the person wouldn't have done it," Malcolm said. "Maybe the person didn't really want to kill Ben."

"No?"

"Maybe they just wanted to send him a message."

"What kind of message?" Bliss asked.

"I don't know," Malcolm said, "something maybe having to do with Ben being a contemptuous person."

"You think anyone hated Ben enough to want to kill him?" Bliss asked.

He didn't answer right away.

"Malcolm."

"Yes?"

"What do you think?"

"If what you say is true, then Owen's girlfriend was sleeping with his best friend," Malcolm said.

"Is Owen a violent person?" Bliss asked.

"He's strong," Malcolm said. "He works out, but he's just naturally strong. He's always been like that."

"But do you think he's capable of violence?"

"I suppose anyone is, to a certain degree. Look at Ben's father, fighting with Owen's father like that. It's like what John Huston says at the end of *Chinatown*."

"What's that?"

"It's when Huston basically confesses to Jack Nicholson that he slept with his own daughter. He says something like—*given the right circumstance, Mr. Geddes, a person is capable of just about anything.*"

They sat for a moment, the detective just looking at him. Malcolm wondered if his fate was being decided at that moment. The detective assembling clues, not from what he had said, so much, but how he answered. The slightest pause carrying more weight, more significance than his words. His words, he knew, were meaningless. It was everything else, all the hidden signals, the gestures, the seemingly insignificant movements of his eyes, shifting contours of his face he may not even have been aware of. The detective relying on some deep part of his brain, something maybe in his spinal cord, like the monkeys he'd read about in bio class, that had been bred in captivity, which had never lived in the wild, but they could tell the difference between a garter snake and a puff adder. The garter snake made them laugh, they'd catch hold of it and toy with it; the puff adder would send them cowering terrified into the farthest corner of the cage, screaming to each other about danger, that death was wriggling on the floor just yards away. That knowledge (if you could call it that) coming from deep in their DNA, seeing not just the shape of the snake, but a *specific* snake, the different markings—one signifying safety, one danger.

So what had the detective detected? What markings had Malcolm displayed in their conversation? Harmless garter snake or deadly adder?

Then the detective spoke.

"You can go now, Malcolm," the detective said. He continued to stare at him, watching Malcolm as he stood up, looking maybe for one last signal, one sign that Malcolm was his man. Perhaps someone had scrawled the letter "M" on the back of Malcolm's shoulder, in chalk, where Malcolm wouldn't notice, marking him, for everyone to see.

"I'll call you if I need to talk with you again," the detective said.

"Okay."

Malcolm turned and walked out.

If there was anything written on his back, the detective didn't say anything about it.

Owen walked into Chantal's room and saw his brother Holden sitting on the floor, his back resting against Chantal's bed, his shoes off, looking cozy. Chantal was sitting cross-legged on a chair, leaning forward, her elbows resting on her knees, her chin resting between her hands, listening to him, listening no doubt to Holden's bullshit.

Between his brother and his girlfriend, on a blanket, the remains of a picnic. Caviar, shrimp, sparkling cider in a blue bottle with a French label. Owen had a weird feeling he'd seen Holden doing the same thing on one of his shows. Surprising a girl he liked with a picnic in her room.

But there was something else here, too, Owen thought. Besides the picnic. There was a feeling that the two of them were sharing something. That Holden was letting her in on one of his Hollywood secrets, all twisted around itself. Trying to dazzle her with the names of the famous people in whose pools he'd taken a dip, in whose blenders he had whipped up drinks filled with tropical fruits and health powders.

Chantal had her hair in pigtails, no makeup, just a T-shirt and shorts. She looked like a little kid. It was like Owen was seeing her for the first time.

She *was* just a little kid.

Holden jumped up when Owen walked in. Jumped right to attention. Not the star now. Just a kid brother doing something he wasn't supposed to.

"Hey, man," Holden said, smiling his perfect white smile that his agents gave him after his pilot was picked up.

Owen didn't respond. He was still trying to take it all in. His brother and his girlfriend alone together, his best friend dead, lying in a coffin, about to be put in a hole.

"Caviar," Holden said, holding out the tin. "Can you believe she never had any?"

"Let me see," Owen said.

Holden walked toward him. "Fourteen and never had caviar," he said. "Good thing I came along, don't you think?"

Owen waited until Holden got close, then he slipped his foot behind his famous TV star brother and pushed him back, the way he used to do when they were kids. Holden fell over. The caviar flew out of his hand. But there was no canned gasp from the audience. No stunt man. This was actually happening. Owen wondered if his brother realized that.

Owen jumped on his brother and sat on his stomach, his knees resting on Holden's arms, pinning him to the ground. He'd done this hundreds of times when they were little, after school, when no one was around.

Holden was yelling at him to get off.

"Phone Mom," Owen said. "Go ahead. Maybe she's at the club."

Holden squirmed and wiggled, trying to push Owen off.

"Owen," Chantal said. "C'mon, Owen."

"This isn't about you," Owen said. "This is brother stuff."

He eased up on one knee and quickly grabbed Holden's wrist. He forced Holden to slap himself.

"Why you hitting yourself? Huh, little brother? Huh?"

"Cut it out," Holden said, his voice starting to crack.

"I'll tell you why. You feel guilty. You want to punish yourself for trying to get some play from a girl who, besides being your brother's girlfriend, is too young to be hit on."

"Dad's going to kill you," Holden said.

"No he's not. You're wrong. I'm protected. Dad doesn't know I exist. So he can't kill me."

"Owen, cut it out," Chantal said.

"This is not for you, Chantal," he said. "None of this is for you."

Then he made his fist rockhard and smashed Holden in the nose. He felt it crunch and when he pulled his hand away he could see Holden's nose crushed to the side, flopping a little, like it was on a hinge. The blood was gushing and Holden was screaming like a baby and Chantal was screaming, too. And the blood was starting to fill up Holden's throat and choke him and he was coughing and gurgling, struggling like crazy under Owen's knees, gagging now, his eyes wide, like someone had a pump to the back of his head, savagely pumping more air inside, more air than he could possibly hold.

Then Chantal was pushing Owen, hitting his head and pushing him and then she ran into him with her shoulder and he keeled over. Holden lurched to the side and spit out a huge mouthful of blood, and then another, smothering the caviar, staining the carpet with a large red blotch. He was moaning now, huge great sobs and moans, crying with complete abandon, his arms flopping helplessly at his side as though some string had broken. Chantal ran in with a towel and put it to his face. Then Chantal was on the phone dialing a number Holden called out to her. His agents, probably. His handlers. They would know what to do. Where to take him, what plastic surgeon would need to be ripped from whatever operation he was doing to attend to their child star. The show would have to be shut down for a few weeks.

But then Owen was struck with the terrible realization that they *wouldn't* shut down the show. They would work it into the script. They would put his broken nose into the episode. Make a joke out of it. A big white bandage. Or have him play a clown that week. *Holden, take that red nose off right now! No, Mom, I want to make the world a happier place. I want to make people laugh! Like Patch Adams.* And the publicity would be stupendous and more viewers than ever would tune in to see his little brother wink and smirk and pout his way to greater fame and fortune.

And then he knew his father wasn't going to "kill him" as Holden said. No, the harsh truth was that Douglas would show up one morning very soon with the limo and escort him to boarding school where he'd finish his semester and then go to college and that would be that.

"Hey Holden," Owen said, "I guess I won't be getting a part on your show now, will I?"

Dom called Rick.

"Hello, Rick," Dom said.

He could hear people in the background.

"Now?" Rick asked.

"It's happening," Dom told him.

"I have people here."

"Rick."

"Yes."

"I'm holding the videotape that shows the man who killed your son."

Silence.

"Rick?"

"Let's do it," Rick said.

Way to be, Rick.

Dom told Rick where to meet him.

"And you'll bring the gun, right, Rick?"

"Yes."

"Because now that we've gotten this far, there wouldn't be any point to turning back."

"No."

Rick hung up.

Every fight told a story. Dom thought. And this one was most definitely his. Now, if only Mae would call again, everything would be going his way. He was feeling strong. He was ahead on points. He threw a quick left in the air. Then two more, then a combination. He smiled at his opponent was lying motionless on the canvas.

They were in Dom's car, parked in a cul-de-sac on 84th Street overlooking the East River near Rick's penthouse. Dom was holding a video camera, showing Rick the tape in the little screen that folded out. It was small, but there was no mistaking Bliss when he turned in the direction of the camera.

"That's him, Rick. That's your man."

Rick was silent, a finger jammed into his mouth at an unnatural angle, nibbling at the nail like a squirrel on a stubborn nut.

"He did it," Rick said between bites.

"It's the only thing that makes sense," Dom said, keeping the pressure on, keeping Rick against the ropes. "No one else came in or out all night but kids."

"Anyone else see this?" Rick asked.

"I wanted you to have it all to yourself. We have to worry about the 'thin blue line.' You've heard of it, right?" Rick nodded. "Cops would find a way to cover this up, have the video disappear from the evidence room, a giant magnet somehow erase the tape—it happens all the time. But a child was killed here."

"Look at him," Rick said, watching the tape.

Rick brought a finger to his mouth.

"This demands a different kind of justice, Rick," Dom said. "You know that, right?"

Rick worked on another nail. He'll be down to the stubs soon, Dom thought. The bone. Guy should take up smoking.

"A different kind of justice," Rick said, lost somewhere, eyes far away, in his corner before coming out for the last round, not listening to his trainer, not feeling the cut man ramming the swab of zinc into the gash under his eye, not really knowing he was in a fight. His body doing it all on its own. Just reacting. Exactly where Dom wanted him.

Dom rewound the tape and they watched the door open again and Bliss leave.

Dom heard a sound, grinding, or ice cracking and he realized it was coming from Rick, from his teeth. Jesus.

"Go back to the house," Dom said. "Back to your guests. I'll call you when everything's set."

Rick didn't say anything. He was already somewhere far away.

"You hear me, Rick?"

Rick didn't answer. He just walked away. Back up to the penthouse.

Jesus, Dom thought he'd better get Rick close to Bliss right away.

The guy was ready to pop.

He called Bliss.

"Lenny, howaya?" Dom said. "Listen, reason I'm calling, two things. One: I need to get in touch with that writer. Mae."

"Mae?"

"Yeah. Mae Stark. The one who was asking for you at the Gelman house."

"You know her?" Bliss said, sounding astonished. Dom didn't realize he was so proprietary with his writers.

"Yeah. I was talking to her. About the job."

"You were talking to her?"

"Yeah?"

"In person?"

"On the phone. About the details. The nitty-gritty. Details are the most important part of a book, you know. I guess I'm more authentic than you. So I was thinking, maybe I could get her number. Call her back."

"I don't have it." Bliss said, scolding him now.

He was lying, but Dom didn't say anything. Dom was going to let Rick do the talking for him.

"Okay. Anyway, the second thing is I got a tape here I copped from the surveillance camera at the Gelmans'."

Bliss didn't respond to that.

"You hear me, Lenny?"

"We like you for Felix," Bliss said. "The super gave you up. 'Dum,' he calls you."

"So, looks like we can help each other out here," Dom said.

"What are you thinking, *Dum?*"

"I'm thinking we should meet. Talk things out."

"Sounds like a plan."

Dom gave him a time and a place.

"So are we good?"

Silence.

"Bliss. I'm wondering, are we good?"

"Yeah."

He felt like Bliss was trying to stare him down. Dom wanted to tell him it didn't work over the phone.

"Last round, Lenny. That means we touch gloves before the first punch."

"Come alone, Dom."

"No problem," Dom said. "See you soon. Oh, and Lenny, it's kind of dark and grainy, but I have to say, you look good on tape. You should think about doing some acting when you retire. And who knows, that day could come sooner than you ever possibly imagined."

Bliss immediately called home. No answer. He left a message for Rachel to call him back right away. It was urgent. He couldn't believe she was talking to Dom.

Then he left to meet Dom, to get back the tape, and do whatever else he needed to do to end this thing and get Dom out of his life.

Dom drove over the Brooklyn Bridge. Traffic was dense but flowing smoothly.

Rick, in the white Saab, was two cars ahead of them.

He had Mae on the phone. She had called him.

"Always try to keep at least one car between you and the mark," he said, feeling authentic. "Two cars are better. But you need to watch out for trucks. And cargo vans. You let a cargo van get between you and the mark your vision is blocked. You won't see his blinker. You could get caught by surprise."

At that moment Rick put on his blinker and moved to the right lane. Dom was pleased to see Rick was following instructions.

"Where do you think he's going?" she asked.

"No idea," Dom said. "That's the thing about tailing some-one. You never know where they will take you."

"Good metaphor," she said, "I'm writing that down. An-other authentic Dom moment. I'm definitely going to thank you in the the acknowledgments."

"The guy who gave you the nitty-gritty."

Of course Dom wasn't really tailing Rick. He knew exactly where Rick was headed. But in Dom's story, he was following Rick and he wanted to stick to the scenario.

"When you get really good at tailing someone, you go ahead of them," Dom said. "The way a good boxer knows what punch his opponent is going to throw before he throws it."

Silence. She must have been writing. Dom was starting to think maybe he should just write the book himself.

Rick was now heading under the bridge, down to the water. Everything was going according to plan. Dom had been wor-ried that Rick would be too agitated to follow the directions, but he seemed to be keeping it together. He hoped Rick would be ready to explode when the time came, though Dom could always nudge him along a little if need be.

"I tried to call you," he said. "You're not listed."

"I'll let you know when the book comes out."

"Okay," he said. Mae didn't like that, him trying to call her. He'd have his friend in the precinct find her number for him anyway.

"Hey, if you need an ending, I have one for you," he said.

"An ending?"

That got her attention.

"Yeah."

The Saab pulled over and Rick parked just where Dom had told him to.

"How can you give me an ending," Mae said, "when you don't know what my story is?"

A fence separated the street from a path that ran along the East River. The Brooklyn Bridge arched over the water, looking massive. There were a few people around. Not many, but enough to serve as witnesses, to corroborate.

"Dom?"

"Yes."

"The ending?"

"I don't need to know the story," he said, "This ending is going to be so good, you'll want to write your story around it."

Rick got out of the car. He was holding the gun in his hand. Jesus, Dom needed to get over there. "Listen," he said, "it's all going to happen soon. I'll tell you everything. We'll talk about it over drinks. On my terrace. It looks out over Central Park. I'll give you lots of nitty. More gritty than you'll know what to do with."

He hung up.

Dom tapped his jacket, feeling for the surveillance tape, just making sure it was there. Later it would be found inside Bliss's pocket. Bliss going into the house, coming out twenty-two minutes later.

He got out of the car and walked quickly to Rick.

"Put that away, Rick," he said. "We don't want anyone getting nervous, calling the cops. They'll come and take away the tape and you'll never see it again and he'll walk away."

Rick nodded, his gaze somewhere far away. But he put the gun in his pocket.

Good boy, Rick.

To the right, through a gate in the fence, was a small park Dom used to come to when he was twelve, to smoke dope and make out with girls who would chew gum between kisses.

"It's time, Rick."

"Yes," Rick said.

The bell rang.

Final round.

Rick bit his thumb. Dom noticed the cuticle was already rimmed with blood.

Bliss walked under the Brooklyn Bridge on the Brooklyn side, the span of the bridge arching majestically above him, the financial district just across the water. He had bungee jumped from the bridge a few years ago, a feat that was supposed to have catapulted him into a new frame of mind. But, like the yoga, it had only made him more certain he was beyond fixing, that ontologically he was a washed-up lounge singer playing a bowling alley bar in a tattered tux that was way too tight.

He followed the path along the water and, just as Dom said, he came upon a small park with a few benches and a rusted swing set. He walked over to one of the benches and sat down. It was a cloudy day. There were only a few people in the park.

He waited, thinking about what this encounter would bring. The whole thing was ridiculous. He felt stupid, getting into such a mess. Dragging his partner down as well.

Then he saw Dom, walking toward him. He looked calm. Bliss watched him closely, waiting until he was about twenty yards away.

"Far enough, Dom."

"Okay."

Dom stopped.

"You packing, Dom?" Bliss asked.

"Not now," he said smiling.

"I'd feel better if you took your jacket off," Bliss said.

"It's Canali," Dom said.

"You don't have to put it down," Bliss said. "Sling it over your shoulder. Like the guy on *Miami Vice*."

Dom complied. It was going too easily.

"The boy," Dom said.

"What are you talking about?" Bliss said. He didn't get where this was heading.

Dom slowly reached inside his jacket. Bliss moved for his piece.

"I'm just doing a little Warner Wolf," Dom said.

Bliss knew what that meant. *Let's go to the videotape.* Dom slowly pulled the video from his pocket. He wiggled it, as if to say "shame on you."

"Why'd you do it, Lenny?" Dom said.

"First let's talk about Felix," Bliss said.

"This is not about Felix anymore." Dom gestured with the tape. "*This* is the story now, Lenny. Once they see this tape, they'll forget about Felix."

Bliss kept his hand on his gun.

"Why'd you kill him, Bliss?" Dom asked, his voice sounding forced, like he was reading cue cards. "That poor innocent boy."

"What are you talking about?"

Then Bliss caught sight of a man in a black suit entering the park. He was moving fast, straight toward him. It took Bliss a moment to realize it was Rick Purdy. Rick Purdy, holding a gun, his arm straight out in front of him, moving toward Bliss like a robot.

Bliss saw the smile edge along Dom's face.

He'll break his wrist if he tries to shoot like that, Bliss thought.

"He was seventeen, Lenny," Dom said, his voice rising, spurring the other man on. "You took away his future."

Rick was now about twenty yards away, closing quickly, his eyes wide and unblinking, the gun in his outstretched arm, like the gun was leading him, dragging him forward.

"You killed my son." he said, his voice calm but intense, like an irate librarian.

"I didn't kill your son," Bliss shouted, his eye on the gun.

"I saw you on the tape!" Rick screaming now, gesturing with the gun. "I saw *you!*"

Rick walked past Dom like he wasn't there. Rick was possessed. A zombie. A zombie with a loaded gun pointing right at him. Bliss realized he was going to have to take Rick down.

"I'm going to do it, Ben!" the guy shrieked. "I'm going to do it!"

Bliss pulled out his gun just as Rick fired. The bullet caught Bliss in the leg. He crumpled over, falling off the bench, his back to Rick, facing the wrong way. He tried to twist his body, to get off a shot. He had his gun in his hand and he was trying to twist his body around, but he couldn't figure out which muscles were working and which weren't.

Then he heard the second shot and he prepared to die.

Dom's elation was short-lived. Bliss was hit, still moving, but down. All Rick had to do was shoot again. There were twelve bullets in the clip. He was bound to connect. All he needed was to pull the trigger. Walk up to the helpless Bliss, put the gun to his head, and pull the trigger.

But Rick wasn't moving. Dom watched in silence as Rick lowered his arm that held the gun. *No, Rick.* Then Rick seemed to freeze, as if he was caught in the invisible force field of some invisible space ship hovering right above his head.

"Rick!" Dom shouted. Rick didn't hear him. Instead Rick started shaking like a broken toy. *Just fire the gun, Rick. Pull the fucking trigger and finish the story. Finish the story the way I planned it!*

Then a wild kind of roar emerged from Rick. Dom couldn't tell if it was the sound of victory or defeat.

Then Rick raised up his gun. Finally. Then he pulled the trigger. There was a loud pop, and Dom watched as the back of Rick's head blew apart, because Rick had stuck the barrel of the gun in his mouth.

Shit, Dom thought. Now he would have to finish it himself. Rick. What a loser.

Dom raced to Rick's body. He'd fallen straight back, his head already swimming in a large pool of blood. Dom put his hand over Rick's. It was still warm. He tried to maneuver the gun in Rick's hand to aim it at Bliss, but it meant the elbow having to move the wrong way.

He wrenched the gun free. He'd pop Bliss and get the gun back in Rick's hand. He'd deal with the prints later. That's when he heard Bliss.

"Drop it, Dom."

He looked across the ring. He saw Bliss on one knee.

One. Two. Three.

Just like the Dominican.

Four. Five.

Bliss was pointing his gun directly at Dom.

Six. Seven.

About to get to his feet. Dom had hit him with all he had and he was getting up.

Eight.

This wasn't the story. This wasn't the ending Dom planned. The wrong guy was out cold. The wrong guy was getting up from the mat. He tore the gun from Rick's hand and swung toward Bliss.

Nine.

Then Bliss toppled over. He was back on the mat. Hah! Bliss was struggling to get up. But he wasn't going to beat the count. Not like the Dominican.

Dom smiled. Dom aimed. Then, perhaps, a handful of neurons registered extraordinary pain for a minute part of a second. Then Dom felt nothing.

Bliss limped to Dom's body. Ward was standing over him, looking down at the large man in the fancy suit he had just shot dead.

"What a waste of worsted," Ward said.

Bliss found the videotape in Dom's coat pocket. He starting scrambling toward the water.

Onlookers had assembled at the entrance to the park. Bliss holstered his gun and pulled out his badge. He showed it to the crowd.

"Call 911," he shouted. "I'm a cop. Call 911 and say an officer's been shot."

A guy ran toward a phone booth. Another took out his cell phone. No one approached him. Which was fine. He had stuff he needed to do. In private.

He felt Ward's hand on his arm, helping to prop him up. Bliss pushed him away.

He limped to the edge of the river and sat on one of the benches, taking a moment to catch his breath. There was a gentle lapping of the water against the concrete wall that ran along the edge of the park.

Rick being there. Rick with a gun. Rick shooting at him. It was not making a lot of sense.

But he knew what he needed to do.

The East River flowed swiftly here by the Brooklyn Bridge. He discreetly dropped the tape in the water. No one saw. He *hoped* no one saw him. The tape floated briefly, moving with the current toward the harbor, out to the sea. Then it sank, hopefully forever.

He heard the ambulance in the distance, police sirens approaching. Then Ward was on the bench next to him.

"He shot you," Ward said.

"He thought I killed his son."

"You okay?"

"No," Bliss said. "Cori is going to be very upset with me."

He put his leg up on the bench. The bullet had passed through his calf. It was starting to hurt now.

"I'll have to lie," he said. "Tell her I was climbing a fence. You'll back me up on that?"

"Why were you here?" Ward asked him.

The uniforms were arriving. The ambulance was driving over the curb and heading down the path.

"Partner," Ward said.

"Yes."

"Why were you here?"

"I'm not sure."

"You have to be sure," Ward said.

The pain was beginning to amp up. His leg felt on fire.

"I was following Dom," he said, wincing as he spoke.

"Why?"

"I don't know."

"You followed Dom because you wanted to talk to him about Felix."

"Okay," Bliss said.

"Say it."

"I wanted to talk to him about Felix."

"Good."

"But why did Rick shoot me?"

"Because his son died," Ward said.

"But why did he shoot *me?*"

"He was deranged. He blamed you. But Rick's dead, now. We'll never know what he was really thinking, what demons were driving him, what evil was lurking in his heart."

"Only the Shadow knows," Bliss said.

"Yes he do," Ward said. "Oh yes he do."

Chantal lay in the hotel bed. Her mother was in the bed next to her.

"It's like a sleepover," her mother said.

"Yeah," Chantal said.

It wasn't anything like a sleepover. Her mother had stormed uninvited into Chantal's bedroom, made her throw some clothes in a suitcase, and dragged her out of the house. Then they took a cab to a hotel. At the front desk, her mother told the clerk they would be staying a week.

"At least a week. Maybe longer."

On the elevator, her mother finally confessed the purpose behind their escapade. At first Chantal thought it had to do with Holden's blood that had pretty much ruined the carpet in her room. But her mother had larger plans.

"We're starting over," she said. She took Chantal's hand. "The two of us." Then she took a deep breath and looked at the numbers, slowly climbing, up and up. Just before their floor she said "I've left your father."

"Have you told him?" Chantal had asked.

The elevator door opened before her mother had a chance to answer.

Once in the room there was a teary session during which her mom confessed to being a terrible mother and that *she* never wanted to stay over Sunday nights in the Hamptons, that she never *condoned* that.

"It was Jerry's idea. It was always Jerry's idea."

Chantal thought that was the first time her mother ever referred to her father as "Jerry." He was no longer "Daddy."

They had dinner sent up—room service, and for a few minutes it was actually fun, they were laughing.

"We're free," her Mom had said.

No, Chantal thought, we're *together*. That's what feels so good. But she didn't say that, didn't feel the need to rub it in.

They had watched a movie and now they were in bed, getting ready to go to sleep.

"Good night, Sweetie," her mother said.

"Good night, Mom."

She turned off the light. Chantal thought about how her mother had behaved that night, curled up on a hotel room floor, in her pajamas, nibbling at her room-service hamburger, giddy from having just left her husband (though Chantal knew they

would all be back together again soon and, except for not staying Sundays in the Hamptons, things would be pretty much the
same), but for some reason Chantal wasn't feeling her usual
anger, wasn't feeling disdain for her mother's transparent attempt
to commune with her daughter, her youth, everything she left
behind. She just felt kind of sorry for her.

Chantal turned in her bed and faced her Mom.

"You weren't a bad mom," Chantal said.

"Really?" her mother said. "You really mean that?"

"Yes," Chantal said.

"That . . . you're saying that means . . ." She didn't finish,
and the words lingered in the air. Chantal turned away and
closed her eyes. After a few moments she heard her mother
whisper.

"Thank you," her mother said.

Soon Chantal heard her mother breathing steadily, sound
asleep.

But Chantal couldn't sleep. The frenzy of the last few days
had her mind reeling. She kept seeing Owen smashing his brother
in the face. She wondered if that was some kind of apology to her,
protecting her somehow. Or was it something Owen had wanted
to do for years. Maybe both. Chantal remembered Owen leaving
her room in the custody of the Gelman family lawyer, head bowed,
dragging his feet, like a bad puppy. She actually felt some compassion for him then. That was the Owen she loved, the innocent boy inside him, the one that emerged after they had sex, who
was quiet and vulnerable and desperately lonely.

But the other Owen, the before-sex Owen, was very different. She remembered the night Owen had tried to force her
to go all the way. She ran downstairs but he caught her at the
front door, apologizing like crazy, saying how much he loved her,

was so crazy about her, begging her to stay. He led her to the couch and held her tight, stroking her hair. But then he was easing her under him and all of a sudden he was right back to where he was before. No, she told him. *Have another drink, some E, a joint.* She tried to leave again, so he said all right and settled for their usual way, not caring if it stained the upholstery. When he was all done, she left.

She hadn't gone right home. She had stopped at a Starbucks, wanting a hot chocolate even though it was spring. She had just sat down and begun to collect her thoughts when she felt someone staring at her. She looked up. It was a guy in his mid-twenties, kind of cute in his V-neck T-shirt and khakis, like one of the mannequins in a Banana Republic window. He smiled, casually yet with purpose, then looked away, as if he didn't care, slyly checking back to see if she noticed him.

She didn't smile back, didn't return the glance, just stared at her hot chocolate, wishing she hadn't looked up in the first place, knowing already, at fourteen, that no stray glance ever went unacknowledged in New York City, that someone, some guy or girl was alert, on the prowl, looking to make a connection. She wished she were home, asleep.

She felt a presence above her, heard him clear his throat, knew it was the guy from the line. Why, she thought. I'm just fourteen, she thought. Doesn't he *know* I'm just fourteen?

"Hi," he said.

Don't look up, she told herself.

But this one must have been used to getting his way.

"Is there anything I could say in the next two minutes that might win your heart?"

She looked up. He smiled in a well-practiced way, unzipping his lips to reveal his white, perfect teeth which he knew were very white and very perfect. The effect was supposed to be charming. His mother probably told him it was charming.

"Hey, how about giving me a chance? Whattaya say?"

All of a sudden she felt a surge of fury rush through her.

"Get away from me!" she screamed, all the pain and humiliation of being with Owen pouring out.

"But . . ."

"Just get away!!" Her voice even louder now because the rest of the shop had gone silent.

"Leave her alone, man," came a deep voice from another table.

"Hey, I just . . ."

"You *heard* her."

The boy turned, indignant now.

"Hey, I don't need you telling me . . ."

"I'm just fourteen!" she shouted. "I'm only fourteen!"

She ran out of the store. She didn't want to hear any more boy talk. She ran down the block and around the corner and then stopped and leaned against the side of a building, hands on her knees, trying to catch her breath. She wished she'd thrown her hot chocolate at him, right in his smirking face.

Chantal sat up in bed.

There was no way she would fall asleep now. She got up quietly, so as not to wake her mother, and went into the bathroom. She shut the door before turning on the light.

She looked at herself in the mirror. She studied her hair, her lips, her breasts. These parts of her seemed to lure her into trouble. Danger. Her breasts were her enemy. Her hair, conspiring against her. She needed to cover them up. Hide them. The only way she could get some peace. They all had to be covered.

She would start with her hair. *Let down your golden tresses,* Holden had said. Her hair was clearly wicked, shimmying and wiggling in some sordid dance without Chantal knowing it, giving the boys the totally wrong idea. Her hair was never quiet. She knew that now.

So she'd start there.

She found a small scissors in her mother's cosmetic bag. She could cut only a few strands at a time, but it didn't matter. She had all night. She started cutting. She could hear the cries of protest from her curls as they landed on the floor, in the toilet, but she didn't stop. She was sick of being betrayed. She wanted it to end.

When she'd gotten most of it off she stopped and looked at herself in the mirror. Her head was now an uneven, ragged mess, like starving insects had gorged there.

It looked ugly. Her hair looked ugly. She liked it ugly. Because it was quiet now. Its coy teasing stilled.

She smiled.

There was a phone in the bathroom. She picked it up and called Malcolm on his personal line, wanting to tell him about what she'd done, thinking he'd be the one person who would understand. But there was no answer. She wondered where he was so late at night. She left a message with her room number and told him to call her tomorrow.

Then she turned off the light and went back to bed and fell immediately into a deep, untroubled sleep for the first time in a long while.

Rachel and Julia stood on one side of the hospital bed, Cori on the other. Cori held her father's hand.

"I shouldn't have tried to climb over that fence," he said. "I'm too old for that."

No one said anything.

"I was never good at fence climbing," he said.

More silence.

Then Julia coughed decorously.

"We already spoke to the doctor," she said. "He told us what's going on."

"Oh," Bliss said.

"The bullet went through your leg," Julia said.

"Clean through," Cori added.

"No souvenirs," Bliss said. "But I guess I'll have the memory."

"That man," Rachel said, "Rick. What was he thinking?"

"He was babbling," Bliss said. "Incoherent. I don't know why he came after me."

"He must have been in great pain," Rachel said. "Losing his son."

"It's better not to think about it," Bliss said, thinking about it, holding Cori tighter.

Anton entered, moved to the bed.

"Lenny," he said. He was dressed in a tuxedo, probably just coming from a fundraiser. "Just heard. A bullet. Where?"

"In his leg, Grandpa," Cori said.

"The leg. Lenny. My fault. I should have told you. Stay away from bullets."

The kids laughed. Rachel, too. It was a good line. Something for the novel. *Stay away from bullets.* Mae's partner might tell her that. Rock, or whatever she was calling him now.

"Lenny," Anton said. "Maybe now. The job. This injury."

"It's not serious," Bliss said.

"Still. A bullet. The job. It's there. Waiting. Lenny. Security. Now more than ever."

The doctor came in, checked the wound, and assured everyone Bliss would be fine, would be walking with a cane or crutch by the end of the week. Then the doctor thought it best if everyone left, so Bliss could get some rest.

They kissed him and said good-bye. Rachel looked at him lovingly. He smiled. She took Cori by the hand and they all left together.

A moment later, Julia came back in, walked close to him, and pressed a piece of paper into his hand.

"Maybe it will help you," she said, "next time you have to climb over a fence."

He looked down and saw he was holding in his hand the coupon for the yoga.

Malcolm leaned his bike against the massive support of the Triborough Bridge. He could hear the unearthly whirring of the cars on the span thirty stories above, a steady stream of traffic even at dawn. Birds filled a small tree bordering the many baseball diamonds wedged into this corner of Wards Island. They chirped madly, in defiance, claiming those few, meager branches as their own.

The East River flowed quietly, slowing as it divided around the island. LaGuardia Airport was just a mile beyond the water. To the west was Manhattan. It was a pleasant bike ride in the morning, one he took often along the promenade adjacent to the FDR Drive, over the East River pedestrian bridge at 110th

Street, a few loops around Wards Island, and then back home.
In all it was about seven miles. A good workout.

If it were the weekend, carloads of kids and parents would
be arriving for little league. Younger kids playing T-ball, older
ones playing hardball in full uniforms, wearing cleats and those
high socks, the brims of their caps set in a rakish curl.

Malcolm did not have fond memories of Little League. His
career, mercifully, lasted only one game. He kept missing the
ball when he was at bat, even though the ball was sitting on a
tee and they gave him far more than his allotted three strikes.
He remembered the extra swings making his humiliation even
more acute. The kids in the field, waiting for him to make contact, kicked dirt with their toes or stared up at the bridge. Some
just sat down and picked at the grass. Finally he hit the ball, list-
less tap that dribbled down the first base line. He prayed it would
stay fair, so he wouldn't have to bat again—ever again. He jogged
to first, slowing down so the first baseman could tag him out.
His coach patted him on the shoulder as he trudged back to the
bench. Everyone breathed a sigh of relief.

Then he had to go out in the field and play defense. They
stuck him in as remote a spot as they could, a bald patch of the
dirt in the outfield surrounded by goose shit and cigarette butts.
Somehow a ball made it through the legs of two other players
and wound up in his glove. He had no idea what to do with it.
The other kids screamed at him—*throw it! Throw it, you idiot!*
but he was frozen. Afraid to do the wrong thing, he did nothing
at all. Finally, one of the junior jocks-in-training ran over and
ripped the ball out of his glove and threw it back to the infield.
Jerk, he said. *Faggot.*

The next day his father bought a shiny new glove and ball
and they went out to Central Park to have a catch. His father

turned out to be as wretched at baseball as he was. His dad would make a bad throw and Malcolm would lunge for it and miss. Then he'd chase down the ball and throw it back to his dad, who would make his own spastic lunge and also miss. Malcolm's glove was still so new that on the rare occasion when he did manage to catch it, the ball would pop out, almost as though it was mocking him.

After one errant throw, the ball rolled to a young couple lying on their blanket reading the Sunday paper. The guy grabbed it and with great fervor, jumped up and got ready to toss it back to Malcolm. As soon as he went into his windup, Malcolm knew he was in for trouble—that this guy, seeing a kid with a glove, must have assumed Malcolm had played catch before, that his dad had been out with him every spare minute, working on their grounders and pop flies. Malcolm wanted to say, *Can't you see my glove is brand new and my dad's an artist and we've never played catch before—and that I'm a jerk and a faggot and I can't catch and I can't throw and I can't hit the ball even when it's not moving?— can't you see?* But the guy couldn't see, maybe because he was too busy showing off for his girlfriend or maybe because (and this was something Malcolm was now beginning to understand in a deeply profound way) guys like that *never* see anything different from themselves. So the guy made an exaggerated wind up and threw the ball at Malcolm. Hard. He had tried to stop it with his glove, not even catch it, just knock it down, or protect himself. Something. But he missed and the ball hit him squarely on the cheek.

He dropped to the ground, curled up and started wailing. The guy ran over and his dad ran over and even the guy's girl-friend ran over. His father picked him up and told everyone it was all right. Through his tears, Malcolm could see the guy who threw it looking all fearful and his girlfriend was calling him an idiot and whacking him on the arm. He clung to his dad who brought him to the shade of a large tree and set him down. It was one of those soft baseballs they'd been playing with, the kind little kids use, so the pain was subsiding and there was no real damage done. His dad brushed away his tears and when he calmed down, took him to get a soda and hot dog from the vendor in the park. They walked around together, his father taking some pictures, and then wound up on Fifth Avenue across from the Frick Collection.

Suddenly his dad's spirit's lifted and he hustled Malcolm across the street and into the most magnificent home he'd ever seen. Only it wasn't a home anymore, it was a museum. His father passed one room after another, knowing just where he wanted to go, striding along the marble floor with ease and lightness. Malcolm couldn't help but be swept along. They didn't stop until they'd arrived in a little room in the back where there were only a few paintings, one of which was of a woman sitting by an open window. *Look at that, Malcolm,* his father said, a tremor of awe in his voice. *Look at the light.* Malcolm was immediately drawn into the mystery of the painting, the way the sunlight leaped out from the canvas, the softness of the woman's face. They stood like that in silence and his father gently took his hand and held it.

They walked through the rest of the museum and it wasn't until they were outside sitting on a bench and eating a Good Humor that Malcolm realized they had left their gloves and their baseball in the park. He didn't say anything about it. Neither did his father.

*   *   *

Malcolm walked to the edge of the river and took off his backpack. He unzipped the main compartment and took out a trophy. There was a bit of blood on the fake marble base. The name on the brass plate read HOLDEN GELMAN. The figure on the trophy was in the process of hitting a baseball.

He reached back and threw the trophy as far as he could into the East River. It made a small splash and disappeared.

Malcolm got back on his bike and headed home.

His life had irrevocably changed. He understood that there was unfairness in the world, that delicate things—delicate *people*—like Chantal, would always be treated unfairly. Violated. And that the only fairness there was, was what you made yourself.

He also knew this was wrong. That once you start making big moral decisions that are for your *own* good and not society's, then bad things happen, like gay boys being beaten and tied to fence rails and left to die. Or abortion doctors getting shot through their kitchen windows.

He thought about the trophy, now at the bottom of the river. It would stay there. Hidden. A dark secret he hoped to somehow completely forget. He wondered if it was possible to completely forget.

But as he rode back home, the morning sun reflecting off the water of the East River, he saw once again in his mind, in a kind of slow motion, the golden boy of the trophy sailing in a gentle arc and landing in the water. And he thought that for a jerk, for a faggot, it wasn't such a bad throw.

ONE MONTH LATER

Bliss handed the coupon to the same pretty Asian girl behind the desk at the Serenity Loft.

"This has expired," she said.

"I know. I was hoping . . . you know, in the yoga spirit."

She smiled and stamped the second square of his card. The Chinese symbol was slightly different from the one he got the first time. The ink a different color. Maybe she remembered him, and this stamp was some kind of warning to the others, that he was Yoga intolerant, the he was one of the un-Zen.

"Been a while," the girl said,

"You remember me?" Bliss said.

"No," she said. "The stamp. We haven't used the waning moon stamp in a few months."

"What's the new one mean?"

"Dawn. Rebirth."

"That's always good, a little rebirth."

She gave him a knowing look and handed him back his card.

"Beginnings are always hard," she said.

"I know."

He couldn't swear to it, but the girl might have had one more earring pierced through her ear than before. They ran up the outside edge, six or seven of them. Maybe they were markers, or badges, that she was one step closer to Nirvana.

Bliss had an impulse to show her the scar on his leg, where the bullet went through, his own piercing, ask her what higher state of consciousness he was getting closer to, but he thought better of it.

He pocketed his card and went into the studio.

He found a place on the floor and looked around for his teacher, but it was a different woman that day. She was young with short hair and taut, lithe arms. She was cute, but carried around her an aura that Bliss immediately sensed made her impenetrable to anything carnal—a toxic combination of deep spirituality and perkiness.

He started assuming Downward Facing Dog, trying to relax his back, trying to relax anything that would relax.

It wasn't going well.

His uniquely asymmetrical approach must have attracted the teacher. She moved to him, her feet barely touching the floor.

"First time?" she asked.

"Second."

"Beginnings are always hard," she said.

"I know."

He gave up the dog and rested on his knees. The teacher gazed on him with pity.

"Too much stress, perhaps," she said.

"Too much bullet," he replied.

"I don't understand."

"I was shot." He pulled up his sweat pants and showed her the scar. "It passed clean through."

He noticed others in the class were watching him, startled by the viscera he had brought into their space.

"I'm a cop," he said.

"Wow," one of his classmates said.

"More cops should do yoga," another said.

He wanted to tell them that Mae Stark did yoga. That she did pretty much everything Detective Bliss did. That they could real all about him in his wife's book, on which she was working feverishly.

"Did someone want to hurt you?" the teacher said. She gently rubbed the back of his neck and shoulders.

"Yes," he said. "But it was a case of mistaken identity."

"I'm glad you're okay," she said.

They started working on Lotus again. Bliss was no closer this time. He felt stiff and foolish.

He decided that just because he wasn't able to assume the proper position, that didn't mean he couldn't assume *any* position. He just needed to name them.

Like the way he was sitting now, one leg stretched, leaning back on his elbows, eyes facing upward, he had assumed the perfect form of Cop in Existential Crises.

He saw some of his classmates had their eyes closed. So Bliss closed his eyes.

The events of the past month were starting to fade. The bullet had passed through his leg. He'd been lucky. He would be back at the job soon, back with Ward, working cases.

Rebirth. Dawn.

He had been happy sitting around the house, listening to music with Cori, meeting Julia after school and taking her for Frappucinos or whatever else she wanted, sometimes with her friends, sometimes just the two of them.

He shifted, so he was resting more on his side, adjusting the yoga pad so he could lean back on one elbow, assuming

Middle Aged Cop Resigned to His Fate. Beginnings are hard, he thought, but endings are harder.

Everyone, the police, the newspaper, had worked overtime trying to figure out why Rick thought a homicide detective had killed his son. It came out that Julia was briefly at the party, but even the most intrepid reporter couldn't find any evidence of Bliss being involved. There was no clear motive. And if they could begin to make a connection between Bliss and Rick's son, Dom's presence at the scene jammed up even the most far-fetched explanation.

Ward said the D.A. was equally frustrated about finding Ben's killer. Too many kids at the party and hardly any had alibis for where they were. *I left the party, came home, listened to music, went to bed. My parents were asleep. My parents were out of town.* And except for Chantal and Billy Dix, no one seemed to have a motive.

So things died down, as they tended to do, unless sex, politicians, large sums of money, or rap stars were involved. The trophy never showed up. No one came forward with new evidence or a confession. Holden returned to his television show. Julia told him that Owen now went to boarding school.

So *Murder on Park Avenue* would have to wait for the TV movie to produce a likely suspect. Or maybe Mae Stark would somehow solve it, and bring the evildoer to justice.

Bliss lay on his back and clasped his hands behind his neck, assuming Man Who Has Given Up on Yoga position. He would go home soon, before class was over. He would not try Lotus today. He had to do the tenor players with Cori that afternoon—Hawk to Chu to Pres to Jacquet to Newk to Trane. And then, where it went next, he'd have to let his daughter decide.

*   *   *

Clara sat at her kitchen table correcting papers. The chairs didn't match and the Formica was chipped in places, but she didn't mind. It was her table. In her kitchen. The water boiling in the kettle was boiling on her stove.

She was working as a substitute teacher now. Next year she was certain to find a regular teaching job.

Her children were upstairs, asleep in their room. For the moment, the two boys had to share a bed, but Clara hoped to be getting another bed soon. The boys didn't seem to mind.

They had wanted to know all about her life in America, but she didn't want to tell them anything. In her bathroom, on the sink, rested a plastic clamshell filled with tiny pastel soaps shaped like little shells. The very one from the Gelmans' guest bathroom. Clara had taken it with her. She and her children and her grandfather would use the seashell soaps until they were gone, dissolved. And then her memories would be gone, too. And then she would throw away the clamshell. And that would be that.

Meanwhile her grandfather sat at the table with her, waiting for his tea to cool. He held one of the curiously colored seashell soaps in his hard, twisted fingers. It made him smile.

And Clara thought, what a beautiful thing, her grandfather's smile.